At her questioning look, Sam grinned mischievously. And before she could protest, he was spinning her around the floor in perfect time to the lively tune.

Lauren was more surprised at the delight she felt than by his actions. He was a faultless dancer, light on his feet, and so adept they didn't miss a step. She was amazed that he was able to whirl her around the store without even so much as brushing against one of her delicate antiques.

The song played for less than three minutes, but Lauren was breathless by the time they stopped. Suddenly embarrassed, she couldn't resist giggling at the fun she'd had if only for a brief, wonderful moment. Self-consciously she tugged at her wrinkled T-shirt with one hand, and tucked her hair behind her ear with the other. "You're very good."

Sam grinned, adding wickedly, "I've been trying to tell you that for the past several days."

JAYMI CRISTOL
Three Wishes

ZEBRA BOOKS
KENSINGTON PUBLISHING CORP.

*For my sister, whose sense of whimsy
and belief in fantasy taught me the wonder
of magic. I love you, Kathleen.*

ZEBRA BOOKS

are published by

Kensington Publishing Corp.
475 Park Avenue South
New York, NY 10016

Copyright © 1993 by Jaymi Cristol

First Printing: March, 1993

Printed in the United States of America

Chapter One

Lauren Kennedy was a millionaire. Even after several weeks, the realization thrilled her. That was the good news. The bad news was she was stuck in New Orleans.

She sighed, not for the first time, as she took a final look around the shop she was going to open for business in — she glanced at her watch — ten minutes. Not bad. In fact, pretty darned good, if she did say so herself. She'd walked into the antique store just six weeks before and had been daunted by the state it was in. Her aunt Edna had been a very successful entrepreneur, but for the life of her, Lauren couldn't figure out how she'd made a penny. The store had been a shambles.

Running a finger over the countertop, she smiled with satisfaction. Not so much as a mote of dust now. All that was left to do before she opened was give the sidewalk out front one last swipe with the broom.

Several people — some tourists, others shop owners like herself—glanced her way, even stared, as she whisked the broom back and forth on the cobbled sidewalk. She smiled tentatively at several of them, but though a few smiled back, most looked at her as though she had two heads.

Probably it was because of the way she was dressed, she surmised, giving her navy gabardine slacks a tug, then self-consciously checking the striped bow at the neck of her oxford shirt. She'd wanted to make a good impression—to come across as a professional businesswoman—but southerners were so laid back. Still, she *was* the epitome of a nineties professional, and her stint as owner of Yesterday's Treasures was temporary. Like it or not, she wasn't going to change.

As she swept, she thought about her aunt, the woman she'd loved almost more than her own mother. Edna had been fun-loving, artistic, and eccentric. Everything she herself wasn't. Perhaps it was their contrasting natures that had drawn them to one another from the moment they'd met, when she was hardly big enough to toddle.

Lauren smiled as she whisked the last particle of dirt off the curb. Her mother had considered Edna, her sister, a nitwit, so she had gasped when Lauren phoned to tell her the amount of Edna's fortune. Lauren chuckled at the memory. And now she was a very wealthy woman.

She tucked a strand of her gleaming pale blond page boy behind her ear, then paused to run her fingers over the glossy shine of the one extravagance she'd treated herself to—a spanking new

BMW. She frowned as she considered the wisdom of parking the expensive car on the street, but her brow quickly smoothed. Just this once, she was going to flaunt it. After today, she'd leave it in the parking lot at the back. But damn it, she was proud of her car, and she wanted the whole world to know.

As she turned back to the store, she glanced around her, willing others on the street to look her way again, see the look of pride that shone in her tawny eyes. She imagined that they gleamed like topaz. Normally a soft brown, she remembered that Aunt Edna had once said that she always knew when Lauren was happy because her eyes always turned golden, like a cat's. Suddenly, she felt the prickle of tears.

She hadn't wanted to come to New Orleans, didn't want to be here now. She missed her life in Chicago, but more, she missed the woman who had loved her enough to entrust her life's work and fortune to. Lifting her chin slightly, she re-entered the store and turned the sign on the door from Closed to Open. She was an extremely wealthy young woman now because of her aunt. And like it or not, she was going to stay until she could sell everything to the right people, people who would love the same things her aunt had. She owed Edna that much.

Lauren turned the key in the cash register, hit the No Sale button to open the drawer, and took a quick inventory of the money she'd counted out an hour before. "Ready to go," she said, squaring her shoulders and glancing around the store once more. Everything was neat and orderly, the time-worn relics polished to a shine and looking almost proud in spite of their sagging, weary faces.

She smiled at the notion of inanimate objects having faces, sagging and weary or otherwise. *Careful, Lauren, you're actually beginning to think like sweet, dotty Aunt Edna.*

The jingle of bells announced the arrival of her first customers. She pulled on her best smile and turned to greet them.

Two elderly little ladies entered almost simultaneously, though with their wide girths, that would have been impossible. After a brief shoving match, one of them was forced to yield and follow the other in.

"Good morning, ladies. Welcome to Yesterday's Treasures." Even as she said the words, Lauren groaned inwardly. Her voice sounded brittle, phony. *Relax,* she ordered herself. "Please feel free to look around," she added before noticing that the two ladies ware already doing just that.

"Oh, Sister, this will never do," one of them whispered just loud enough for Lauren to hear.

"Indeed it will not," the second chucked. "Oh dear, dear, imagine what poor Edna would say if she could see her beloved store in this condition."

Lauren frowned. What did they mean, "What would poor Edna say?" She'd probably say, "Everything looks wonderful, Lauren. You've got it all shaped up the way it never was when I was running things." Lauren bit her lip to hide her annoyance as she followed the women down a recently created aisle. "Is there anything in particular you are looking for?"

The women—sisters apparently, judging not only by the marked likeness of their round faces, but by the title one had used earlier—smiled at each other as if sharing a private joke. The taller of the two, by an inch or so, turned to look at Lauren, her pale, rheumy eyes almost squinting in their bold appraisal of her.

"Oh no, dear, we just wanted to see how the old shop looked. Goodness, we've been waiting for weeks for you to get the door open. We promised Edna, don't you know?"

Lauren could feel her annoyance growing and fought to keep her tone bland. "As a matter of fact, I don't know. What exactly did you promise my aunt?"

"Why, that we'd check up on things; make sure you got off on the right foot. But I can see, Sister and I should have come in long ago. Why, this simply will never do. Everything is too . . . what's the word, Sister?"

"Neat. Everything is too neat."

"That's bad?" Lauren asked.

The shorter sister pursed her lips at this piece of sarcasm. And her ladylike southern accent grew more pronounced as she struggled to find a polite way of putting the new proprietress in her place. "No, that's not bad, dear. Not if you don't want to sell anything. If you're only intendin' to fritter the day away sittin' around, then I suppose it's good."

9

Lauren suppressed a smile. But she still didn't understand what they were talking about. She was about to ask when the other sister suddenly shrieked.

"Oh, mercy me, Sister, would you look over here in this box under the table. Why, Edna must surely be doing somersaults in her grave."

The second gasped, and her hand flew to her mouth as she followed her sister's pointing finger.

Lauren was tall—almost five-eight—but she couldn't see over them or past them to find out what had disturbed them. She was about to ask when both women spun around indignantly.

Lauren cut them off before they could deliver the diatribe she knew was coming. "Could we start over? Who are you, and what are you both so upset about?"

The women colored slightly, and the shorter one actually giggled in embarrassment as she answered. "Oh, dear me, I do believe we've forgotten our manners. I'm Matilda Crocker and this is my sister, Petulia Le Point, although our friends call us Tillie and Toots—as you may, dear. We are your neighbors, both widow ladies, don't you know, just like your dear aunt Edna was before her passing last summer."

"I'm Lauren Kennedy, as you obviously know, and I'm delighted to meet you, but confused as well. Aunt Edna's attorney told me that her death came unexpectedly, but you both act as if she'd known she wasn't going to be around and asked you to oversee things."

"Not oversee, dear, just follow up. Your aunt had the utmost faith in your abilities. But she knew you didn't know the first thing about running an antique shop, so she asked us to come in and just offer advice as you needed it. We would have come sooner, but we didn't want you to think we were meddling. We thought we'd wait until you at least had a chance to open the doors. I suppose we should have suspected something was wrong when it took you so long."

"But I still don't understand what *is* wrong," Lauren said with exasperation.

"Perhaps wrong is too strong a word, Sister," the one called Toots said tactfully.

Matilda ignored her sister and explained. "People are funny about antiques, Lauren. If everything is too orderly and clean, they automatically assume your prices are going to be too dear as well. They like to think of shopping for antiques as bargain-hunting or junking."

Lauren considered this, then shook her head. "I understand what you're saying, and it makes perfect sense, but I've done a lot of studying in the past few weeks, and Aunt Edna has some very valuable pieces here. Surely, no one would confuse them with junk."

Tillie and Toots exchanged a look that said all too clearly that they both thought Lauren a mite slow.

Toots took it upon herself to explain. "Why, of course you've got some wonderful pieces here! Some of them have come from our very home,

11

don't you know? You want to get a good price for them, but you must create the impression of giving something for nothing. Antique dealing is a very practiced art, and illusion is an important part of it." She leaned forward to pat Lauren's shoulder. "But don't you worry, dear. We'll help you. We gave our solemn promise to Edna, after all, and a lady's word is golden."

For the first time, Lauren smiled, charmed by their old world southern gentility. "And I appreciate it." She remembered their gasps of horror of a few minutes before and changed the subject. "A few minutes ago you both seemed particularly upset—"

"Oh, yes, Sister, you must explain about the lamp," Toots told the shorter sister.

"We noticed a box you've tried to hide underneath that table in the corner. You were quite right in your assessment that most of the contents are truly pieces of junk, Lauren dear, but one piece—a bronze lamp—was your aunt Edna's most treasured possession. In fact, she wouldn't even consider selling it, and would never have tossed it into a box. I think you should give it a place of prominence in loving memory of Edna, if nothing else."

Was that all? If it would appease the two sweet busybodies, Lauren thought, she'd hang it from the ceiling in the middle of the room. She hurried to the table, and stooping retrieved an oddly shaped lamp from the box. Holding it away from her so as not to soil her clothes, she examined the tarnished bronze piece. "Is this the one?"

Both ladies smiled and nodded briskly.

The lamp was shaped almost like an hourglass, with a spout, a pointed top, and a hinged curved handle that opened the lid. It was made of bronze and etched with flowers and leaves. Though in another time or culture, Lauren supposed it could have been considered attractive, its oriental look didn't appeal to her at all. "It's certainly different, but I don't recall anything in the catalogues that would suggest it was particularly valuable."

Toots answered. "We didn't say it had a market value, dear, but to Edna, it was priceless."

Well, if all it took to win the two ladies' approval was giving the lamp a place of honor, she'd gladly do it. Walking over to the counter, she placed it on a shelf directly behind the cash register. "How about here?"

"Why, isn't that remarkable, Sister?" Tillie asked. "Isn't that almost the exact spot Edna always kept the lamp?"

"I believe it is," Toots agreed as she beamed her approval at Lauren. "Now, if you'll just muss things up a bit here and there, and let the dust settle back into place, I think you'll be a very successful entrepreneur, Lauren dear."

After the two women finally left, Lauren considered their counsel. Maybe they were right. What did she know about antiques, anyway? She'd always hated old things, preferring the simple, sleek lines and gleam of modern lacquered furnishings, silk flowers, and chrome accessories. She was definitely a woman of the nineties. Perhaps clutter

13

was in order here, no pun intended. She looked around her, then back at the lamp sitting on its new perch. But dust? She'd have to draw the line there.

Picking up the lamp, she found a rag under the counter and began wiping it vigorously. She'd have to get some cleaner and shine it up, too. She'd—

Whatever she'd been about to decide was quickly snatched away as a swirl of smoke began flowing from the spout. She nearly dropped the lamp, but remembering the sisters' words about her aunt's attachment to the thing, quickly set it on the counter instead.

She blinked, thinking the swirling cloud a trick of the light, but the smoke continued to flow from the lamp and then take shape. A man's shape!

Lauren stifled a scream with a fist pressed between her lips. Was she losing her mind?

The smoke—or man—was taking on color and losing his transparency.

Lauren closed her eyes as she sank dizzily into the chair beside the cash register. *I'm finally going over the brink,* she thought. Sobs shook her shoulders, and she buried her face in her hands as she gave way to the emotions she'd too long denied herself.

She'd never wanted to come to New Orleans; never wanted to do anything but stay in Chicago at her advertising job and marry Charles. When she'd been passed over for two promotions, and Charles, who had started with the company a year after her, had continued to move up the ladder, she'd felt almost devastated. She'd been happy for

Charles. She loved him, after all. She'd clung stubbornly to reason, arguing that she was still young enough to make her mark, even find a new company if necessary. But she'd been forced to admit that things were not progressing as she had hoped. Charles seemed resistant to announcing their engagement, and her career had become stagnant. When her aunt's attorney had called to tell her of Edna's bequest, she'd almost dared to hope that putting distance between herself and the many problems plaguing her might be the answer. But all along she'd been deluding herself. Nothing had gotten better. In fact everything appeared worse than ever.

"Yo, mama, it can't be as bad as all that."

Leaping to her feet, her shoulder brushed a glass bottle on the shelf. But before it could fall, the man who'd spoken to her somehow managed to cross more than five feet in a split second and rescue it.

Lauren backed further into the corner of the sales nook. "Who . . . who are you?"

The man grinned, his smile almost splitting his face in two. "Eugene's the name. Magic's my game."

Lauren felt her knees sag with relief. "Oh, thank God. You're a magician." She laughed weakly. "For a few seconds, I really thought I was losing my mind."

The man didn't answer but continued to grin at her as he pushed himself up onto the countertop, crossed his legs, folded his arms, and studied her.

"So, Lauren, what's happenin'?"

Lauren's small smile faded like breath off a mirror. "How do you know my name?"

"Edna told me."

"You knew my aunt?" Lauren asked as she took in the man's strange appearance. With his shaggy brown hair, thin craggy face, wire-framed glasses, and goatee, he looked like a cross between Maynard of Dobie Gillis fame, and Woody Allen. His loose-fitting embroidered shirt and bell-bottom pants were a costume from the sixties complete with straw sandals. Why in the world would Aunt Edna have befriended such a strange person? Why, he looked like a Woodstock leftover, and though she'd just witnessed some amazing magic illusions, he hardly looked successful.

"Edna and I go way back. She was one far-out lady, your aunt. Knew how to go with the flow."

Far out? Cool? He *was* from another era. "But when . . . I mean, how did you meet my aunt?"

Tugging absently at his goatee, Eugene seemed to consider his answer carefully. "You might say I just appeared one day. Back in sixty-one, I think. Yeah, that's right. She was just setting up her shop here. We stayed together ever since. Doesn't happen that way often. I'm kind of a ramblin' dude, you might say, but Edna was hip and knew just the right words to keep me around. 'Sides, it was real peaceful here. Your aunt had a live-and-let-live attitude, kind of in keeping with the whole movement then. I dug her and the new era. Decided to adopt both."

16

Lauren rubbed her brow, confused and, though it was still early, more than a little tired. She had thought today would be exciting, but the visitors she'd had so far this morning had exhausted her.

"Well, I'm delighted to meet you, Mr. — ?"

The man grinned. "No mister, just Eugene."

"Okay, Eugene. As I was saying, I'm delighted to meet you, but I've really got a lot to do."

Eugene looked around the shop, shaking his head. "Looks like you've already done too much, mama."

Another critic? Terrific! Lauren's fingers found the spot in her temple where a headache was beginning to throb and rubbed it, her fingers making tiny circles. "Look, Eugene, two of Aunt Edna's friends just stopped by and already pointed out my mistakes, so if you don't mind . . ."

"Hey, it's cool. You're the boss, after all."

Lauren started to smile, but squeaked with surprise when the strange man suddenly appeared beside her, sitting on the counter near her arm. "Look, I know you're a magician, and that's great . . . I think, but you're really a bit disconcerting. Please stop doing whatever it is that . . . that . . ."

"Makes you crazy? Hey, that's groovie. Like I said, you're the boss, but I think you should understand, I'm not really a magician, at least not in the way you think."

Lauren tried to take a step back but she was already standing in the corner. "Then what are you?" she asked carefully.

"I'm a genie. Eugene. Genie. Get it? Name used

17

to be Ali Simm Simm, but I got hip in the sixties and realized the name was outdated. Edna helped me pick out a new one."

Lauren's knees would no longer support her. Slowly, she sagged to the floor where she drew up her legs and buried her face against them. "Oh, God, it's true. I really have flipped out."

Eugene was instantly beside her. "Hey, mama, you don't look so good. You're white as a ghost, and believe me, I've known quite a few in my time. White as paste, most of 'em, and you could pass for one right now." Tapping her on the shoulder, he said, "Here, maybe you'd better drink this."

Lauren raised her head and looked at the man now hunkering at her side only inches away. He'd produced a glass of brandy out of thin air and held it out to her, his dark eyes watching her kindly. She started to protest, but changed her mind. If she was truly mad, then what difference could drinking brandy at nine-thirty in the morning make? It wasn't real anyway. She choked and sputtered as the hot, fiery liquid went down. It certainly had a real enough effect on her, she realized as it began to warm her, and she began to calm down.

After a few minutes, Eugene offered her a hand and helped her to her feet. "Better?" he asked.

"I think so. At least I'm not dizzy now. But I'm still confused."

"Hey, well that's cool. Not every day a genie comes boppin' into your life, right? I can dig it. Your aunt Edna was a tad shocked, too." He scratched his head, then grinned. "Napoleon was the worst case I ever met. Damned near jumped out a window when he rubbed my lamp and I appeared. I try to be more subtle about it nowadays, but I can't figure a way around the smoke thing."

Lauren knew her mouth was hanging open, but for the life of her she couldn't seem to close it. "Napoleon? As in Bonaparte?"

"The same dude."

"You really knew Napoleon and were his genie and granted him three wishes and all that?"

Eugene nodded. "Hey, that surprises you? You don't think a beauty like Josephine would have given that jive turkey the time of day without a little help, do you?"

It might have been the aftereffect of the brandy, or maybe she really was nuts, but Lauren believed him. Propping an elbow on the counter, she rested her chin in her hand. "If you were really there, how did he go wrong at Waterloo?"

Eugene seemed to take offense at the implication. "Hey, now, mama, don't go laying that trip on me. I tried to warn him that he only had three wishes, but he was one determined dude. Wired, ya know? Never stopped to think things out. He had one elephant-sized ego. The man thought he could do no wrong. But the pressure! Whoa, now that was something fierce. He was an insomniac and had terrible ulcers. That's why he was always walking around with his hand stuck in his jacket holding his stomach. The pain was something awful, but he wouldn't listen. I told him to slow down, take it easy, but he used up his wishes same way he

19

did everything. Too fast. Then he shipped me off—bottle and all—to America, so none of his enemies in France could get hold of me."

"What other famous people in history did you grant wishes to?"

Eugene blushed. "Now you're asking me to brag, mama, and that ain't cool. I'm just a modest ol' genie who's into Janis Joplin and The Mamas and the Papas when I'm not on call. Love music. Can you dig it?"

For the first time that day, Lauren really laughed. How had she been lucky enough to get stuck with a time-warped genie from the sixties? "Yeah, Eugene, as a matter of fact I can dig it just fine."

Eugene returned the smile, then looked around the shop. "You know, mama, Tillie and Toots are right. You got this pad lookin' so fine nobody's gonna buy a thing from you."

Lauren followed his gaze, then shrugged. "Since I have you, maybe I don't have to worry about that. You're prepared to grant me some wishes, aren't you?"

Eugene frowned, tugging at his goatee again. "You wantin' to make them already? Didn't you hear what I said about that Corsican? He wouldn't have lost the battle at Waterloo if he hadn't been so impetuous."

"But I hate this antique shop. I hate old!" She gasped in embarrassment as soon as the words were out of her mouth. "Oh, I didn't mean you. You are very old, aren't you?"

"Age is a state of mind," Eugene huffed. "I don't feel a day over thirty, but if you're going to get personal, I just celebrated my birthday a couple of months ago. Two thousand thirty years to be exact."

Lauren couldn't help it, couldn't check it. "Wow!"

"Look, here's the deal," Eugene said, his back to her, but his annoyance still clear in his tone. "Take some time, mama. Think about what you want to wish for. I'll be in my pad. You decide on something, you just rub the lamp, and I'll come runnin' . . . actually smokin'."

"Don't go, Eugene! I want to ask you some questions about all of this."

But Eugene had disappeared in the blink of an eye. Lauren was surprised at how quickly she missed him. She sighed, sorry she had offended him, then jumped when he called to her from behind.

"Back here, mama. Thought I'd better change this sign in the window if you want to talk. No sense getting interrupted by customers right in the middle of everything."

Lauren looked at the sign which now read Closed. "Good thinking. Besides, as I said, now that you're here to help me, I don't know if I want to open the store anyway."

Eugene was immediately sitting behind her again on the counter.

"Don't do that, Eugene! At least not until I have a chance to get used to you."

"Sounds to me like you're plannin' on wishing me away right now. So what's it gonna be?"

"I'm not in that big of a hurry. But I want to understand. I get three wishes, right?"

Eugene nodded. "Used to be more. Aladdin got as many as he wanted, but people got greedy so we unionized in the twenties—nineteen twenties, that is. One of the first things we did was set a limit."

"Okay, but can I make some test wishes? You know, just feel you out? I mean, is that allowed?"

Eugene seemed not to hear as he studied a tattoo on his forearm that read Peace, but he surprised her by answering unexpectedly. "Yeah, I suppose that'd be cool, but you gotta be careful how you phrase 'em. You can't just say, 'I wish' 'cause I'll have to grant 'em. But you can say, 'What if I wished?' "

Lauren smiled. Really smiled, as she hadn't in weeks. This was going to be fun. "Okay," she said. "What if I wished that I was back in Chicago at my job at the ad company with a big promotion?"

"That's easy. You'd have it all. You could even wish that you'd be their star, dreaming up the best ad promos in the business. That's what would happen. But, Lauren, you wouldn't be happy, because in granting your wishes, I can't change the will of others."

Lauren's hopes sagged. "So what you're saying is, even if I got the promotion and became their star exec, Clifton Hedges would still think women should be relegated to the home and kept barefoot and tending babies, and the men would still be try-

22

ing to cut my throat at every turn."

"Right on, mama."

"And if I were to wish that Charles and I would get married, same thing?"

Eugene shrugged "Afraid so, but the question is, why do you want to tie yourself up with an uptight dude like Charles Edmund Dumont, anyway?"

"You know about Charles? Do you know everything?"

"Now don't get mad, but your aunt asked me to check out this Charles. I went up to Chicago and looked him over. One uptight dude if I ever met one."

"You actually met him?" Lauren asked. And when Eugene nodded, she had a fit of giggles. Just the thought of Charles talking with someone as offbeat and different as Eugene was hilarious. Charles would certainly seem like a stuffed shirt to Eugene, she supposed. Still, she ought to be offended; after all, they were practically engaged. And Charles *was* what she'd always wanted. He represented everything that was important to her — stability, security, predictability.

As her giggles subsided, a sense of depression enveloped her. She sighed as she sank into a chair and bent forward to hug her calves. "Oh, Eugene, I'm such a mess. All I ever wanted was to be successful and happy and loved. I was for a while . . . successful and happy, at least. Two out of three's not bad, I guess. Then Aunt Edna left me all this money and I thought I was home free. I bought that BMW out there, and I'm going to use a chunk of the money for the society wedding we'll have in a year or two. That is *if* Charles and I ever become officially engaged. He's very cautious. And sometimes I can't help wondering if we got together just because he thought I could help advance his career."

"Dudes like him are a dime a dozen and not worth your worry," Eugene said softly. "I know we just met, but your aunt Edna told me a lot about you. You deserve someone special, someone who would be mad about you just for *you*, even in spite of you, you dig?"

Lauren could feel her eyes misting and a lump had formed in her throat, so she merely smiled her gratitude at the compliment. It wasn't just that she appreciated Eugene paying it, but also that it reminded her of the kindness of the aunt she had loved so dearly and lost. Too, she thought about the happiness she had known when Charles first started courting her. He'd made her feel important, needed, as if her opinions mattered. But she couldn't quite forget that that had been in the beginning. Recently, since his rise in the company, he'd seemed too often annoyed by any show of independence. Take her trip to Louisiana, for instance. He'd been downright rude, ridiculing her determination to fulfill her aunt's wishes. What if Eugene was on target about Charles Dumont? What if she'd been too hasty in selecting him as a life-mate? She sighed, then almost in a whisper, spoke her fears aloud.

"Well, if you're right about Charles, I wish I'd

meet that special someone, Eugene."

Lauren didn't realize she had made the wish until she saw Eugene close his eyes, fold his arms, and give a mighty shudder which ended with a snap of his head.

She opened her mouth to protest as she suddenly understood that this was part of the ritual he went through in the process of granting wishes. "No, no," she wanted to shout, but a loud crash in front of the store checked her words.

Eugene was at the window before her. Glancing back over his shoulder at Lauren, he said, "I think Prince Charming has arrived."

Chapter Two

"Oh, no," Lauren said, "Tell me that crash wasn't what I think it was."

Eugene's wide smile spread across his thin face. "Hey, now, the situation called for drastic measures. 'Sides, it's hardly more than a scratch, and nothing I can't fix with the blink of an eye."

Lauren sighed in exasperation and was headed for the front door, when it was flung open.

"I know you're closed," began the stranger who had just entered, pointing over his shoulder at the sign on the door. "But I'm trying to find the owner of the beemer that's parked out front."

Lauren was surprised at the tears which sprang to her eyes. Surely she wasn't going to cry! Yes, she was! She was going to sit right down here in the middle of the floor and sob her heart out. She was going to kick and scream and throw a childish tantrum such as her mother had never even seen in all the years of her turbulent childhood. It just wasn't fair. Please, not her new car!

Suddenly, the tears dried as quickly as they'd appeared, replaced by a hot surge of anger. "Look, mister, if you've so much as scratched my car, I'll sue you for everything you have." Now her anger evaporated as a giggle escaped her lips. *Sue him for everything he had?* From the looks of him, that probably amounted to pocket change. Obviously, she was still teetering on the verge of some kind of breakdown. One second she'd been about to cry, then been so angry she'd been about to strike something, and then she'd actually giggled. Why, she hadn't giggled in years.

Looking from one man to the other, she ran a shaking hand through her hair. "I'm sorry, I don't think I can handle this right now. Eugene, would you please talk to this . . . this gentleman. Go out and see how much damage there is to my car—you *did* hit my car?"

The stranger tucked his thumbs into his jeans pockets and rocked on his heels. "Afraid so, although for the life of me, I still can't figure out how. One minute I was thinking about my kid's birthday—what I should buy her, you know. And the next, pow." He offered a crooked grin and a shrug of what must have been intended as apology. "It's really not too bad though. If you'd just come outside and take a look, I can give you the name of my insurance company. We

27

can get this all settled in a matter of minutes."

He'd turned his attention to Eugene, obviously preferring to deal with the strange-looking man sitting Indian fashion on the counter than trying to reason with this flaky girl.

Eugene was at the door so fast both Lauren and the stranger looked bemused. "Be back in a flash with the accident report, mama. You just hang loose." Eugene flung the door open, waited until the newcomer had left, then said to Lauren, "Not bad, huh?"

Lauren opened her mouth to scream with rage, but Eugene was already gone, so she muttered a curse instead. "Why?" she asked the room. "What have I ever done to deserve any of this? Just tell me that!" she said, making her way to the front window and peering through the blinds.

Her frustration mounted as she realized that from her vantage point it was impossible to determine the extent of damage to her car. She diverted her attention to the faces of the two men. Eugene was laughing for heaven's sake. And the stranger . . . why he was grinning from ear to ear, shrugging his shoulders and talking a mile a minute.

Focused on him now, she recalled Eugene's parting shot and reiterated his comment.

Not bad? No, not if you were into reprobates. And this one fit the bill. Holes in the knees of his jeans might be fashionable on a teenager—

and the way he filled his out. . . . Well, enough along those lines, she silently chastised herself. And what about that T-shirt? *Jazz musicians do it with rhythm.* His near-black hair was only a few inches shorter than hers, and he clearly hadn't shaved in a couple of days. He glanced up at her just then, flashing her a dazzling smile. She jerked back from the window as if burned. Okay, Eugene, so he does have the most magnificent mouth I've ever seen, but even you can't argue with what Aunt Edna used to say: "A man's soul is reflected in his eyes." This guy's eyes—for all that they were the most startling green she'd ever looked into—definitely reflected the soul of a devil.

She craned her neck and saw his car. It was parked at an angle, its front bumper apparently resting against her left front fender. Her eyes widened with incredulity. She had expected a relic from a junkyard but instead found herself staring at a candy apple red Vette convertible. Okay, so she'd been wrong. He wasn't broke, but you didn't have to be penniless to be a bum.

She frowned as she saw the two men laugh. Exactly what was so funny about a dent in her car? It'd taken her two years to save up enough just for the down payment. She was about to go out and give them a piece of her mind when they started toward the shop. Eugene was talking a mile a minute and the handsome stranger was laughing again.

"Well?" Lauren asked as soon as they entered. But the stranger's attention was on Eugene, who was once again seated on the counter, his legs and arms folded in front of him. "How does he do that?" he asked Lauren.

"He . . . he . . . oh, never mind. Tell me about my car."

He scratched his head. "I'm not sure what to tell you. When I hit the beemer, I got out and checked the damage. It wasn't extensive to either car, but they definitely bore battle scars. But when we went to check out the damage, there was hardly a scratch. They were fine. That's great news, I guess, but I still don't know how I could have . . ."

Lauren couldn't prevent the smile that stole across her face. She turned it in gratitude on the genie, who grinned like the Cheshire cat and gave her a conspiratorial wink.

"Well, what say you two go out and celebrate?" Eugene suggested.

"Celebrate?" Lauren and the stranger both sputtered in unison.

"Why not? You're closed for business, Lauren. And you, my man, have just had the great fortune of running your car into the vehicle of New Orleans' prettiest new resident. Being a native of the nation's most hospitable city, I don't know how you could refuse buying my boss a cup of coffee."

"Don't pay him any attention. He's got a bad

habit of interfering," Lauren said, at the same time casting Eugene a stern look that said all to clearly 'Butt out.' "

The man tucked his thumbs once again into his jeans pockets and began rocking on his heels in the way Lauren had noticed before. She wished he wouldn't do that, but couldn't stop her gaze from traveling downward to his legs and noticing how his jeans tightened against his straining thigh muscles in a way that was just too enticing.

"Look—" she began.

"No," the man interrupted. "You look. Eugene's absolutely right. We lucked out with the damage—bumpers must have run interference. But I did scare you almost to tears. The least I can do is buy you a cup of coffee. Besides, it'll be a novel experience for me. I don't think I've seen New Orleans before noon in three years."

Lauren hardly registered the invitation. She was too busy fighting the blush she could feel spreading up from her neck. *He'd seen the tears!* He must think her an idiot. But why did she care what he thought? She already detested everything she'd decided he stood for.

"Well? What do you say?"

Lauren blinked. Why, what did he think she'd say? No, of course, but before she could get the words out of her mouth, her "assistant" answered for her.

"Hey, dude, she says yes."

The stranger unhooked his thumbs and took her elbow, the gentlemanly gesture provoking an arched brow.

Lauren stood her ground, refusing to budge until he'd answered a question or two. "Before we go, what is your name?" *Before we go?* Where had that come from?

The man laughed, and this time he received more than a mere raised brow. The rich, deep sexy timbre of his laughter inspired a glare directed at Eugene. Well, she'd show them both. It took more than a hot bod, terrific eyes, and a sexy voice to turn her on. She was much more into the cerebral than the physical, and in spite what Mr. Eugene Genie thought, he'd clearly goofed with his matchmaking this time. She smiled as she waited for his laughter to subside. She couldn't wait to hear his name. Probably something straight out of a romance novel.

"Sorry. As I said, still too early for me." He let go of her elbow and stuck out his hand. "Sam North," he said.

Lauren couldn't resist the satisfied grin. Yep, straight out of a book. Then she frowned. Maybe that was exactly where her aunt's friend had found him—in a romance novel. Well, she had news for Mr. Genie. She might be twenty-nine years old and well on her way to spinsterhood, but she wasn't desperate enough to want some fictional character conjured up from a book.

"Now that all the formalities are out of the way, you ready to go?" he asked.

"Umm, would you mind if I spoke with my, ah, assistant for just a moment?"

Sam hunched his shoulders. "Fine. I'll just go on out and move my car off the road." He turned to the man perched on the counter. "Stay cool, Eugene."

Eugene grinned and unfolded his arms long enough to salute the musician with his fingers spread in a vee. "Peace, man."

Lauren rolled her eyes, but as soon as the door closed, she whirled around to glare at the genie. "All right, Eugene. Enough's enough. I know I wished for a man, but I didn't mean it . . . and even if I did, Mr. Sam Smooth out there isn't him."

"What's wrong with him, mama?" Eugene asked, his eyes widening with almost comical amazement. "He's handsome, smart, talented — a musician, did I tell you? And he definitely thinks you're something special."

He does? No way, Lauren. Don't let Eugene sidetrack you with flattery. "Looks are unimportant."

"Yeah, guess I should have figured you felt that way when I met ole Chuck up in Chicago."

Lauren ignored the dig. "And as for him being a musician . . . why, that alone would turn me off. I prefer responsible adults who *work* for a living. I'm sorry, Eugene, but you bombed it this time." She grabbed her purse from behind the counter, paused to give Eugene a smug can't-win-'em-all smile, then walked to the front door. She paused. "Besides, even if he was everything I could ever desire, I'd want him to be someone *real;* not someone you conjured up from your imagination."

"Hey, mama, he's real as rain. Genies are good, I'll give you that, but even we can't make a man up out of smoke."

"Oh, come on, Eugene, you said it yourself. He's just a little too good—in the looks department, anyway. So, a word to the wise. Next time you're gonna mumbo jumbo someone up, try to come up with a name that's not so . . . so . . . Oh, never mind."

The sound of Eugene's amusement followed her out the store.

Just three blocks from the antique shop, Sam eased the car to a stop in front of a small cafe.

"Well, I guess this is it," Lauren said. A small, tentative smile slipped away with his next words.

"Yep. Make the best chicory coffee in the state of Louisiana. And it's even better laced with a jigger of brandy. I've only slept three hours. I need something to get the juices stirring."

Well, this was just terrific. An alcoholic rogue

musician! When she got back to the shop, she was going to make sure Eugene was fired from his union. In the meantime, she would just keep everything light. Be polite and distant. Bore him to tears and maybe he'd slug his brandied coffee and get her back fast. "Oh, I'm sorry. Why did you only get three hours' sleep? I mean, I know you're a musician, so of course you sleep days—"

"Had to get up and take my kid to the dentist."

"You're married?" Lauren asked, then immediately regretted her tone. So what if he was? She was never going to see him again, anyway, and sharing a cup of coffee hardly constituted a violation of marriage vows.

"Divorced."

Before she could even register a reaction to this pronouncement, Lauren found herself being escorted from the low-slung car and into the restaurant.

The room they entered was like so many other small cafes she'd visited in the weeks since her arrival in the Big Easy. Like the city, the ambience of the restaurant was one of casual ease. Autographed pictures of local celebrities, including Pete Fountain, several Saints football players, and Paul Prudhomme, the famous chef, lined the walls. She recognized the man standing behind the small corner bar—his narrow bearded face could be found in most of the pictures as well. Obviously the owner. Several plants which had all seen better days lined the wide windows, and the tables were covered with graying plastic cloths. Lauren tried to hide her distaste by fidgeting with the napkin-wrapped place setting in front of her.

"Coffee straight, chicory, or brandied?" Sam asked.

"Brandied," Lauren replied, then almost gasped in surprise. Well, why not? Scarcely three hours into her day, and she'd already had enough upsets to unsettle a demolition expert. Then more firmly: "Definitely laced."

Sam grinned and winked. "That's my girl." He signaled the man behind the bar, then turned his attention back to his breakfast partner. "How about some beignets? You know. doughnuts. Pierre's absolutely melt in your mouth."

As soon as they were served, Sam asked Lauren about her move to New Orleans. "Your friend, Gene, tells me you're from Chicago. How'd you decide to settle in New Orleans?"

Lauren swizzled the heavy cream into her coffee as she answered. "My aunt died a few months ago. She'd never had children of her own, so she left everything to me—house, business, the whole shebang. Ordinarily, I would never have considered moving here, but events in my life seemed to conspire against me."

"Ah, and are you glad? Do you like New Orleans?"

"Like it? I hate it!" Seeing the way his eyebrows drew together, she immediately regretted her candid outburst and tried to soften her words. "I mean, it's so different from what I'm accustomed to. I'm afraid I'm a bit of a stickler for order, and there doesn't seem to be much of that in Louisiana."

Once again she could feel her face heat as his slow, deliberate gaze trailed over her body, and his tone as he answered. "Yes, I can see that you can be a real pain in the backside about that. Bet all your shirts even face the same way on the hangers in your closet, huh?"

"Well, of course—" Lauren began, then broke off to glare at him as she raised the mug to her lips. She cried out in the next instant as the coffee burned her tongue, then almost poured the scalding liquid on his head when she caught his grin.

Apparently Sam realized he might have pushed her too far, for he offered a truce of sorts with his next words. "I love this zany city, but I guess it's not for everyone. But I don't understand. If you hate it, why not put the shop and house up for sale and move back north? By the way what did you do in Chicago? Obviously you weren't into antique sales there."

"I'm an account executive with a prestigious advertising firm. But it's not that simple. For one thing, like I said, my life was in a state of upheaval when Aunt Edna died—but I don't

37

want to get into that. Besides, it was her dying wish that I at least give it a try. She left me everything. I feel I owe her that much."

Sam grinned at her answer, and holding his mug, leaned the chair back on two legs as he studied her insolently for a long moment. "So let me get this straight. Your delicate senses are offended by lack of order. You drive a beemer, so you've got bucks. Obviously well-educated and ambitious. And self-sacrificing to boot. Lady, I think you're just too good to be true."

Lauren's eye's widened at the insult, and she could feel self-pitying tears threatening, but she wouldn't give him the satisfaction of seeing her cry. "Obviously, Mr. North, this was a mistake." She pushed her chair from the table, grabbed her purse, and stood up. Quickly extracting a five-dollar bill from her purse, she tossed it onto the table. She was tempted to leave without another word, but vanity got the best of her. "I happen to think I'm a very together person; a woman of the nineties. Something a caveman such as yourself clearly has had no experience with."

The front legs of Sam's chair thudded to the floor with a bang. "On the contrary, honey, I've had enough experience dealing with your type to last me a lifetime. My ex was *Ms* Superwoman, too. That's why she's my ex."

"A very lucky woman, your ex" was Lauren's parting shot.

By the time Lauren got back to the shop, she was livid. She would have refused Sam's offer to drive her back had he made it, but the cad had just sat there when she walked out.

It was only three blocks between the cafe and her store — or should have been, but she'd taken a wrong turn as soon as she stepped outside. What should have been a five-minute walk had turned into a sixty-minute exercise.

Her feet ached.

Her head was pounding.

She was furious, and Eugene had better have crawled back into his bottle if he knew what was good for him.

Obviously Eugene was not concerned with his physical well-being, for he was seated atop a large chest playing host.

For a few seconds Lauren forgot her pique with the handsome stranger and even Eugene as she realized he had a guest. Lauren looked at the strangely clad woman seated across from Eugene on an old dresser, legs folded, the wide hem of her embroidered muumuu drawn around her knees. The woman, not young by any means, nevertheless wore her faded blond hair in long pigtails that were tied off with beaded strings. Lauren tried not to stare, but she could swear the woman had a small gold loop in her nose, and her peace-sign earrings were as large as tires.

Another genie? Lauren wondered. Wonderful! Simply terrific!

Pressing a hand to her forehead and covering her eyes, she leaned against the counter. If she didn't know better, she'd swear she was caught in the "Twilight Zone" and had just been beamed back thirty years into the sixties. A voice to her left made her jump.

"You all right, mama?" Eugene asked.

"Damn it, Eugene, don't do that!"

Eugene backed away, his hands held up in surrender. "Sorry, mama. Guess I forget you're not used to the way I move. I'm so used to Edna and Lovey, here, I forgot myself."

"Lovey?" Lauren mouthed as she took her hands from her eyes and glanced questioningly at the strange woman sitting on the dresser.

"Oh, sorry, you don't know Lovey." Eugene made the introductions. "Lauren Kennedy, meet Lovey True. Lovey owns the health food store, The Spice of Life, next door. She and your aunt Edna were good friends."

Well, at least she *wasn't* another genie, Lauren thought as she managed a weak smile before turning her attention back to Eugene. "Think you could whip up a couple of aspirin and a glass of water?"

Both water and pills appeared almost immediately in Eugene's outstretched hands. "Your

40

wish is my command, mama."

"Lauren . . . please, just call me Lauren."

Lovey and Eugene exchanged tolerant grins that annoyed Lauren further. "While we're on the subject of wishes, Eugene —"

"Oh, yeah, how did it go with our musician friend?" Eugene asked. "He came in a few minutes ago. Didn't seem too happy. Just picked out a doll — the ceramic bridal one — and left. I was going to ask him what he thought about you, but he seemed to have a headache, too, so I didn't push it," Eugene told her.

Lauren frowned. "He came back by here? He bought a doll?" She shook her head, more confused than ever. "I don't understand. I thought he came in because you caused him to hit my car."

"Seems he hit the car when it suddenly occurred to him to buy his kid an antique doll for her birthday," Eugene explained.

"Well, anyway, as I was saying, you certainly blew my first wish. Prince Charming turned out to be the biggest toad I ever met."

"Impossible," Eugene replied genially. "Sam North is Mr. Right, guaranteed."

"Sam North ia a rude, insufferable jerk, and a *big* mistake on your part. You might be great at getting rid of dents, producing water and aspirin out of thin air, and moving around in the blink of an eye, but as a matchmaker, you're a failure. Trust me, Eugene, if that's the best you can

41

do, you'd better turn in your genie papers."

Lauren was truly upset by the musician's rude comments earlier and more than a bit unsettled by all the morning's events. But she had intended to lighten the situation by being overly dramatic, so she was surprised at the look that Eugene and Lovey exchanged. She could swear they were both afraid. But of what? Before she could ask, Eugene yawned and stretched exaggeratedly, excusing himself to return to his bottle for a nap. He was gone in a whiff of smoke.

Lovey immediately unfolded her spindly legs, and scooted her bulky torso from the dresser top. "It was nice meeting you, Lauren. Hope you'll like it here. If I can help in any way, you know where to find me."

Lauren's frown quickly mirrored the one on Lovey's face. "Wait a minute, Lovey. What happened? What did I say? Did I hurt Eugene's feelings because I told him he had botched it with Sam North? He did, but it's okay. I'm really not in the market for a man right now anyway. I didn't mean to upset Eugene though."

Lovey stared down at a place on the floor following the circle her foot was tracing. "I really should get back to the shop. I just hired a new salesgirl, and I don't know how well she'll do on her own for more than a few minutes."

Exhausted from the wild and crazy morning, Lauren surprised herself with her burst of energy as she pushed herself away from the counter. In a few quick steps she crossed the space between them to grab Lovey's shoulder. "Please, wait. I've really offended Eugene, haven't I?"

Lovey glanced up, then back down again. "I don't know if Eugene would want me worrying you."

"Look, I'm not too up on genie rules, but it seems to me if I remember correctly, the person who rubs the lamp or bottle or whatever it is he lives in, is his boss in a manner of speaking. Is that right?"

Lovey shrugged. "I suppose so."

"Then shouldn't I be told if something is seriously wrong?"

After a few more words of persuasion, Lovey let herself be led to the back of the store, where she reluctantly admitted the truth to Lauren.

When Lovey was finished, Lauren shed her mantle of uncertain store owner and pulled on the more familiar cloak of authority she'd worn as a corporate executive. "Okay, let me see if I have this straight. Genies don't die, they just fade away. But before they fade away they show signs of illness by not being able to deliver wishes. Is that about right?"

Tears shone in Lovey's brown eyes, and her lips trembled as she nodded. "Eugene's getting up there in genie years, and lately there have been, well, signs. Nothing as serious as a botched wish, but if he is wrong about your

Sam North, then this could be the first major indication that he'll soon be . . . ah, leaving us."

"Your very fond of Eugene, aren't you?"

"I've loved him since I first met him years ago."

"Isn't there anything we can do?"

Lovey didn't answer, but the bright fuchsia flush which covered her face was a dead giveaway.

"There is! What?"

But Lovey shook her head. "There's nothing I can do, no."

"Because you love him?"

Lovey nodded, then noisily sniffed back tears.

"Which means there's something *I* can do, but you can't tell me, right?"

Lovey set her lips and looked at the floor once again, refusing to say more.

Grabbing her hand, Lauren pulled Lovey after her through the store. "Come on, let's take a walk and talk about it."

Once outside, Lauren began counting off suggestions. At each one, Lovey became more and more dejected, though she refused to comment. Finally, Lauren offered the one she was most reluctant to suggest. "Okay, so you can't tell me, but what if I was wrong? What if Mr. Music and I merely got off on the wrong foot? What if Eugene isn't starting to fade at all?"

For the first time, Lovey raised her gaze from the pavement. Her face actually lit up when she met Lauren's eyes. "Oh, Lauren, do you think that's possible? You sounded so adamant before. I mean, even Poor Eugene was convinced he'd bombed."

Lauren was mentally cursing herself for even suggesting the possibility. She *knew* she wasn't wrong. Sam North was everything she detested in a man. But maybe she could pretend she was mistaken until she figured out what she could do to save Eugene. She couldn't believe it mattered so much to her. After all, she'd only met the strange little man a few hours before, and he'd already complicated her life more than anyone had a right to do. But in spite of her resolve not to like anything or anyone in New Orleans, she had to admit he was an endearing genie—not that she had any basis for comparison, of course.

She became aware that Lovey was speaking to her. "I'm sorry, what did you say?"

"I asked if you'll go see Sam again and find out. It's terribly important, Lauren."

"Of course I will, Lovey," Lauren lied. *Find* the man again? No way! There had to be a better way. She squeezed Lovey's hand. "Look, I've got to get back to the shop. But don't worry. We'll work this out, I promise."

Lovey smiled, still with sadness in her eyes, but Lauren thought she detected a glimmer of hope as well.

Once back at the shop, she quickly summoned

45

Eugene with a brisk rub on the lamp. When the smoke billowed from the spout, she realized that she was already calmly accepting the bizarre ritual. Perhaps she was more resilient than she'd believed, but Eugene's dejected expression quickly brought her thoughts back to the matter at hand.

"Sorry to bother you, Eugene, but I've been thinking. It wasn't entirely your fault that Sam North appeared suddenly at my door." Casting him a sidelong glance as she paused, she noticed his slumped shoulders and the woebegone, hangdog look in his eyes. Intensifying her sales pitch, she began to pace at the same time, waving her hands much as she'd done not so long ago in her job at the ad agency. "I mean, at least consider this. I was making test wishes. The slip of the tongue about finding Mr. Right was just that, nothing more. Don't forget, there is Charles waiting impatiently for me in Chicago." She stopped in front of him, spreading her arms. "So what do you think?"

Eugene smiled halfheartedly, reaching up to pat her shoulder. "I think you're a very nice young woman just as Edna said you were, and I appreciate you trying to make me feel better."

"No! It's not that. I really believe your subconscious confused my slip of the tongue with my test wishes. Can't we start over? You could give me my three wishes from here, and we'll both just forget all about Sam North. What do you say?"

With a halfhearted shrug, Eugene agreed. "Sure, Lauren, we can play it that way. But I'm going to turn in for now. I'm suddenly exhausted."

Lauren frowned. "What happened to 'mama' and hip words like 'crash' instead of 'turn in'?"

Eugene gave a weary grin. "Just too much effort right now, I guess. Don't worry, I'll feel better after a nap."

"But what if I decide on a wish? If you're sleeping, you won't even know that I've settled on one. How can we prove you're as good as new that way?"

"I'll know," he said. "No matter where you are, I'll hear your wish."

"You sure?" Lauren asked, not convinced.

"Tell you what, you make a wish, I'll send a signal to let you know it's been granted." At her deepening frown, he added, "Trust me, Lauren, I'll hear it, grant it, and you'll realize that I've given you your heart's desire."

Lauren felt suddenly unexpectedly close to tears. She should never have agreed to come to New Orleans. She should have just put the estate up for sale and let the lawyers and real estate agents handle it all. Why, she couldn't even help this poor genie feel better. Instead, he was trying to cheer her up.

As if reading her mind, Eugene seemed to

rally long enough to appear at her side. Putting his arm around her, he asked if he might give her a piece of advice. Feeling sorry for herself, Lauren sniffled and nodded.

"Listen, kiddo, I know a lot about you from your aunt. For example, I know that security is at the top of your list of priorities, that you are cautious by nature and afraid of risk. Kinda up-tight for my taste ordinarily, but your aunt Edna had faith in you—she left you her fortune. So now you have the security you've always craved, but life is about more than money." The genie paused, shrugging his wiry shoulders. "I trusted Edna's judgment more than anyone I've met over the centuries, so I don't really believe you're going to need my magic. I'll do my best to grant your wishes if you do, but I think you need only to learn to loosen up a touch, learn to enjoy life, experience it, and trust your emotions."

A few minutes later the genie had disappeared into his bottle once again, and Lauren decided to close the shop. The entire day had been a bust, and she felt more depressed than she had since coming to New Orleans. "But damn it, I'm going to find a way to help you, Eugene," she said as she passed by his bottle to close out the cash register. As she moved about the store, turning off lights and securing the doors, she thought of ways to go about keeping that promise.

Maybe if she made her wishes real easy . . .

but that wouldn't work. He *did* mess up with Mr. Sam North, so unless she found a way to save the genie, it didn't matter what she wished for.

She was just getting into her car when Lovey True beckoned from across the street. "Yoo-hoo, Lauren, wait a second."

Lauren waited, a smile in place as the other woman approached, for she suddenly sensed that it was as important to keep Lovey as encouraged as Eugene. "Leaving early," she said as Lovey crossed the narrow road in her direction. "Got some thinking to do."

"About Eugene? Bless you. He kind of gets under your skin right away, doesn't he?"

Lovey's face had brightened with her wide smile, which Lauren found irresistible. "Gotta agree. He's a special man." She patted Lovey's plump shoulder as she opened her car door with her other hand and started to slip inside. "We're going to find a way to keep him around, too. Don't you worry."

"Oh, I'm not," Lovey said. "Ever since you mentioned that you were probably wrong about Sam North, I've felt better. Guess I'm just a worrywart."

Lauren groaned inwardly but kept the smile plastered in place. "Well, he certainly is the handsomest man I've ever met." This was said quickly, and just as fast, Lauren changed the subject. "I was wondering about your name

49

Lovey. Did you make it up? It's so different, and clever, too."

Lovey laughed, a delighted little-girl giggle that flitted around them in the breeze. "No, my parents get the blame for that one, as well they should. They were at the Beatles concert when my mother went into labor with me. They were playing my mom's favorite song, 'Love Me Do.' They named me Lovey in tribute. Guess it could have been worse when you consider all the Beatle hits. Think about it." She waved and turned to go in, but quickly turned back to face the new shop owner. "Oh, Lauren, I almost forgot why I stopped you. Sam North."

Lauren almost flinched, but she managed to work interest into her expression and tone. "What about him?"

"I didn't tell you where you can find him. I know him. He's a regular in my store. Plays the piano at The Jazzy Lady every night. Oh, and he's your neighbor."

Chapter Three

Sam rubbed sleep from his eyes then squinted through the fading light at the clock on the far wall. Six-thirty already. He'd promised his daughter, Casey, and the aunts that he'd join them for supper before leaving for the club. He tried most evenings to spend a couple of hours with his daughter but wished he could skip tonight. He'd only had a little over three hours' sleep. But of course that was out of the question. Today was Casey's birthday.

Tossing back the covers, he climbed from the bed and groggily struggled into his jeans. Padding barefoot across the oak flooring, he went into the bathroom to splash cold water on his face. He met his dripping reflection in the mirror and was surprised at the scowl. It had been a rotten day all around. Not that he had anyone to blame but himself. The aunts had offered to pick up Casey's birthday gift for him, but he'd insisted on doing it himself. Mistake number

51

one. If he'd let them, he wouldn't have met the new owner of the antique shop.

His second mistake had been inviting Ms Chicago for a cup of coffee. He'd let his hormones override his judgment. In spite of the fact that he'd been immediately attracted to her, he'd realized she wasn't his type. Not that he didn't go for saucy, lithe blondes. Hell, he liked women in general — blonde, brunette, redhead, bald — but not uptight executive types like the one he'd been married to for four years.

He toweled this face, pulled a clean T-shirt over his head, then ran a brush through his hair, all the while going back over the doomed morning. He'd actually made it to bed by noon after picking Casey up at the dentist. But sleep had eluded him. And the damnedest part of it was that he had only himself to blame.

Admitting that the disastrous ending of his coffee with Lauren had been his fault was what had kept sleep at bay.

It wasn't her fault that he'd been married to a workaholic, obsessive man-hater with the ego the size of Lake Pontchartrain. Nor had his comparison of Lauren to his ex-wife been fair, he admitted. And neither was she to blame for not liking New Orleans or for being ambitious and wanting more than a small antique business. It was just all too painfully familiar. Didn't he have the same conversation every time he talked to Casey's mother?

"How can you stand it, Sam?" she'd said when she called the night before to arrange Casey's flight back to New York next week for the new school year. "To be out of the mainstream, stuck in a societal swap—excuse the pun, darling—playing bar music for tourists, for God's sake!"

At that point he'd hung up.

No, he definitely hadn't been fair to Lauren. He'd been a cad to let her walk out of the restaurant without offering her a ride back. He'd calmed down by the time he'd finished his coffee, even admitted his guilt in provoking her. He should have waited for her when he'd gone back to the shop to pick up the doll. Better still, he should have gone to look for her when he realized she had probably lost herself in the look-alike streets. But he'd done neither. Just bought the doll from that weird hippie and left. Well, he'd certainly paid for his mistake. His conscience had niggled at him all afternoon, and he'd be miserable at the club tonight after losing so much sleep.

He pulled a fresh dinner jacket, slacks, and shirt from the closet and flung them on the bed. He was about to set his shoes out when a ping on the window stopped him. Grinning for the first time since he'd awakened, he crossed to the window to signal to his daughter that he'd be right down. Should never have encouraged her to wake him with pebbles against the glass, he thought. When she'd come to visit last year at Mardi Gras, she'd barely managed to hit the crepe myrtle growing up the side of the garage apartment he'd claimed as his own since the aunts had moved into the main house. Now she rarely missed hitting the windowpane squarely in the middle.

He was moving away from the window when he noticed the light of the setting sun flash on pale gold hair on the walkway next door. Pressing his face close to the window, he strained for a closer look. Surely his eyes were playing tricks on him. The woman leaving the house couldn't be Lauren. Wouldn't his aunts have told him if someone had moved into Edna Jarrod's house?

But snatches of conversation immediately began to come back to him:

"She's quite a pretty thing, our dear Edna's niece."

And, "I wish we could go to the shop and help her get everything organized, but I know Edna asked us to let her do it herself."

And what had Casey said just the day before? Something about the neat lady who lived next door and had taken her fishing for crawdads.

Skipping down the stairs and hurrying through the front door, he nearly ran into his daughter.

"Whoa, Dad. Where ya going?"

"Sorry, kid." Sam paused long enough to rub the top of her blond head, but his gaze was fastened on Edna Jarrod's house. "How's my girl?"

"Better after she's opened her presents," Casey teased, her nose wrinkling up prettily with her smile.

Sam stopped, slapped his forehead, then gathered his daughter to him in a tight hug. "Sorry, Case. Guess I'm still half asleep. Happy birthday."

"Thanks, Daddy."

"So how does it feel to be a mature woman of ten?"

Casey groaned and rolled her eyes.

"So when does the big celebration kick off?" Sam asked.

"Not till after dinner," Casey said, pretending to pout. "So get awake so we can eat, will ya? Gosh, I thought you were going to sleep all day."

Sam tousled his daughter's hair playfully. "Hey, give the old man a break, will ya? I didn't get more than a couple of hours' sleep. Had to go shopping for a certain special present this morning."

Casey giggled. "Give me some clues so I don't die from frustration while I wait?"

"Not even one."

"Party pooper," Casey moaned.

"Dinner ready?"

"No, not for another fifteen or twenty minutes, Aunt Tillie says."

Sam's gaze drifted to the house next door,

55

then back to his daughter. "Hey, Case, the lady you went crawdad-netting with yesterday, what was her name?"

"Lauren. Why?" But before her father could answer, Casey saw the object of their discussion exit the side door of her house and turn toward the levee. "Oh, I get it. You must have seen her from your window. Pretty sexy, huh?"

"What would you know about sexy, kid?" Sam asked, but thinking to himself that sexy wasn't exactly the word he would have used. At least until now after he'd just seen her dressed in halter top and shorts. But *crawdad-netting?* Now that was an image he couldn't reconcile with the uptight Ms Lauren Kennedy.

Casey skipped past him, pushing open the heavy door. "Dinner's in fifteen minutes, Dad. Don't forget."

"Okay. Go on in and get washed up. Tell the aunts I'll be in in a few minutes. We'll scarf it down so you can open the loot." He gave her a wide grin and wink. "I think I'm going to wander down to the levee, kind of work out the kinks from my nap."

Casey giggled with childlike glee, but the look in her eyes belied her youth. And her parting statement, just before she pushed the door shut behind her, could only have come from a ten-year-old going on thirty. "Walk south, Dad. You'll have to hurry to catch her, but it'll definitely help you work out the kinks."

Sam didn't have to hurry to catch up with Lauren. She was seated just a few yards past the boundaries of her backyard on a dried smoke-wood weather-whitened log. She sat with elbows propped on her knees, her hands cupping her face. A gentle summer breeze stirred tendrils of hair around her cheeks and eyes, but she didn't seem to notice as she sat watching a ship round a bend in the river.

"Hi," Sam said too loudly. He was immediately sorry when she jerked around, her eyes wide. "I didn't mean to startle you. Are you all right?"

Lauren immediately turned her back to him, obviously not thrilled with his intrusion. "Hi," was all she said.

"Mind if I join you?"

Lauren ignored the question. "So it's true. You are my neighbor."

"Yeah, so I just learned."

"Small world," Lauren murmured.

As Sam sat on the log at her side, he chuckled. "Don't sound so thrilled."

"Oh, sorry," she said, turning to meet his eyes for the first time. "I guess that did sound rude. I didn't mean it. Guess my thoughts are somewhere else."

"Not in a happy place judging from your melancholy tone."

Lauren shrugged. "As a matter of fact, just the opposite. I was thinking of happier times at this place right here. I used to come down here every year when I was a child and spend the summer with my aunt. Uncle Paul was always away on business trips, so Edna and I'd come out here to net for crawdads or simply spread a blanket and eat dinner under the stars and smell the night jasmine. I really miss her today."

Suddenly Sam was laughing, but only for an instant, for the glare Lauren turned on him was sobering. He held up his hands. "I'm sorry, Lauren. I wasn't laughing at you. I was laughing at a memory and at how crazy today has been."

Lauren didn't answer but continued to stare at him through angry eyes. She folded her arms over her chest.

"Look," he explained, "today I came into your store just to buy my kid a birthday present. When I hit your car, I forgot the present. At the restaurant I made a complete ass of myself. Then when I remembered the doll, I came back, but I should have waited for you. Guess that proves just how big a jerk I am." He paused, staring down at the ground where a colony of ants were busily at work. "I really am sorry for the way I acted, by the way. I was going to come by the shop tomorrow and apologize, but when I glanced out my window I saw you. Then it all came together, pieces of conversation my aunts have been dropping around me for the past few weeks, and Casey, my kid, too.

And just now, the most incredible of all coincidences hit me between the eyes. I *know* you."

Lauren's frown changed from one of anger to perplexity. "What are you talking about? Of course you know me. You met me this morning, but I don't see what's so funny about that. If I remember correctly, you don't seem to like what you know. As a matter of fact, you made that abundantly clear."

Sam was chuckling and shaking his head at the same time. "Like I said, I'm sorry, but when I talk about knowing you, I don't mean just from this morning. I've known you for years. I just didn't remember the name. Guess that's 'cause you were always Wendy to me."

"What are you—" She gasped suddenly, then covered her mouth with her hand before mumbling, "Peter?"

"Yeah! Peter Pan, that's me. We must have played that game for what, two or three summers." He grabbed her hand and suddenly pulled her to her feet "Look, over there. See between those trees? That was our Never-Never Land, and over there," he said, steering her left to a small inlet of water, "Mermaid Lagoon."

Lauren was laughing now, too. "I can't believe it. I guess I was too young to remember your name. I couldn't have been more than seven or eight the last time I saw you."

"Eight, I think. I was twelve when my parents decided I was ready for military school. After

59

that I usually went to summer camp."

"What ever happened to John and Michael?"

For an instant, Sam seemed confused, but his eyes suddenly widened with understanding. "Ah, my brother, Scott, and the little kid from up the street. What was his name, anyway? Oh, well, doesn't matter. Scott, uh, that'd be John to Wendy, died two years ago of a heart attack."

"Oh, Sam, I'm sorry. How old was he, for heaven's sake?"

"Only thirty-two," Sam muttered, his eyes no longer amused, but staring out at the Mississippi as if seeing his lost brother there.

Neither of them spoke for a few minutes. Lauren turned away, allowing him a moment to himself as she reclaimed her seat on the log. The silence hung in the air as heavy as the scent of night jasmine.

"Where are your parents?" Lauren asked after a few minutes.

"Dead, too. Mom passed away when I was still in high school. Cancer. Dad had a stroke two years after I graduated from college." He had been speaking with his back to her, but he suddenly turned and surprised her with a dazzling smile that she recalled all too clearly from her encounter with him that morning. "I can't believe I've found Wendy after all these years." He came over to sit beside her again. "You know, I never would have believed that the lady I met today was that little tomboy. Looks like you changed your mind and decided to grow up, after all."

Lauren hugged her bare legs, resting her chin on her knees. "If you remember the story, Wendy always did intend to grow up. It was Peter Pan who refused."

"And I guess you think I've lived out the fantasy pretty well, huh?"

Turning her head so that her cheek was resting on her knees, she gazed up at him. "Oh, I don't know. You went to college, got married, had a child. Must have decided to try it for a while."

Sam didn't answer, but sat hunched over staring out at the water.

"So why didn't it work?" Lauren asked.

"What? Growing up? Sometimes it's not all it's cracked up to be. People grow up too fast, they have heart attacks and die."

"And that's when you decided to come back to Never-Never Land, when your brother died?"

"Not quite, but something like that." Sam stared into Lauren's blue eyes for a long moment, before standing up abruptly. "Well, I think I'd better go in and make peace with the aunts. They're having a special birthday dinner for Casey and are probably not too pleased that I didn't come to the table."

"The aunts?" Lauren asked, knowing who he was talking about of course, but momentarily thrown by the sudden change of topic.

61

"*My* aunts, I should say. Tillie and Toots to everyone who knows them. I can't believe they haven't been over to introduce themselves to you. I've heard them talking about you, though, I didn't really pay attention until I saw you tonight."

"Oh, but they have. Just this morning, as a matter of fact. Although I didn't know they were your aunts or that you were my neighbors until later."

Sam surprised her by smiling. "Quite a day, huh? Even for New Orleans, I'd say it's been unusually wacky. Knowing how you like order, I guess you must have really hated today."

He was only teasing so he was surprised by the sudden flare of anger in her eyes. "Hey, it was a joke, okay? Lighten up, lady."

Lauren was immediately on her feet. She walked a few feet before turning back to meet his gaze. "Sorry, I don't see the humor. I don't like being made fun of. Contrary to what you think, some of us were glad to grow up." She turned her back on him, but looked back over her shoulder long enough to add, "Don't let me keep you. Go on back and have your celebration dinner. I know you must have to get to the club in couple of hours."

Sam had stood up with her, and now he stared at her back, but didn't answer. A muscle flexed in his cheek as he fought his annoyance at her arrogance. Who did she think she was sitting in judgment of him? She didn't know anything about him or his work or his dreams. He opened his mouth to defend himself but clamped it shut again. To hell with it. "You know, Lauren, you were a nice little girl. I wish we could still be friends."

Lauren spun around on her heel, kicking dirt up as she approached him. Stopping at his side, she raised her eyes to meet his gaze which seemed sad. But maybe that was just a trick of the sun meeting the emerald of his eyes. "Unfortunately, we're not children anymore, Sam. Neither are we still pretend friends in a fairyland playground. Real life is not just fun and games."

Sam chuckled, shaking his head. "No, I certainly can't imagine that you find much fun in life much less enjoy playing games."

Lauren was immediately furious again. "Don't you dare judge me! You're so bent on escaping reality you wouldn't know if real life hit you square between the eyes."

Sam folded his arms and grinned. "You're sure one hell of a good-looking woman, Lauren Kennedy—especially when you're all heated up like you are right now. Passion—even passionate anger—is very becoming. Too bad you can't find a better way to direct all that heat."

Too infuriated to even answer, Lauren turned her back on him. She heard the crunch of sand as he started to walk away, but then there was only silence. What was he doing? Why was he just standing there? She started to turn around, but it was too late by then. She heard him returning, and then his hand grabbed her arm, completing the pivot she'd only begun. She opened her mouth to question him, but her eyes widened as she realized his intention, and her voice refused to cooperate as he lowered his head and kissed her.

He held her firmly, one hand clasped at the back of her neck, his other still holding her arm, but he needn't have worried that'd she try to pull away. She was too shocked to move . . . until his tongue slipped between her lips. A jolt of electricity ran the length of her, and a gasp escaped her lips. She would have pulled away then, but he suddenly released her without warning.

"See what you're missing, babe," he said, turning on his heel again to walk away.

How dare he? Who in the hell did he think he was?

But the question that was really making her crazy was why his kiss had affected her the way it had. She loved Charles, was practically engaged to him. Charles was the man of her dreams. Handsome in a conservative way, reliable, respectful, ambitious, and when he held her in her arms and kissed her she felt safe. Sam's kiss had made her feel anything but safe.

She put her hand to her lips and realized she

could still feel the pressure of his mouth, still taste the mint of his breath, and feel the heat of his darting, probing tongue. "I wish he'd try that again," she muttered angrily, kicking sand with the toe of her sandal and turning back toward home.

She shrieked as she ran into the rock wall that was Sam North standing just two feet behind her. He looked surprised at the words he'd overheard, but then a wicked gleam began to shine from his eyes, and his cocky grin spread too easily into place. "With pleasure, ma'am," he murmured.

Before Lauren could protest that she hadn't meant the words, his lips found hers again, and this time she could not ignore their command. She didn't think. She couldn't reason. She could only let her body respond of its own will as one hand gripped his forearm, while the other found the hard muscle of his shoulder, and she leaned into him.

In the distance, she heard the toot of a tugboat. Ordinarily she might not have noticed, but it was not merely the lonely warning to other vessels on the water but a patterned toot-toot-toot that she recognized as the genie's signal. She groaned.

Sam groaned once, too, before letting her go again. But this time he didn't say anything. His eyes questioned her, but she didn't know what they asked. So she merely brushed past him, controlling her pace until she was out of his sight and could break into a confused, angry run.

Both aunts looked up as he entered the dining room. "Did you have a nice visit with Lauren, Sam?" Toots asked.

"We had a visit," he replied with a smile as he pulled out his chair. "I don't know if you would call it nice, exactly. Strange is more like it." As he heaped his plate with potatoes and meat, he looked at his daughter's empty chair! "Where's Case?"

"She's already finished, dear. We excused her to go into the den. She wanted to watch "Growing Pains" until its time to open her presents and have cake and ice cream. It's her favorite, don't you know?"

Sam smiled at his aunt Tillie. "I seem to recall that, yes."

Toots turned the conversation back to their new next-door neighbor. "Don't you like Lauren, dear? Edna was so sure you would. What exactly was it she said about Lauren and Sam, Tillie?"

"She said she always thought the two of you would be perfect for each other."

"Yes, that was exactly what she said, Sister."

Sam swallowed a bite of roast then chased it with a sip of wine, watching the two women exchange satisfied grins. "Well, Edna was a smart lady, all right, but she missed this call. By the way how is it I didn't know Edna had left everything to her niece?"

"Why, I suppose it's because you never listen, dear," Tillie said gently. "You're a good boy, but you could have spent a little more time with Edna before she left us."

"I suppose you're right," Sam agreed before stuffing his mouth again.

"About Lauren, dear, don't you agree she's lovely?" Toots pressed him, once again sharing a secret smile with her sister.

Sam looked from one of his father's sisters to the other as he continued eating his dinner. They were acting oddly. And then it dawned on him. They were trying their hands as matchmakers. No doubt, judging from the comments about Edna Jarrod, they'd discussed all of this with her before her death. Giving both of them a smile and wink, Sam tossed his napkin onto his plate and pushed his chair back. "Well, guess we'd better go let the kid open her presents. Dinner was great, ladies. Sorry you had to hold it for me."

Tillie and Toots were on their feet at once.

"You are going to try to get to know Lauren better now that you've met her, aren't you, dear?" Toots asked.

"I don't think that's the best idea," he said as he kissed both aunts on the cheek. "The lady doesn't seem to approve of me."

Toots shook her head, but it was Tillie who provided the argument. "Oh, no, dear, that can't be. Any woman would love you. Besides, there's magic in the air. I can just feel it. Can't you, Sister?" She winked at Toots who quickly agreed.

"Most definitely, and you know what they say, Sam dear. Where there's magic there's love."

"I thought the expression was 'Where there's smoke there's fire,' " Sam teased on the way into the den.

Tillie patted his arm. "Same thing, dear. Same thing."

Chapter Four

Lauren slammed the kitchen door behind her with enough force to rattle the windows. "Eugene!" she howled, then nearly jumped when he suddenly appeared. "You're going to scare me to death one of these days."

"Sorry," Eugene said, but he looked anything but repentant as he stood wearing his Cheshire cat grin.

"Just what exactly do you find funny?" Lauren demanded.

"Nothing, everything, you, me. This morning I was certain my days were numbered, then you mumbled your wish out there on the levee, and here I am as good as new."

Lauren walked to the kitchen window to stare at the house next door. "I'm glad for you, Eugene. I mean, it's really wonderful that your powers all seem to be intact, but I've got serious problems here."

In the blink of an eye, Eugene was seated at her side on the countertop, his spindly legs folded in front of him. "Hey, Lauren, you got to learn to relax. Ain't nothing so terrible about your situation. You're young, healthy, loaded, and you've just been kissed by the super hunk of the century."

Lauren gave him a look of incredulity on the last point, but turned her eyes back to her neighbors' house, deciding that arguing would be wasted breath. Her genie's mood was too euphoric to be reasoned with. "I *blew* my first wish, Eugene. Sam North might be a terrific kisser, but I had intended to save my wishes until I could make them count for something."

"Lauren, Lauren, Lauren," Eugene said, sounding amazingly like Aunt Edna when she'd been about to deliver one of her famous lectures. "I told you today that you don't need magic, but since you're uptight about it, let me remind you that you still have two more wishes. Just be careful the way you say things." He frowned slightly. "What surprises me is that you're so impetuous. Your aunt always described you as so . . . cautious. Guess no one really ever knows another person."

"I am cautious or maybe prudent's a better word. I'm careful about the things I do, the decisions I make. I rarely suffer slips of the tongue as I have today. It's got to be this crazy city affecting me."

Eugene grinned. "Well, if that's it then, I'll be getting back to my pad."

He was gone from his seat on the counter almost before the words were uttered, but Lauren cried out with surprise when he spoke from just behind her. "Eugene!"

"Sorry. I was halfway home when I remembered to ask you, what did you think about the signal I sent you? Pretty creative, don't you think?"

Despite her pique, Lauren grinned when she remembered the tugboat, but her smile disappeared when she turned to face the genie. He wore a bright blue and green striped shirt and denim bell-bottom jeans, but she could actually see the dusty rose print of the paper on the far kitchen wall through his clothing. Eugene was really fading. She could see right through him!

"What's wrong, Lauren? You're as white as ol' William Tell's boy when his dad shot the apple from his head."

Lauren started to ask if he'd actually witnessed the feat, but she couldn't tear her thoughts away from what was happening before her eyes. Eugene was growing dimmer and dimmer by the minute.

The strange little man's face sobered as he followed her eyes to his shirt. "Guess the celebration I was planning was a bit premature," he muttered. "If you'll excuse me . . ."

He was gone before Lauren could find any words of encouragement. "Poor Eugene," she murmured, turning back toward the window and giving a cabinet door a vicious kick. "Here I was worried about blowing a wish on that overgrown escapee from Never-Never Land, and he's about to vanish into oblivion."

Tears burned behind her eyes as she opened the freezer door and pulled out a TV dinner. She didn't even bother looking to see what the meal was, but ripped open an end and stuck the cardboard container in the microwave. She dashed away a tear, set the timer then hoisted herself up on the counter to sit where Eugene had been perched only moments before.

Well, maybe she was making progress. At least she wasn't crying for herself. With that thought it occurred to her that she'd been pretty self-centered of late. Perhaps, in searching for a way to save the aging genie, she'd forget some of her own troubles for a change.

Ten minutes later, she was seated in the cozy booth her aunt had installed, picking at her dinner, which turned out to be Chicken Kiev but tasted like the cardboard package it came in. She was racking her brain for a solution to Eugene's dilemma when the doorbell sounded. Only then did she remember her neighbor.

"Whatever you're selling, I'm not buying," she called out.

A little girl's giggle answered her.

Lauren scooted quickly from her seat to open the door to Casey. "Hi! What brings you over here? I thought you'd be knee-deep in birthday presents by now."

A smile lighted up Casey's face. "Not yet. Dad and the aunts just finished dinner. I talked them into letting me eat early so I could watch my favorite show." She smiled and her big eyes sparkled with mischief. "Mom says I'm spoiled rotten, but I always take advantage of Christmas and my birthday to get every minute's worth. That's why I'm here. I asked the aunts and my dad if I could invite you over for the party."

Lauren found the girl's allure impossible to ignore. She chuckled. "And of course, how could they refuse you?"

"Yep, exactly. So will you come?"

"As a matter of fact, I bought you a gift. Nothing big, but something I thought you'd like. I was going to bring it over in the morning before you left for the airport."

"You got me a present?"

Lauren couldn't help but laugh at the girl's exuberance. "Just a tiny one. Come on in. I'll run upstairs and get it."

But Casey shook her head. "Nope. If you're going to give me a present, you have to bring it to the party. That's the oldest birthday rule of all."

"Case—"

The child's nose wrinkled up as if with distaste, but her eyes twinkled with mischief. "You sound just like my parents when they're about to tell me no. That's when they shorten my name to 'Case.'"

"Oh, sorry."

"That's all right, as long as you hurry up and come. All the ice cream will be melted by the time we get back. It's fudge ripple, my favorite. Aunt Tillie says it's your favorite, too."

"How does she know that?" Lauren wondered aloud, her brow wrinkling when it occurred to her that Eugene might had told her. Maybe the genie was faking his fading spells just to soften her up, but Casey's answer proved her suspicions groundless.

"She said your Aunt Edna told her to keep a lot of it on hand in case you got sulky. She said it always used to work when you were a kid like me."

Lauren laughed, shaking her head as Casey took her hand and led her out the door. She stopped as she remembered the birthday gift upstairs. "You go ahead. I'll get your present and be over in a minute."

"Hurry! Fudge ripple's not good if it melts. Then it just looks like mud."

Casey ushered her guest into the living room five minutes later. "You look real pretty. How come you changed?"

Lauren fingered the eyelet ruffle of Casey's party dress as she answered. "Now how could I come to a birthday party looking like I did." She held out the small gaily wrapped present just as they entered the room.

"Sit there next to Dad," Casey commanded, falling to her knees among an impressive pile of presents.

Lauren murmured a tentative greeting to the

man she'd been instructed to sit beside, her smile widening as she said hello to the two aunts. For the most part, however, all eyes were focused on the birthday girl, for which Lauren was thankful.

It took Casey less than thirty minutes to unwrap all the gifts, but Lauren noticed the look of rapture that lit the girl's face when she held up the doll her father had selected for her.

"Ohhh," Casey breathed. "Isn't she beautiful?" Still holding the delicate china bridal doll under her arm, she jumped to her feet and carefully stepped over gifts to hug her father with her free arm. "I love you, Daddy. It's the best present of all." Then to Lauren, she said, "She looks kinda like you. I think I'll call her Lauren."

"I'm honored," Lauren told her. And so she was, as well as touched by the obvious love between father and daughter.

"You've still got one more to open," Sam reminded Casey.

"I didn't forget. It's from Lauren." She held the doll out to Sam. "Would you hold her for me while I open it? But be careful. She'll break."

"Yes, ma'am," Sam said with a smile that he directed Lauren's way. It was almost the first time he'd looked her way since she'd arrived, and she couldn't resist its magnetism.

In less than thirty seconds, Casey had the small jewelry box free of its wrappings. Casting them aside, she lifted the lid then squealed with delight. "Crawdads! Oh, Lauren, thank you. They're absolutely perfect!"

"Crawdads?" Sam asked, raising one of his dark eyebrows.

"Not just *crawdads,* silly," Casey answered. *"Gold* crawdads. They're earrings. Now I have a real souvenir to show off when I go back to school." Scrambling to her feet, she scampered across the room to hug Lauren and kiss her cheek. "I love them, Lauren. They're special because they'll always remind me of you."

Lauren was touched by the girl's affection and returned the hug with ardor. "You're more than welcome, sweetheart. I'm glad you like them."

"Well, who's ready for cake and ice cream?" Tillie asked.

"None for me," Sam said, standing up. "I've got to practice before I go to the club." He tugged at his daughter's ponytail. "But first, seems to me there's one song I've been practicing all week. Let's all gather around the piano to sing 'Happy Birthday.' "

If the singing was a cacophony of flat tones and offkey notes, Casey's exuberance and the perfection of the piano accompaniment made up for it.

Afterward, Sam went into the dining room long enough to watch Casey blow out the candles on her cake. Everyone applauded as all ten flames vanished in one great huff, but Lauren was touched by the scene that followed.

76

"Guess you know what I wished for, Daddy?"

Lauren saw his eyes glitter even as he ducked his head.

"Think Mom will ever let it come true?" Casey asked in a wistful voice.

"She wants to come live with Sam," Toots whispered in Lauren's ear.

Lauren had surmised as much, and felt tears start into her eyes.

Sam lightened the mood in the next second, provoking laughter from the small group. "Of course she will. Don't forget Cinderella, Case. Even the wicked old stepmother couldn't keep her from the ball. At least your mother doesn't have warts on her nose."

Casey giggled. "No, she's pretty neat. She just doesn't understand that I'm as southern as Aunt Toots's raspberry dumplings."

"I'll remind her of that when I talk with her tomorrow. Now, you'd better get to your cake and ice cream. Got a kiss for your old man before he goes to work?"

Lauren knew it was rude to stare, but she couldn't tear her eyes from the pair as father lifted daughter in a bear hug, kissing her ear and neck and making her giggle. Dressed as he was in formal black and white tux—obviously his "work" attire—he was impossibly dashing and handsome. But what touched her was the expression of pure, undisguised love that shone from his green eyes. No matter what she thought of him as a man, it was clear that he was a devoted father—a definite plus on the so far blank credit side of the balance sheet she was mentally keeping on him.

As attention was turned back to the party, Lauren tried to hold up her end of the conversation. But she couldn't help letting her thoughts drift toward the next room where strains of music were born.

"Pretty good, huh?" Casey asked, seeming to read Lauren's mind.

"Very good," Lauren admitted.

"You ain't heard nothing yet. He always starts with the classical stuff. Says it loosens him up, gets his soul involved. Just wait till he breaks out the rhythm and blues. He's the best."

And Casey was right. Sam North was damned good. Though not a professional herself, Lauren considered herself a fair judge of musical talent, and she didn't think he missed a note.

"So how did your first day go, Lauren?" Toots asked as they finished the last of their dessert.

The question startled Lauren. The music had stopped a few moments before, and she'd discovered herself bracing for the reappearance of the attractive man who played such a large part in upsetting the day. She struggled for a smile and was inordinately proud of herself when she came up with one, however thin. "Different. Definitely different."

But the aunts weren't to be denied.

"How so dear?" Tillie asked.

78

"Well," Lauren began tentatively when she saw Sam appear in the doorway and lean against the jamb, his deep-set eyes focused on her . . . and laughing. She'd read about eyes that laughed. Now she knew it was really possible. To the two elderly ladies seated to her right, she said, "I met the strangest man. You know him well, I imagine. Eugene?" There, that should fix Mr. North. She was certain he'd expected her to mention her encounter—no, make that plural, encounters.

"Why, of course, we know Eugene. He's a darling, darling boy. He was so devoted to Edna, God rest her soul."

Toots nodded her agreement to Tillie's analysis of Eugene, then leaned forward, her round face animated. "Tell us, Lauren. Has he agreed to stay around and help you out as he did Edna."

Lauren was reminded of Eugene's troubles. "I don't know, Toots. I think he wants to, but he's feeling a bit under the weather."

"Oh, dear me, we can't have that. Is there anything we can do?" she asked, then without waiting for an answer, she said to her sister. "Perhaps you could take him one of your honey crumb cookies, Till. They seemed to work miracles on Father DeGass last year when he was feeling so poorly."

"I'll bake a batch in the morning," Tillie promised.

"I'm sure he'll appreciate them," Lauren said.

"So what else happened, dear?" Toots asked. "You said it was a strange day. Surely, you don't mean just meeting Eugene?"

Lauren couldn't resist glancing at the doorway, and she felt the blood rush to her cheeks. "I got lost in the Vieux Carré for about an hour, and then I met Lovey True who runs the health-food store across the street.

"Well, I imagine getting lost could be unnerving, but you can't ever get lost for long in Nawlin's, honey," Tillie told her. "Folks here are just too friendly to let that happen. You remember that if you ever make another wrong turn. All you have to do is ask anyone for directions."

"Thanks, I'll remember that. It wasn't too bad really. I found my way back eventually, and in truth, the walk did me some good." She hesitated, turning her gaze fully on Sam. "I seem to rise to challenges, and by the time I got back to the shop, I was feeling quite well about how I'd mastered the problems of the morning."

"Edna said you were a stubborn little thing. I'm not surprised at all that you didn't let an upset like getting lost unnerve you, dear."

Lauren smiled sweetly at Tillie, then turned her face to include Sam. "You play quite well, Mr. North."

Sam bowed. "Thank you, Miss Kennedy. Maybe you'll come out to The Jazzy Lady and catch the show before you head back for Chicago."

Lauren was about to decline politely, but Casey interrupted.

"You're not staying in New Orleans, Lauren? I thought you'd still be here when I come back at Thanksgiving."

"I'll be here for a while, sweetie. But I'm afraid my heart's up north. I have a good job there," she said, adding a wink and last jibe for the girl's father. "Not to mention a special man who's waiting for me."

"Why don't you just convince him to move here?" Casey asked.

"Oh, I don't think Charles would like New Orleans too well. He's very much a Yankee at heart."

"Sounds like my mom," Casey said with a pronounced wrinkle of her nose. "I wish I could live here all year round. I'm a true Southerner in my heart." She giggled at a sudden memory. "Daddy even wanted to name me Scarlett."

Lauren chuckled. "You would have made a fine Scarlett. She was very passionate and full of vigor like you."

Sam left a few minutes later after kissing his daughter and each of the aunts. For Lauren, there was only a faint nod and brief goodbye, but she noticed the amused glance he cast her one last time. She wondered what he found so damned funny.

She was still asking herself that question when she let herself into her house two hours after leaving it. But as she showered later, she had forgotten his laughing eyes and was thinking about his kisses on the levee. Her lips even tingled with the recalled memory, and she gave herself a good mental kick. "You're letting his sexy looks override your good sense," she told her image as she stood before the bathroom mirror, lathering her face with night cream. "He's a rare, handsome man, but he can't hold a candle to Charles. Charles is a man in all the ways that count."

As she dressed for bed then slid between the covers, she recounted all of Charles attributes. Responsible. Dependable. Ambitious. Organized. Predictable. Financially set.

Sam North was a rogue — a talented, charming, sexy rogue, but a rogue nonetheless. He was a mongrel. A rebel. A ne'er-do-well.

Turning on her side, she willed the image of dark hair, tanned skin, and amused, deep-set green eyes from her mind. Punching her pillows, she ordered up the more common looks of her soon-to-be fiance. But try as she might, she couldn't quite conjure the picture she wanted. Sleep was a long time coming as she fought the long losing battle. At last, with a sigh of defeat, she gave into the image that intruded on the movie screen in her mind, and went unstruggling into dreams of Never-Never Land and a teasing overgrown Peter.

The next morning, Lauren was backing her

car from the garage when a squeal stopped her. Glancing in her rear view mirror, she was relieved to see that she hadn't been about to mow down a child. Casey was running across the lawn toward her car.

"Lauren! I was just coming over to tell you goodbye."

Lauren got out and allowed herself to be grabbed in a bear hug. "I'm going to miss you, Casey. You were my first friend in New Orleans." She kissed the girl's cheek, hugged her once again, then stepped back to admire the tiny gold earrings molded into the shape of crawdads. "They look good."

"Dad said they suit my personality," Casey said with a giggle. "I told him I was going to get him a bear to wear around his neck. He's been grumping since I woke him up this morning."

Lauren was about to reply but the sudden arrival of the "bear" from his garage apartment, checked her. "Hi," she greeted him, intending to turn her attention immediately back to Casey. But for the life of her, she couldn't tear her eyes away.

He was dressed in wrinkled, faded jeans and a "New Orleans Man — Big and Easy" T-shirt. But even disheveled, his hair standing up in sleep-snarled spikes, his jaw dark with five o'clock shadow, and his eyes red-rimmed, his raw animal magnetism begged not to be ignored. "Rough night?" she asked, a smile tugging at the corners of her mouth.

"Good night, bad morning," he replied in a gravelly voice.

"All mornings are bad," Casey said. "Mom says he was probably descended from vampires."

"The lady should know whereof she speaks. Her father was the famous Count Dracula himself," Sam countered, tugging on his daughter's ponytail. "You ready to fly, brat?"

"All set." Then to Lauren, she said, "Promise you'll still be here at Thanksgiving when I come back?"

Lauren hesitated. How could she make such a promise when she hoped to be gone long before November. Sam interceded.

"Give the lady a break, Case. Just looking at her, you can see she's not cut out for life in the Big Easy. Tell me the truth, when was the last time you saw anyone going to work in the Vieux Carré dressed in pinstriped slacks and black squared-toed patent shoes. This lady, my dear daughter, intimidates even the best yuppies."

Lauren bristled just as he had intended. She suspected that his damned green eyes were laughing at her again. She couldn't be sure, though, for he'd pulled on a pair of black-tinted glasses. She decided to disappoint him and smiled as she spoke to Casey. "I'll more than likely still be here. If anything changes, I'll write and let you know. But in the meantime, I'll look around for that bear you want to give your father. Everyone should have a talisman that reflects the soul."

"And yours would be a saint, no doubt," Sam muttered just loud enough to be heard.

"A saint? I hadn't thought of it before. But you know, I think you're right. Maybe Saint Agnes," she said, letting her eyes travel from the top of his head to his sandaled feet. "She didn't fall breathless at the feet of pagan gods either."

Not giving him a chance to reply, Lauren bent to give Casey one last hug and kiss, then hurriedly climbed into her car and started out of the drive. She was stopped once more by Tillie and Toots just before backing onto the street. She tried to escape with a wave, but they hustled to the car, motioning her to let down her window. With a faint sigh, she smiled and greeted them.

"Don't mean to detain you, dear," Toots huffed, out of breath from hurrying. "We wanted to wish you well at the store today. We know you got off to a poor start yesterday, but just you have patience. Everything's going to get better for you, Lauren. Your aunt Edna was so positive you were going to love it here once you got accustomed to everything."

Lauren chuckled. "I appreciate your faith in me, but not to worry. I'm unflaggingly optimistic this morning. Yesterday wasn't the best way to start off, it's true. But what the heck. If business doesn't pick up in a few days, I'll just put everything up for sale, lock, stock, and barrel."

"Surely you don't mean the house, too, Lauren dear?" Tillie asked.

Lauren let her gaze wander over the house where she'd spent so many happy years as a child before looking back at the sweet sisters who were so concerned with her welfare. "I love it. I can't deny it. I was even thinking that with a few changes here and there, I could stay the rest of my life in the old place. But I have my life in Chicago to think about. Let's face it, if I can't get the business off the ground, there won't be any point in keeping the place."

"Oh dear, I don't suppose so, no. Do you, Sister?"

Tillie, who looked as if she might start weeping at any second, only shook her head.

"Well, I've got to get going. I'm sure not going to sell any antiques sitting here. You all have a safe trip to the airport, and kiss Casey for me again."

Tillie and Toots had taken their lemonade to the back verandah that afternoon as was their custom when they listened to Sam practice the music he would perform that night at The Jazzy Lady.

"You seem fairly well lost to another world, Sister," Toots said to Tillie.

"Thinking about Lauren, of course. What else?"

"What else, indeed? Do you suppose we should pay Eugene a visit? Edna would be so sorry if Lauren left New Orleans without even giving it a chance."

Tillie shook her head. "No, I don't suppose that would do at all. Eugene can't *make* her stay, for all his magic. He's bound by Lauren's wishes, and I hardly think she's going to wish to stay here. I really do think Edna made a mistake giving him to Lauren. We could have been so much more effective."

"You know, Tillie, you amaze me sometimes. You're absolutely right. I hadn't thought about it before, but we could have accomplished everything our dear Edna would have wanted. We could have wished Lauren to love New Orleans and her new business."

"And for her and Sam to fall in love," Tillie added.

"And even for our sweet Casey to be able to live with us all the time."

Tillie nodded, her rocking chair flapping noisily on the rickety boards beneath her feet. "It's too bad we didn't think of this before Edna passed on."

"Well, we may not have magic, Sister, but we're hardly two useless old women without a constructive thought in our heads. I think if we put our minds to it, we might just find a way to keep Lauren here. I firmly believe, as did Edna, that time will make the difference."

"Perhaps with the shop, but I'm not too sure

about Sam. They did seem to get off on the wrong foot."

Toots chuckled. "If I recall, you and that handsome captain you married couldn't abide one another when you first met. When he went off to Europe to fight for our country, it seems to me you quickly changed your tune."

Tillie's smile of fond memories quickly changed to a perplexed frown. "Why, whatever are you suggesting, Sister? Are you saying that if Lauren goes back to Chicago, perhaps she'll suddenly realize how much she misses Sam?" She shook her head firmly, then answered her own question. "Oh, no, Sister, I think that would be far too risky."

"Now, Tillie, I wasn't saying that at all. I was just observing that time has a way of changing things. No, I think we just have to find a way to slow our pretty neighbor down until some of Eugene's magic can take hold."

"Maybe if she started selling the antiques, she'd realize that she likes what she's doing," Tillie said.

"Why, that's a marvelous idea. We can even help. I've been thinking about buying that beautiful mahogany chest for some time to put my linens in. And I know you've fancied that table with the hidden drawer. The mahogany one. Remember?"

"I certainly do. And, you know, Toots, Martha Ambrose mentioned to Edna that she had a fondness for beveled mirrors. I'm sure we could talk several of our friends into buying something from Lauren. Most of their money is getting so stale, it's starting to smell musty anyway."

Tillie held up a finger, her ear cocked toward the kitchen door. "Sam's finished practicing, Sister. We mustn't let him hear us talking about this."

"Mustn't let me hear you talking about what, Aunt Tillie?"

Tillie and Toots both jumped in their chairs at the sound of Sam's voice at the kitchen door.

"Oh, Sam, we didn't know you were there," Toots said, feeling herself blush.

"So I realized," Sam teased. "What are the two of you scheming."

"Scheming! Why Samuel North, southern ladies do *not* scheme. Besides, we weren't even talking about you. We were talking about Lenny Pack, our gardener. We were only observing that he missed a spot when he was trimming the hydrangeas last week. But we wouldn't hurt his feelings for the world by letting him overhear us."

Sam looked suspiciously from one to the other, then shook his head. "Whatever you say. I'm going up to the apartment to wash up before I go to the club. See you both tomorrow afternoon."

"All right, dear, but try to get to bed early; we might need you to help us pick up some items we're thinking of purchasing tomorrow."

89

"What kind of items?" Sam asked, his brow furrowed with mistrust.

"Just some odds and ends, dear," Tillie said, barely suppressing a giggle.

The sisters waited until Sam had gone back into his apartment before clapping their hands with glee. "Oh, Tillie, that was so clever of you to tell him we ware talking about poor Lenny."

"Well, I certainly don't countenance fibbing, but as Mother used to say, 'Bending the truth for good is making use of the devil's tool for the Lord's work.' "

Toots looked troubled. "I agree with what you're saying in principle, Sister, but it worries me that we're being such busybodies. Are we certain that it's for Lauren's good to stay here? She did say she has a fellow in Chicago she's very fond of."

"I understand what you're saying, Sister," Tillie said with a nod. "But we can't forget that Edna knew her niece better than anyone, and she met this young man of Lauren's and found him entirely unsuitable. Called him a cold fish, if you remember. She said Lauren had even forgotten how to have fun when she saw her last, so profound was his influence."

"That's true, so I suppose she'd want us meddling if it'll save sweet Lauren from a disastrous relationship with that Yankee she's set on marrying."

"Not to mention that Sam needs a good swift kick in the britches as well. I do declare, Sister, young people aren't as smart as we used to be. Thank goodness they've got us."

Toots giggled and her eyes twinkled. "And don't forget Eugene. Lauren's got magic working for her as well."

Tillie pushed herself from her chair, straightening the bodice of her dress and squaring her shoulders. "Well, let's get to work calling the girls. Magic's all good and well, but I've always put a great deal in store in the love bug. We've got to do our part in keeping Lauren here until he can bite."

Chapter Five

Lauren was just rinsing her coffee cup and preparing to leave for the store the following morning when the phone rang. She caught it on the second ring.

"Good morning, darling," Charles greeted her, his baritone voice warm and smooth as the chicory coffee she'd just drunk.

"Charles! What a pleasant surprise!"

"I know I told you I'd call on the weekend, but I felt impulsive this morning."

Lauren simply smiled into the phone. What a wonderful way to begin the day. She'd admired Charles Dumont from the beginning; found his cool demeanor charming, but she had to admit that she agreed with Eugene. His cautious nature and predictability bothered her at times. How many times had she wished that he'd do something off the cuff? Spur of the moment? On a whim? And now he was. He was calling her on impulse because he missed her. Her smile widened only to be erased with his next words.

"I couldn't resist the urge to call and brag. You're talking to the new vice president of sales, Lauren. Clifton conferred the honor on me ten minutes ago. Everyone's going to be pleased, of course, but I knew how thrilled you'd be. Now, darling, when you finish all this nonsense in Louisiana, I want to plan our wedding. I think you should call Hedges today and tender your resignation. Between all the money your aunt left you and my promotion, we can start a family right away."

It was a full ten seconds before Lauren could reply. She felt like a fool standing there, blinking and swallowing convulsively, but she couldn't find words to express her . . . her what? She wasn't even sure what she was feeling. Happy for Charles, of course. Even thrilled as he'd known she'd be. But as for the rest . . .

"Lauren, are you there?"

"Yes, Charles, I'm sorry, you caught me by surprise. I'm so excited for you, sweetheart. I hate it that I'm not there to celebrate with you." At once she brightened with a new thought. Maybe that was exactly what they needed, for him to come to New Orleans over the weekend. They could celebrate his promotion, and she could explain that though she wanted children eventually, she didn't want to give up her career. "I've got a wonderful idea, Charles. Why don't you—"

"Sorry, Lauren, I've got to hang up. Clifton needs to see me. I'll call you in a few days, okay? How about Friday night? Make it ten o'clock."

"Charles, I—" She was interrupted by the whine of the disconnected line.

With a muttered curse, she slammed the phone back in its wall cradle, grabbed her purse, and stormed from the house. As she walked toward the garage, she stopped to glare up at Sam North's apartment. "Men!" she raged, then grinned, feeling better for having one near enough to take her annoyance out on. It didn't even matter to her that he was probably sound asleep and unable to hear. Her step was lighter as she approached her car, and she was still smiling when she pulled out of the drive.

Sam was smiling, too, as he sat on the side of his bed watching her back her car onto the street. He didn't know why he'd awakened so early. Ordinarily a hurricane wouldn't shake him from sleep, but he was glad he'd been up to see Lauren leave her house.

Damn but she was a beautiful woman, even more so with color high in her cheeks, as it was this morning. He'd stood back from the window out of sight when he heard the bang of her kitchen door, but he'd been able to see her clearly. Her blue eyes flashed daggers, and judging from the way she'd spit out "men," he'd guess she'd just had a run-in with one of them.

Stretching as he stood up again, he chuckled. Apparently Ms Kennedy wasn't the cool lady she'd have everyone believe. Fire flowed in those delicate blue veins, he thought as he took a can of soda from the refrigerator and popped the lid. Maybe he'd find an excuse to pay her a visit later. He liked playing with fire, and he was good at stoking flames.

The phone rang as he was about to lie down again. It was his Aunt Tillie reminding him he'd promised to help them pick up some things later that day.

"Care to be more specific?" he asked.

"Toots and I were talking to some of the girls last night, dear. Lauren's name came up, and we started discussing the beautiful antiques Edna had bought. We're all going to go over to Yesterday's Treasures this afternoon and pick up a thing or two before Lauren sells the place. It would be just like us to let something we've wanted get away by waiting too long. So bring the truck, Sam."

When Sam hung up, he chugged the cola then flopped down on his back, arms beneath his head. So the aunts had decided to bring in the troops to keep Edna's niece in town. Fine with him. But he couldn't help grinning as he imagined Lauren's reaction to their "help."

Lauren was worried about Eugene. She hadn't seen him even once the day before, and though

95

she'd already been at the shop for more than two hours today, he still hadn't made an appearance. Several times this morning, she'd considered summoning him but thoughts of Charles's high-handed assumptions had kept intruding, distracting her. By noon, however, she'd managed to talk herself out of her pique. Charles was a wonderful man; everything she'd ever dreamed of finding. He loved her and wanted only to take care of her, protect and support her, and make her happy. If he was a bit old-fashioned, that was better than carefree and irresponsible like her neighbor.

She cursed herself for making the comparison. Sam North should never be considered in the same thought with Charles Dumont. Okay, so he was handsome and talented and wickedly charming. Those were hardly the kinds of qualities she'd always admired. She forced the image of mocking green eyes, gleaming, too-long dark hair, and lean, sensual body from her mind, struggling for the image of the man she planned to marry. Physically, Charles was the loser in the competition—*if* there was a competition—but she and Charles were cut from the same cloth. Both planned for tomorrow rather than living for the day, as did that overgrown child next door. Aunt Edna had given her a brighter future with the fortune she'd left, and Lauren was thankful she had a man like Charles who would help her invest it. Sam North would probably use it to open some risky business like a piano bar. Obviously, he'd never saved a penny, otherwise why else would he be forced to live in his aunts' garage apartment?

Her thoughts were interrupted by the jingle of the bell over the front door. She smiled when she saw Lovey walk in.

"I'm glad you're here, Lovey. I haven't seen Eugene for a couple of days. Maybe you can roust him out of his bottle."

Lovey's brown eyes showed the sadness she was feeling, but she tried valiantly to smile even as she shook her head. "I don't think so, Lauren. I came by last night after you left the store. Hope you don't mind. We have a signal— Eugene and I. When I tap on the window with a certain code, he brings me into his bottle. He didn't answer last night. I . . . I'm afraid he might have already faded away."

Lauren immediately felt ashamed. Here she was selfishly worrying that Charles didn't appreciate her own ambitions, which amounted to hardly more than a small hurdle they'd have to get over. And Lovey might have lost the man she loved forever! She hurried behind the sales counter to grab the genie's bottle from the shelf and give it a couple of brisk rubs. She and Lovey nearly sagged with relief when smoke billowed from the spout.

"Yo," Eugene said as soon as he'd taken shape. "What's up?"

"We were worried sick about you, Eugene Ali Simm Simm! Lovey thought you'd . . . well, she thought you might be sick! How dare you scare her like that."

Eugene's narrow shoulders hunched in apology. "Guess I was feeling a tad under the weather. Kind of feeling sorry for myself, too, Lovey. Didn't want to worry you."

Tears stood in Lovey's eyes, and Lauren felt like a voyeur. She was about to excuse herself, say something about moving some things around the back of the store, when she saw Tillie and Toots and several other elderly women approaching from across the street. "I think we're about to have some company. Why don't the two of you go visit in your bottle, Eugene? I'll see that you aren't disturbed."

They disappeared in the usual whiff of smoke, which still startled Lauren though not as much as before. She was saddened by the seriousness of the genie's condition, and again resolved to think of a way to save him. But that was the last thought she'd have time to give him for the next several hours.

Tillie and Toots must have raided an old folks home, Lauren decided as the group of elderly women filed into the store. She greeted each one of them warmly, her mind spinning as she fought to remember names. She needn't have bothered, for it seemed they had come on a mission. As Lauren stood dumfounded in the middle of the store, the old women—short, tall, plump, lean, withered, and proud—took off in different directions. Within minutes each was back, the object of their search either in hand or claimed, and staked with a purse, umbrella, or shopping bag left on top as a marker.

"What in the world is going on?" Lauren asked Tillie as she rang up the sale for a costly crystal vase.

"Why, whatever do you mean, dear?" Tillie asked, her hooded eyes suddenly wide with innocence.

"You know perfectly well what I mean. I've been in business for three days. The first two days I didn't have a dozen customers and three modest sales all together. Suddenly, you and Toots show up with every senior citizen south of Mississippi, and I'm in danger of not having enough stock to stay in business until tomorrow."

Toots had arrived at her sister's side and answered the implied charge of conspiracy. "Why, it's really quite simple, Lauren. The ladies belong to our card club. Every month we set aside a day for lunch or shopping or the like. We've all been customers of Edna's for years. Why, every one of our houses is just brimming over with collectibles we bought from here. When you mentioned yesterday that you might sell off the store and house, Till and I simply called the girls and suggested that if there was anything they wanted to buy, they'd better get a move on. We decided to change our weekly Friday outing to today."

"Well, I appreciate the business, Toots. Truly I

do, but I didn't mean I'd be closing the doors right away."

"Well, now you won't have to close them at all. You can see by the turnout how many of our ladies value priceless pieces of craftsmanship that just can't be reproduced today."

Lauren smiled. "I certainly can, Toots, but you've forgotten that I know next to nothing about antiquing. I've read a lot about the items Edna had here in the shop, but I wouldn't know how to go about buying more. So you may well have helped me close up sooner than I'd hoped." She turned her attention back to another blue-haired customer, missing the look of consternation that passed between the sisters.

Lauren was just coming from behind the counter to help another of the elderly ladies when the bells above the front door chimed. She groaned when she saw Sam North standing there.

"Don't tell me, you aunts suggested you might want to come and purchase an antique for your apartment," she said. "And like the obedient nephew you are, you came rushing over to oblige. Well, sorry, you should have crawled from your bed an hour earlier. I've been practically bought right out of business."

Sam rubbed at his eyes with the heels of his hands before tucking his thumbs in his jeans pockets. "You've got the obedient nephew part right, but I'm not into antiques any more than you appear to be. I've been roped in as a delivery boy. So if you'll just stick a piece of paper with name and address on top, I'll start loading up the loot.

"Some of this is heavy," Lauren pointed out. "You couldn't possibly handle it all by yourself."

"Thought of that," Sam countered with a smug grin. "Got a couple of friends from the band waiting outside to help."

"Such a dutiful nephew. But I guess anything to keep a roof over your head, huh?" Lauren muttered as she went after pen and paper.

"Whatever did she mean by that?" Tillie asked her sister.

"I'm sure I wouldn't know, but whatever she meant, Sam has that ugly look in his eyes."

Tillie pivoted slightly to follow her sister's gaze to where their nephew stood glaring. "Better get him busy carrying the ladies' acquisitions out of here, Sister. He does look like he's considering murder, and I do believe Lauren is his intended victim."

Sam was bone tired by the time he backed the truck into the garage. For the first time that he could remember, he was going to skip his routine practice session at the keyboard before going to the club. He wanted only a long shower and a couple of more hours in bed. But as he left the garage, Tillie and Toots came rushing down the back veranda stairs, yoo-hooing. He gave a good healthy groan before managing what he hoped was an acceptable smile of greeting.

"Everything delivered, Sam dear?" Toots asked.

"Every last stick of wood, shard of crystal, and chunk of porcelain."

"You're a precious boy, Samuel David North," Tillie said, patting his arm. "All of the ladies were so grateful to you and your friends for helping. Sarah Sheridan even suggested that we pay you tomorrow. I told her you wouldn't accept money for helping, but she'll probably offer anyway. Sarah's always had so much pride, don't you know?"

"Whoa, back up. What were you saying about tomorrow?" Sam asked.

"Oh, I guess I forgot to mention that we need your help again tomorrow afternoon, dear."

Sam looked from one aunt to the other. "But there's nothing left to buy, Aunt Tillie. You saw the store when we were finished. Except for a couple of dresses and dolls and a table or two, ya'll managed to buy Lauren out."

Both women nodded vigorously. "That we did, Sam," Toots said. "And when we all got home with our new treasures, we discovered that our own homes are looking overcrowded. So tomorrow, we need you to go pick up some furniture that the ladies are going to sell to Lauren."

It was all suddenly clear to Sam. The aunts

were determined to keep Lauren in business. First they'd decided to help by buying up her stock. When they'd realized they'd practically bought her out, they'd found a way to restock her store. He rocked on his heels with laughter. "You two are too much."

"Too much what, dear?" Toots asked.

Sam put his arms around their shoulders, steering them back toward the house. "You might succeed in keeping Edna's niece in business, but you may very well lose me a band when I tell the boys I need their help again tomorrow."

"Oh, dear, that won't do," Tillie said, worried.

"I was kidding, Aunt Till. They'll grumble, but I hardly think they'll walk out. I pay them damned good wages. Much better than union scale."

"You take care of everyone, Sam. You're a very good boy."

"I love you, too, Till." He squeezed her shoulder then planted a kiss atop Toots's head. "You, too. But do me a favor. After tomorrow, why don't we let Lauren run her own business?"

"But that's the problem, dear. Lauren doesn't seem to know what she's doing. We're only buying her some time until she figures it all out. She's a very bright young woman."

Before Sam could answer, Toots asked, "What do you think of her, Sam?"

"I think it's not nice to gossip," he said and

103

quickly changed the subject. "And I think I'm going to fall over on my face if I don't get some sleep."

"Aren't you going to practice this evening?"

"Nope, and don't hold dinner for me. I'll catch a bite at the club."

Tillie was about to protest about his eating away from home, when she heard their neighbor's car turning into the drive. "There's Lauren now. Would you stop by on your way to the apartment and tell her how pleased everyone was to meet her today, Sam? You might also let her know that we'll be bringing in a few things tomorrow."

Sam shrugged his acquiescence. "You got it. Only hope the lady realizes that civilized people no longer slay the messenger bearing bad tidings."

Tillie and Toots smiled politely as they shooed him on his way. They were quite used to their nephew's humor, even though it made no sense to them.

"What ever do you suppose he meant by that?" Tillie asked Toots as they walked back toward their house.

"I never understand his jokes, Sister. I just hope Lauren understands him better than we do."

"I think she must, Toots. Remember that remark she made at the store earlier about keeping a roof over his head. Sam seemed to understand what she was saying, though it was lost on me."

"But I don't think she was making a joke," Tillie observed. "Sam didn't seem amused by it."

"It's a new generation out there, Till. Maybe tomorrow we can follow Sam over to the store and speak with Eugene. He seems able to translate what everyone's saying without trouble."

"Wasn't it strange that we didn't see him today?"

"It most certainly was. I don't remember a time when Edna was there that Eugene wasn't sitting around somewhere always ready to be of help."

Just inside the kitchen door, Tillie stopped dead. "You don't suppose Lauren is already using up her wishes. Why, she might have had him out seeing to one of them while we were there."

"Now that's an unpleasant thought. I do hope she's not that hasty. Edna seemed to think her niece was too prudent to waste her wishes without careful consideration, but maybe she didn't understand young people any better than we seem to."

Toots nodded her agreement as she crossed the large room to the refrigerator. "We'll seek him out tomorrow and put a stop to all this guesswork."

Lauren, too, was thinking about Eugene when she spotted Sam crossing the yard next door in her direction. She'd been wondering what would happen to the poor failing genie if she did in fact close up the shop, now practically bare after the day's run on her antiques. She had to find a way to delay her departure from New Orleans until she could find the secret to making him mortal and keeping him around. But how? And what would Charles say if he found out she was staying long after she'd been bought out?

She registered Sam's arrival at the side of her car but barely acknowledged him as she considered the problem.

He bent slightly, peering in and waving a hand in front of her eyes. "Earth to Lauren."

In spite of her worrisome thoughts, Lauren smiled at that. Getting out, she apologized. "Sorry, I was miles away."

"Not in Chicago, I hope."

Lauren was tired, but it felt good to talk about nothing, just relax for a few seconds. At least Sam was a pleasant diversion. "Good for something." She hadn't realized she'd said it aloud until she saw puzzlement in his eyes. "Nothing. Don't ask," she said. "Like I said, I'm off in la-la land."

"Whatever, but like I said, I hope it's not Chicago, because my sweet, dear aunts are plotting fast and furiously to keep you here. As a matter of fact, they've already cooked up a scheme to restock your store tomorrow."

Lauren laughed, a short ha of amazement.

106

"How are they going to manage that?"

"I think I'll let them explain that to you, but keep in mind I'm only the errand boy."

"But I think it's great," Lauren said.

Sam crossed his arms over his broad chest, making the muscles in his arms flex. He stared hard at her, making her blush.

"What are you staring at?" she asked uncomfortably.

"Just trying to figure you out, see if I can't look inside and get a glimpse of what makes you tick. Two days ago you were sitting across from me in a quaint cafe telling me how much you hated it here. You couldn't wait to get back to the sanity of Chicago and your orderly, upwardly mobile life as an ad exec. Now you look relieved not to have an excuse to take off." He scratched the back of his head. "Oh, well, I can't figure it, and I'm too beat to worry about it anymore today."

Lauren didn't answer but gave him a little wave in response to his own as he walked away. When he was halfway across the yard, he stopped at the edge of the drive and called out, his eyes dancing with mischief. "Why don't you come out and play tonight, Lauren? I kinda have a thing for puzzles. Might be fun taking you apart and putting you back together again."

"I don't think so, Sam. I like puzzles, too, but I think we'd both be bored to tears. You've already figured me out, remember? I'm a materialistic yuppie too much like your ex-wife for your liking."

"And what am I?"

"I thought I told you."

"Tell me again," he dared. "It's okay. I can't touch you. Against the rules. Besides, I'm on my side of the game board." He looked down at his toes inches from the boundary line of her property. "You're safe."

Lauren was suddenly angry, and more so because she didn't know why. He looked as if he was really just having fun, but she had the feeling it was at her expense. "You are a man chasing rainbows and freeloading off your aunts who are too generous and good-natured for their own good. You're talented, I'll give you that, but you should be working at a profession that would enable you to stand on your own two feet so you could support your daughter. Maybe then you'd have some pride in yourself and stop running down the rest of the world just because most of them happen to care about getting ahead."

Sam was still smiling but Lauren could see that she'd made him angry. It showed in the way a muscle rippled in his cheek and the way his green eyes darkened from bright emerald to murky jade. She felt a flash of remorse, but before she could soften her words, offer an apology, he laughed.

"Gosh, Lauren, you're going to have to loosen up, learn to get your feelings out. You're just too uptight."

In a flash of fury, and without thinking, Lauren made a suggestion that would have made her mother faint and shocked even her. Only she should have been more specific about whom he do it with, for Sam merely lifted a brow and said, "Anytime, babe. All you gotta do is holler."

Chapter Six

By noon Thursday, Lauren decided the day had all the makings of a Shakespearean farce.

First the air conditioner had gone kaput. It wasn't quite ninety degrees outside, but the humidity was registering eighty per cent according to the radio meteorologist. By ten o'clock, Lauren had pulled her hair up on top of her head using two pencils to secure the haphazard knot. She'd dressed more practically than days before in cotton T-shirt and jeans. By eleven, the shirt had been knotted below her breasts, baring her midriff, and the jeans turned into cutoffs. At eleven-thirty, Sam and his group of merry men arrived with a truckload of furniture—quality antiques, she judged at once.

Though not one piece grazed a wall or scuffed the floor, by the time the last of the bounty was placed, Lauren was certain she was in the early stages of a nervous breakdown . . . and she wasn't even sure why.

Maybe it was the damned heat. Or maybe it

was that the trio of musicians managed to have fun despite the sky-high temperatures and tedious chore. She glanced sidelong in Sam's direction as she fled to the rear of the store, noticing again that he'd pulled off his shirt. But she firmly refused to consider that the way muscles rippled in his powerful shoulders or the way sweat turned his skin to gleaming bronze had anything to do with her reaction to his presence.

"Chill out, Lauren," Sam said when he found her hiding behind the counter, sitting on a low footstool, her face buried in her hands. "I know it's hot in here, but the man from Igloo Air Conditioning promised to be out here right after lunch."

"I can handle the heat," Lauren growled. "What I can't handle is your attitude."

"What attitude? What's wrong with my attitude? I've been so cheery Santa Claus couldn't fault me."

"Exactly! For two days, you've invaded my store, whistling like Harpo Marx, cracking jokes with your two establishment reject friends, Malibu Jones and Hanky Panky—"

"His name's Hank Patty. The best damned clarinetist in the business, incidentally."

"Good for him. That doesn't change the fact that your cavalier attitude has just about wrecked my emotional well-being. Your aunts and the other ladies entrusted you with some very valuable pieces, and the three of you act

111

like you're auditioning for a comedy juggling routine."

"We didn't so much as put a scratch on anything," Sam pointed out with enough patience to earn him points toward sainthood.

"So miracles still happen," Lauren bit out sarcastically, standing up to face him, her chin raised in defiance at the angry glint in his eyes.

"Hey, lady, lighten up. In case you haven't noticed, our time is donated. I agreed to deliver this stuff because my aunts have some harebrained notion about trying to keep you happy so you'll stick around. My friends are simply doing me a favor. In case you aren't aware, my eyes don't normally look as red as stop lights. We work until two every morning. For the past four days, I haven't had more than four hours' sleep. Mal and Hank haven't done much better. They both have families, and when they're not sleeping or rehearsing, they like to spend time with them. Instead, they're here helping me. If they made the best of a bad situation by trying to find some humor in it, I'd think you'd appreciate it."

Lauren felt properly shamed, but her pride was stinging. Refusing to back down, she turned her back on him as she opened the cash register and extracted three crisp fifty dollar bills. "Here," she said, holding out the bills. "I apologize for my ingratitude. Please share this with your friends and thank them for me."

Sam didn't take the money but stood staring at her, disappointment in his eyes. "You're a piece of work, Lauren Kennedy. We don't want your money. The thank you will do. I'll pass it along, but in the meantime, you really ought to take a look inside yourself. I don't think you're going to like the person you meet there."

With a gasp of hurt, Lauren brushed past him, hurrying to the back of the store where she stood quivering. After a few seconds she heard the bells over the front door tinkle Sam's departure. Only then did she let the tears come.

She slumped onto a crate and gave in to waves of self-pity. She'd been rude and unreasonable. She realized that, but damn it, she wasn't accustomed to dealing with men who acted the perpetual child no matter what the situation.

One thing was certain, she didn't belong in New Orleans. If she'd started thinking otherwise, this morning had certainly cleared away that crazy notion. New Orleanians clung too tenaciously to the adage *Laissez les bon temps roule*—let the good times roll. Especially Samuel North!

She stood up so abruptly she tipped the crate and would have fallen to her knees, if she hadn't caught herself with a hand against the far wall. She stomped her foot. "Eugene!" she wailed.

Five seconds passed, then ten, but the genie

didn't materialize. Instead, she heard footsteps approach from the front of the shop, and turned to meet the green eyes of her irritating neighbor. "I thought you'd left."

Sam shook his head. "Naw, the boys are waiting for me in the truck. I was just checking the receipts you wrote out against the merchandise we delivered. Everything looks in order, so *adios*." He turned and almost ran into a withered old man dressed in a long white caftan and leaning heavily on a cane. Sam cast a quizzical glance at Lauren, but she seemed equally surprised by the old man's sudden appearance.

"I'm sorry, I didn't hear you come in," she said. Her voice sounded polite, even kind to her own ears, for which she was grateful *and* surprised. Never in her life had she seen anyone so ancient.

The little man wore his snowy-white hair long—much longer than Sam's shoulder-length style. His beard extended to mid-chest, and his face was as withered and wrinkled as a potato she'd once played Mr. Potato Head with then forgotten in her toy box for several months. "May I help you?" she asked, her eyes on the gnarled fingers gripping the head of the cane as if every ounce of his energy was focused there.

"You called, mama?" the man asked in a voice so familiar that Lauren jumped.

"Eugene!"

"Eugene?" Sam mimicked.

"At your service," Eugene croaked in the craggy voice of an ancient.

"Don't you move," Lauren said, pointing a stern finger at the genie. "I'll be right back as soon as I see Mr. North to the door."

Eugene gave a slight nod, but it was enough to make him teeter precariously. Sam and Lauren reached out to steady him, then settled him on the crate Lauren had occupied only moments before.

"Now don't move," Lauren ordered.

Sam couldn't resist looking back at the frail old man who couldn't possibly be the same man he'd met only four days before. "This is a joke, right?" he asked as he followed Lauren reluctantly to the front of the store.

Lauren stopped and ran a hand over her brow as if trying to erase the headache that had begun like an insistent tattoo just above her eyes. "Yes. A joke is exactly what it is. It's a costume; Eugene's idea of fun. Apparently, you're not the only one who insists on spicing up my life with bits of hilarity."

"Well, don't be too hard on the old guy. He looks like he's on his last leg."

There was that laughing glint in his eyes again, the one that made them sparkle like bits of bottle glass in sunlight and made Lauren's heart quicken. At least he'd bought the 'costume' excuse, but she had to get rid of him so she could go see to Eugene. *Then* she was going to get in her car and drive deep into the bayous where she could scream until she had no more voice left. After that . . . no, she couldn't think about what she'd do after that. She wasn't sure she was even going to make it that far. Tears were already burning behind her eyes again.

"You sure you're okay?" Sam asked, the humor in his voice replaced by a sensitivity that made her jerk her head up to meet his gaze. Yes, it was there but quickly gone again as he smiled and winked. "Yep, there's still fire. Your eyes are the color of smoldering wood. You'll make it."

He was gone before Lauren could find a reply. Just as well, she thought. She'd noticed an itch in her hand she'd never experienced before. It was the itch that came with the need to slap something.

She marched to the back of the store, ready to deal with the other man who was making her life crazy. Naturally, he was gone. She started to call his name again but it quickly turned into a screech of fright when she nearly stepped on him. He was stretched out on the floor behind the crates, only his head visible, lying inches from her toes. She dropped to her knees, touching his brow tentatively as she whispered his name. "Eugene?"

Blue eyes met her gaze in an instant. "Yo."

"Don't you 'yo' me! I thought you were dead! You scared ten years off my life."

The genie was on his feet so quickly she could have sworn she hadn't seen him move. "Not so feeble suddenly, are we?"

Eugene leaned heavily on his cane, but his boyish, guileless grin was that of the spry magic man she knew. "Just trying it on for size. Figured if I'm old enough to fade away, I should look the part."

"You look like Howard Hughes in his last days."

The genie's grin widened with satisfaction. "Exactly the look I was after. Now *he* was a man I admired. Eccentric, no doubt, but a true, rare genius."

"I am not amused, Eugene. I'm having a deplorable day. I don't need you adding to it. So blink, shimmy, or whatever it is you have to do to turn back into yourself." His thin, pale lips formed a straight stubborn line, and Lauren felt the last of her control snap. "Now!"

The metamorphosis was accomplished in the blink of an eye. Lauren was startled as always, but she managed to hold onto her sanity long enough to tell him, "I need you to man the shop for a couple of hours. I've got to get out of here for a while. Think I'll go junking or something the way Aunt Edna used to talk of doing. A man is coming to fix the air conditioner. You can pay him out of the register. If I'm not back by six, close the shop."

Without waiting for an answer, she walked

117

away but only as far as the door to the front of the store before stopping. "Look, I'm sorry, Eugene. I know you've got problems. Serious problems. I don't mean to seem insensitive, and I really am still trying to find a way to keep you from fading away, but I have to get out of here for a bit. Will you be all right?"

"Right as rain, mama. You just get your head on straight. By the way, you shoulda called earlier, I can fix your air conditioner in a flash."

For the first time that day, Lauren smiled, then laughed. "Of course you can. See what I mean? I didn't even remember how handy you are to have around. Just let me have a couple of hours. I'll pull it together, then come back. But, Gene, I think you should know. I've just about got my last two wishes figured out. As soon as I find a way to keep you from departing this planet, I'm going to be calling on you for them, okay?"

At this, Eugene's eyes took on the woebegone look of the hound dog pup Lauren had once discovered hiding under her car in Chicago. "Don't look like that, Gene. I'll find the answer to save you, I promise."

"Wasn't thinking about myself, Lauren. Guess, I just pretty much know what you're going to ask for, and it makes me feel kinda blue. Edna and I thought you'd adjust and learn to like it here."

Lauren didn't answer as she pulled her purse

118

out from under the counter and rummaged through it for her keys. Her aunt had loved her, there was no doubt about that. But she'd heard love in the genie's voice just then as well, and she was busy swallowing a lump in her throat.

"Guess we can't change the way you feel about this place," Eugene said, "but your aunt would have been proud of how quickly you learned."

Lauren looked up then. Eugene was studying the price tags she'd put on some of her new acquisitions. She couldn't help feel a spark of pride. "I've been studying some of the books you gave me. Think they're priced within reason?"

"I think Edna herself couldn't have done better."

Lauren hugged him to her in an impulsive gesture that seemed to embarrass him as much as her. "Thanks, Gene. I take back everything I said earlier. You are the one bright spot in this entire miserable day."

Sam fell into bed shortly after noon and slept like a man drugged. He didn't awaken until nearly six o'clock. Even then, knowing that he couldn't avoid at least an hour of rehearsal before getting ready for the club, he moved with languid slowness from the bed to the shower. For the first three or four minutes, as the hot

119

spray of water pelted his back and shoulders, his mind remained groggy and murky. Eventually, slowly, the fog cleared and memories of his visit to Yesterday's Treasures filed into the forefront of his thoughts. He recalled the way Lauren had looked upon his arrival with the antiques his aunt had gathered for delivery.

The normal flawless perfection of dress and makeup missing, he'd thought her never before so beautiful. A sheen of perspiration on her cheeks and brow, tendrils of damp hair around her face, dark eyes snapping with frustration and annoyance, all combined to give her a look of sensuality she normally hid behind a veneer of cool reserve. He pictured her stretching to place an expensive cut-glass vase on a high shelf out of harm's way, and his mind focused on the small muscles in her arms, the taut flesh over her rib cage and stomach, and her long, toned legs defined by her stance on tiptoe. In that instant, he'd thought her the most exquisite woman he'd ever seen.

Laughter churned deep in his throat as he recalled the way she'd turned then to catch him watching her. Color had flooded her cheeks, and her brown eyes had caught fire and threatened to sear the smile off his face.

As he toweled himself, his memory jumped forward an hour or so to the tears he'd seen still standing in her eyes, and the marks left on her cheeks when he'd gone to the back of the

120

store to say his farewells.

Without even thinking about what he was doing, he walked to the bedroom window over-
looking the rear of her house. No lights burned
in either the downstairs kitchen window or
above in the bedroom, as they did most
evenings.

He frowned as he glanced at the clock on his
nightstand. She was normally home by now.

While he dressed, he found a hundred reasons
for her absence. She could be rearranging the
store. Knowing her need for order, that was
probably what she was doing. Or she might
have decided to stop at a restaurant for dinner.
Perhaps she'd gone grocery shopping. The possibilities were endless, and he knew it was silly to
worry. Neither was it any of his business what
she did after work. She'd made it abundantly
clear that he had *no* business in her life.

His spine stiffened when he remembered how
easily he irked her. He stepped into his shoes
and faced the mirror to comb his damp hair
back into the ponytail he wore when working at
the club. He grinned and was rewarded with a
response from his reflection. He wished it was
that easy to win a smile from his beautiful
new neighbor. "Might as well wish for the
moon, buddy," he told the man in the looking glass. "The lady clearly is immune to your
charm."

As he tied his hair back, he vowed to push

121

thoughts of Miss Lauren Kennedy from his mind. But an hour later, a quickly eaten dinner and forty-five minutes of practice on the piano behind him, he couldn't resist glancing at her house again as he backed his car from the drive. Though late summer, a storm threatened and darkness had settled earlier than usual over the ocean port city. Still no lights burned in the house next door.

He switched on the dome light and glanced at his watch. Eight-ten. He started playing at ten, though he was usually at the club by eight-thirty, nine at the latest. Tapping the steering wheel with restless fingertips, he made his decision and headed out.

Fifteen minutes later, he sighed with relief when he pulled his red convertible into the small lot behind Yesterday's Treasures. Her BMW was parked exactly where he'd seen it this morning. He started to reverse, stopped, pulled back up once again, and got out.

He was going to invest five more minutes to make sure she was all right, then get on over to the club.

The back door was unlocked. He frowned. When it came to crime, New Orleans couldn't hold a candle to New York City. But it existed, and nobody in their right mind would leave a door unlocked after hours.

Fear twisted in his gut as he rushed into the store, and his imagination played out all sorts of ugly scenarios.

He didn't call out, was afraid he'd startle her. No, he admitted, that wasn't the truth. He was afraid that she might not answer, might not be *able* to answer. And then he became aware of the music playing somewhere in the front of the store. Stopping, he cocked his head, listening, trying to identify the source, and then it came to him. It was a music box and the tune repeating itself over and over was "Glow Little Glow Worm."

Anger washed over him. He'd been worried about her! Hardly been able to concentrate on his music for wondering if she was okay! He'd driven twenty minutes out of his way to check on her, and she was listening to a music box. He called out her name in an angry bark, "Lauren!"

"Out here," she called as calmly as if she'd been expecting company for tea.

"Out here" wasn't as easy to find as he'd have thought. One lamp with a low-watt bulb was on in the store. It sat on a shelf behind the sales counter and succeeded only in bathing the store in eerie shadows. There was enough light to make out the different pieces of furniture and shelves of glassware, dolls, lamps, and chinaware, but still he couldn't find Lauren. He followed the sound of the music and located her sitting on the floor, cross-legged, head bent, in front of a large square box.

"Hi, Sam," she greeted him simply without

123

bothering to look up.

"Hi, Sam?"

She did look up now, but only long enough to grace him with a brilliant smile. Then she focused her attention on the music box again. "Isn't it exquisite?" she asked.

As Sam stared at her, he silently agreed that exquisite was exactly the word he would have used. She still wore the same cutoff jeans, the same T-shirt, though it was unknotted now and wrinkled in the front. Her hair hung loose around her shoulders, unbrushed and tangled, reminding him of the carefree little girl he'd played with as a child . . . and loved as young boys do their first sweethearts.

"It's a calliope. I found it at an estate sale today." She lowered the lid to run her fingers over the smooth wood finish and the etched drawing of a dancing girl. It was made in Leipzig, Germany, almost a hundred years ago. I got it so cheap I felt almost like I was stealing it." The song that was playing came to a stop, and she opened the box again to remove the large, round, grooved disc. "That was the *'Glühwürmchen Idyll.'* "

"Could've fooled me," he said with a hint of amusement in his voice. "Sounded like 'Glow Little Glow Worm.'

Lauren did laugh. "Translated, that's it." She removed another disc from a round carton at her side, placed it on the player, and announced the name of the next song. Though it, too, was in German, Sam recognized the word polka.

He surprised her by putting his hands under her elbows and lifting her to her feet. At her questioning look, he grinned mischievously. "Never could resist a polka." And before she could protest, he was spinning her around the floor in perfect time to the lively tune.

Lauren was more surprised at the delight she felt than by his actions. He was a faultless dancer, light on his feet, and so adept they didn't miss a step. She was amazed that he was able to whirl her around the store without even so much as brushing against one of her delicate antiques.

The song played for less than three minutes, but Lauren was breathless by the time they stopped. Suddenly embarrassed, she couldn't resist giggling at the fun she'd had if only for a brief, wonderful moment. Self-consciously she tugged at her wrinkled T-shirt with one hand, and tucked her hair behind her ear with the other. "You're very good."

Sam grinned, adding wickedly, "I've been trying to tell you that for the past several days."

Lauren saw the devil in his eyes and felt a shiver run up her spine. Turning away, she crossed the floor and knelt down in front of the calliope again. "Why are you here?" she asked.

Sam hesitated. He hadn't expected that. What should he say? That he was worried about her?

125

That he'd seen the tears in her eyes earlier? Instinctively, he knew either answer would anger her. "Noticed you weren't home. I thought I'd stop by and see if you got everything squared away after we left. I'm glad they got the air-conditioning fixed for you."

"Right after you left today," she said, keeping herself busy packing away the discs and locking up the music box.

"Well, then, I guess I'll be getting on to the club."

"See ya," she said with a glance up at his face as she tried to stand and lift the discs at the same time.

Sam came to her rescue. "Heavier than they look, huh?"

Lauren accepted his help without answering, motioning with her chin to a shelf in front of them. She followed with the calliope. "Just put them there for tonight. I'll decide where to display them tomorrow unless I decide to take them home."

Sam did as directed then moved aside to allow her to place the music box beside the carton of discs. As he watched her, he thought again what a beautiful woman she was. Not his type. Not by a long shot. She was too uptight, too rigid and unbending, too controlled. Too much like his ex-wife. Then she stepped back, bumping into him, and he was reminded of how soft and right she'd felt in his arms when they'd danced. "Come to the club tonight, Lauren," he said, and was as amazed by the invitation as she seemed to be when she turned to face him.

"Dressed like this?" she asked with a nervous titter.

"You look great to me."

Her gaze slid over his impeccable white shirt, black bow tie, and crisp tuxedo pants, and she raised a brow.

"Okay, so drive home and change," Sam said. "You've got time. We don't start playing until ten."

Stepping past him, she answered with her back to him. "Thanks, but no thanks. Not tonight. I've still got some things to arrange here. I found an old spinning wheel today and a wonderful pie safe. I want to check them over, see if they need any touching up." She gave him a friendly smile that she hoped disguised the inexplicable nervousness she suddenly felt.

Sam merely nodded. "Okay, but don't stay too late. There's a storm brewing. Streets will be particularly slippery after the past week of no rain." At Lauren's nod, he turned away, but stopped after only a few feet. "Walk me to the back door so you can lock up behind me. It's not safe to leave the door open so any Tom, Dick, or Harry can wander in."

"Oh, Lovey—the lady who owns Spice of Life across the street—stopped by. I guess I forgot to lock up after she left."

At the door, she said good night, then pulled back to let him pass. "Thanks for the dance. It was fun. Really."

Their eyes met, holding in an embrace neither had the will to break for the next several seconds. He was disappointed when Lauren was the first to look away. "Better be careful, Lauren, you might fall in love."

That got her attention, but he couldn't read her expression. Was it anger or thrill he saw flashing in those dark eyes? He wished he dared push his luck, but he thought it best to back off . . . at least for the moment. He gave his head a slight jerk in the direction of the store. "The antiques," he explained. "I think you're starting to care about them."

Chapter Seven

Lauren heard the first drops of rain pelt the windows as she checked the locks on the front door. Emptying the cash drawer, she thought back to the visit she'd enjoyed with Sam. Pleasant, friendly, easy. She sighed, then started to hum the tune to the polka they'd danced to. She could almost feel the pressure of his hand on the small of her back, the coolness of his small gold earring against her cheek, even smell the rich scent of his cologne.

As she counted the money, balancing it against the receipts and tucking the bills and deposit slip into a bank bag, she wondered what Charles would have said if he'd witnessed the impromptu dance, heard her laughter. Probably nothing. Charles Dumont was nothing if not secure. She doubted that even Sam's uncommon good looks would intimidate him. For the first time in her nearly two-year relationship with Charles, Lauren felt a twinge of doubt. Oh, not that Sam was the cause of it. It had nothing to

129

do with the green-eyed devil. She just couldn't help thinking that Sam North would be very proprietary about the woman he loved. A long sigh escaped her lips. What was she thinking? Wasn't it Charles's cool reserve, his arrogant confidence, his poise under fire that had attracted her to him in the first place? Still, the dance had been fun. The unexpected visit, flattering.

The rain was coming down heavily now, and she tore her thoughts from both men as she pulled her purse from beneath the counter and searched inside for her keys. Reaching behind her, she fumbled for the light switch, but jerked her hand away with a start when the odd-shaped brass lamp on the shelf began to rock. What was Eugene doing in there?

Suddenly she was grinning, for the faintest sound of voices filtered through the narrow spout, and she *knew* exactly what he was doing in there . . . and with whom. No wonder she'd forgotten to lock the door behind Lovey. Lovey hadn't left at all.

Lauren was still smiling as she made the short dash to her car. Less than four yards, and she was soaked, but a glance in the rear view mirror confirmed what she already suspected: the rain hadn't blemished her appearance. Guess a drowned rat wasn't really less comely than a dry one, she thought, recalling the way she'd looked before. She laughed. At least the wrinkles were

130

gone and her dripping blond tresses definitely tamed.

As she drove by the bank, depositing the leather pouch, it occurred to her that she'd rarely laughed as much as she had this evening. She discovered something more. It felt damned good.

Deciding against driving directly home, she turned back in the direction of the Vieux Carré. The rain fell steadily, but it hadn't yet turned into one of the wild storms New Orleans was famous for. She drove slowly and cautiously, allowing plenty of room for stops, but she was taking her time as much for her own pleasure as for safety.

For the next thirty minutes, she drove up and down the streets in the French Quarter taking in the beauty of old buildings constructed by the descendants of romantic Frenchmen and Spaniards who had settled the port city. The rain had driven all but the most daring indoors, so she was able to proceed at her own pace.

She had to admit that Chicago had none of the Big Easy's ambience.She loved the intricately woven wrought iron of the balconies and verandas that circled the brick buildings, the vines that wandered up the walls, the courtyards, the cobbled roads and walkways. Neon signs blinked over storefronts and billboards capitalized on advertising, but oddly, they didn't detract from the special feel of a time long lost.

At the edge of the French Quarter, she caught sight of a gold-lettered sign announcing The Jazzy Lady. She jerked the car to a stop. The building occupied a full corner of the street, its entrance facing the intersection beneath a red awning. She opened her window a crack, but against the steady drumming of the rain, she could make out no sound of music. Still she stared. Like many other establishments in the famous district, it had a quaint, antique facade, but offered promise of a lavish interior. She imagined Sam sitting at a piano inside — no doubt a baby grand — enjoying the music he created with such ease and brilliance. For an instant, she wished she could watch him perform, work his magic on his audience, for she didn't doubt that he had that ability. Talent and charisma were a powerful combination.

But, she reminded herself, she hadn't taken the drive to think about Sam North. In fact, just the opposite.

Shifting into drive, she pulled from the curb without looking and earned a wrathful blast of a horn from the car she'd almost hit. Though the driver probably couldn't see her through the rain-streaked window, she shrugged an apology. As she drove away, she gave herself a lecture about keeping her attention where it belonged, which was *not* inside The Jazzy Lady.

She circled back to arrive at Jackson Square, remembering another visit there, long ago with her mother and aunt. Now she imagined it filled with tourists as it had been then, some merely meandering, others sitting for the artists who congregated there seven days a week. She stopped her car on the east side to look out over the river. Lights from one of the riverboats danced on the water, and laughter was carried back to her by the rain and wind. She was filled with a sense of belonging that shocked her, yet thrilled her, too.

Wouldn't Aunt Edna be surprised?

No, Lauren realized, she wouldn't. Edna had remembered, as she herself had not, how much she'd loved the city as a child. Well, her heart might belong to New Orleans, but her life was clearly committed to Chicago . . . and Charles.

With a sigh, she pulled the car back onto the street and started for home.

By the time she reached the house, the rain had all but stopped, but a glance at the clouds scurrying overhead indicated a lull before the storm. Pulling the shiny new BMW into the garage, she paused to admire its quiet elegance, and remember the pride of ownership she'd felt when she'd purchased it less than two months before. Odd, how little it mattered to her now. It was beautiful, comfortable, and reliable; but after all, for all its shiny chrome and rich leather, it was only a car.

The air, as she stepped from the garage into the night, was sweet with the scent of jasmine and magnolias, roses and honeysuckle. She stopped a few yards from the kitchen door to pluck a gardenia. Holding it to her nose, she inhaled deeply just as the phone pealed inside the house. She quickly tucked the flower in her hair over her ear and fumbled to unlock the door.

"Hello," she gasped into the phone.

"Lauren, for heaven's sake, I was getting desperate. Where on earth have you been?" her mother demanded without preliminaries.

"I worked late at the store, Mom, then took a leisurely drive around the French Quarter."

"Alone?"

"Just me and the beemer," Lauren said with just a hint of rebellion in her tone.

She heard the all too familiar cluck of her mother's tongue, but no lecture followed, which almost made Lauren groan. Judith Kennedy rarely missed the opportunity to chastise, which meant she had something more significant to rail about. With a sigh, Lauren stretched the phone cord to the kitchen table, plunked down her purse and keys, and pulled out a chair. "Are you still there, Mom?"

"Of course I'm still here, Lauren. I was waiting for an explanation, but since one is obviously not forthcoming, I'll get to why I called."

"Shoot," Lauren said, then smiled, glad that her mother couldn't see her even if she could detect the flippancy in her tone.

"I just spoke with Charles."

"And?" Lauren asked, feeling the first inklings of exasperation. Why couldn't her mother ever just spit it out? But she knew the answer. Lectures were always more painful if eked out in painfully slow doses.

"*And* he's quite frustrated by how long it's taking you to wrap things up in Louisiana."

"I spoke with him yesterday, Mom. He didn't sound frustrated at all. Actually, quite the opposite. He just received a promotion. Vice president. Did he tell you?"

"Of course he told me, and that's just my point. You should be here celebrating with him instead of down there trying to handle everything yourself. Your aunt had competent attorneys who could well wrap everything up without you."

Lauren ignored the last. They'd been through this before. "I'm sure Charles will be happy to celebrate with me when I come home. In fact, he's calling me tomorrow night, and I'll suggest a party for when I do get back to Chicago."

"I doubt very seriously that he'll be phoning you tomorrow night, Lauren. Hedges & Marshall—the same company who has so generously granted you a leave of absence—has planned a dinner in honor of his new position. Charles called to tell me that, as you're away, he had no choice but to invite Natalie Wolfe to accompany him. *Now* do you see what your stubbornness is doing?"

135

"Natalie Wolfe is not a threat, Mom. She's just a friend who happens to work with him. Actually, I think it's perfect. Natalie isn't seeing anyone, and Charles knows I wouldn't mind."

They talked for ten more minutes, her mother piling accusations at her feet, Lauren knocking them down. By the time she hung up, she was exhausted.

She'd planned to fry some okra, heat up some greens she'd cooked a few days before, and slice a tomato. She opted for a crisp Granny Smith apple instead.

As she made her way slowly up the stairs, she mimicked her mother, "If I remember correctly, Lauren, Natalie Wolfe is a very attractive young woman. Do you really believe you can afford the risk of her capturing Charles's attention?" She champed into her apple, not sure if it symbolized her mother's head or Natalie's. Then she halted at the top of the staircase. Funny, it hadn't occurred to her to be upset with Charles. Her mother was right. Natalie was an extremely handsome woman. Exotic, clever, bright, witty.

He *did* need a companion on his arm for the Hedges & Marshall dinner party. She'd attended many of them, and knew they were always lavish sit-down affairs that one didn't attend alone. Of course Charles could have invited Linda Pray or Marla Wallace. They, too, were young, single ad execs, though definitely not in Natalie's league.

So why wasn't she as upset about it as her mother?

Because, Lauren promptly reasoned, *she* understood Charles. *She* realized, as her mother did not, that image was important to a young executive on the move.

That settled, she finished her apple and dropped the core into a wastebasket with a promise to dispose of it in the morning.

By the time she had slipped between the cool sheets, the forecasted storm had arrived in full force. She snuggled beneath the security of her down comforter and flicked off the light. Her last glance before the room went dark was directed at the gardenia she'd placed on the dresser earlier, and she gave a fleeting worried thought to the flowers outside, hoping they'd survive the onslaught. She didn't give another thought to Charles or Natalie before sleep claimed her, but they refused to be pushed from her mind, turning up dutifully in her dreams.

Charles was whirling the tall exotic dark-haired beauty around the floor, and then there she was herself, dancing as well, and also in the arms of someone tall, dark. The room spun as they matched the frantic tempo of the polka. She smiled at Charles and Natalie as they passed, but when she looked into the eyes of

137

her dance partner, Sam North, her smile was far more dazzling and intimate.

The next morning, Lauren awakened late, but when she started to jump from the bed, she discovered her muscles were sore and stiff. Trying again, this time more gingerly, she climbed from the bed and moved toward the shower.

As she stepped beneath the steaming spray of water, she urged it to work its magic, and promised herself she wouldn't try to rearrange her entire stock in one night again.

When she finally got out of the shower, Lauren felt only slightly better. But she was determined not to open the store a minute late. So, except for an occasional involuntary groan, she resolutely ignored the aches that accompanied every movement. From the closet she selected a yellow sundress to brighten the overcast day. The loose flowing skirt would be the kindest thing for her protesting muscles.

She tied her hair into a neat ponytail with a matching ribbon and put on gold stud earrings as her only other adornment. Sliding her feet into a comfortable pair of sandals, she took the stairs slowly, babying her aches and pains.

Thank goodness she'd worked so hard to get everything arranged last night. She'd have little to do today except wait on customers.

A glance at her watch told her she had no

time for coffee. She'd just have to wait until she got to the store and brew some. And then she had an idea. Perhaps she could "radio" Eugene through his telepathic receiver to make a pot. With her fingers to her temples—though she was sure it wasn't necessary—she closed her eyes. "Okay, Gene, here goes. I'm late and hurting. Please make me a pot of coffee so I can revitalize myself as soon as I get there."

She opened her eyes and chuckled self-consciously as she looked around to make sure no one was watching her. Of course, that was silly. Who would be able to see her?

Pulling her purse strap over her shoulder she took a step, stopped, took another, then laughed with delight. The soreness had disappeared. And then she smelled it—the rich, aromatic scent of freshly brewed coffee. Spinning on her heels, she saw the steaming mug sitting on the kitchen counter. "Oh, Eugene, I think I love you."

Her spirits were high when she walked into the store less than twenty minutes later. She started to call for Eugene to thank him for the coffee and the added miracle of erasing her pain, but saw a note taped to the front of his lamp.

Gone fishing.

Eugene.

Lauren frowned. What the hell did that mean?

In five minutes she'd have to open the store, but first she had to find out what the genie's strange note meant.

She dashed across the street to Spice of Life. A Closed sign still hung in the window, but she knew someone must be inside. She tapped insistently on the window, and after a moment she saw Lovey coming to the door.

Lauren waved in greeting through the glass, but the smile she wore slipped at the sight of her friend's tear-stained face.

As soon as the key was turned, Lauren barged in. "What the heck's going on?" she demanded. She didn't give Lovey a chance to answer but grabbed her by the shoulders and steered her toward the rear of the shop, talking all the while. "First I come into work to find an enigmatic note from Eugene. Then I come over here to ask you to explain it to me and I find you've been crying. Don't tell me 'Gone fishing' is his way of saying farewell. He hasn't faded away, Lovey. Tell me he hasn't."

Lovey sniffled, at the same time scooting her rotund bottom onto a high stool in the kitchenette at the back of her health food store. She shook her head. "No, not yet, but it's getting near. At least I suspect it is. He won't admit it. Keeps insisting there's still time, but last night . . ." She stopped, unable to finish her sentence as a blush washed over her face.

"Go on," Lauren nudged with rare gentleness.

"Last night we spent the evening together. It was the same as always. Eugene was funny, regaling me with stories about people he's known over the centuries. We laughed and joked and . . . and shared some tender moments, and right in the middle of . . . everything, he, ah, started fading." Tears sprang to her eyes. "Oh, Lauren, you have no idea what it's like to watch the man you love literally wash out in your arms."

Lauren shook her head. "No, I don't suppose I can, although I have witnessed the fading. It is quite traumatic. But, Lovey, where is he today? What the hell does 'Gone fishing' mean?"

Lovey plucked a tissue from a decorative container on the counter in front of her and dabbed at her eyes and nose. "He really has gone fishing, Lauren. Says Mark Twain—Samuel Clemens, you know—taught him to appreciate how much can be resolved when one's alone on the water or hunting. Of course Eugene is opposed to hunting. I don't think he'd ever even consider keeping a fish he might hook. So, I imagine he's thinking." She laughed unexpectedly and hiccuped. "Probably doesn't even use a hook if the truth be known, he's that gentle and good-hearted."

"Then he thinks he might be able to find an answer to prevent himself from fading away if he has time to think?" Lauren asked hopefully.

141

Lovey shook her head, her eyes once again brimming with tears. "No, umm, he's just trying to come to terms with . . . with the inevitable."

"Okay, now, Lovey, you have to stop this crying. You're not doing yourself any good, and you're certainly not helping Eugene."

"I know. I just feel so helpless. I love him so much, and I can't bear the thought of losing him."

Lauren began pacing around the small room. There had to be something she could do. But what? Suddenly she stopped, turning to face Lovey who sat weeping, head bowed and lost in her own thoughts. "Lovey True, stop this crying right this second! We've got to talk."

Lovey made a valiant try and even managed a slight smile.

"Okay, that's better," Lauren said, her tone kinder. "Now, if I remember, when we first met you said there was a way to save him, right?" At the other woman's nod, she pressed on. "You know what it is, but you're forbidden by some kind of genie law from telling me, right?"

"I could tell you," Lovey said, "but then you'd be bound not to help, the same as me. You have to find the way yourself, Lauren, and I hope you can. I *really* hope you can."

"I'm going to try, Lovey, I promise, but I need your help."

"But what can I do?"

"Well, first I have to get him back here. Then

142

I have to find someone to man my store for me. Can you suggest anyone?"

"Sure. Me. I have a girl working for me. She'll be here in about thirty minutes. I'll go over to Yesterday's Treasures and stay there as long as you want me. But where are you going?"

"If I can bring Eugene back, I'm going to take him for a drive. We might be gone for several hours, Lovey, but I think if I spend some time with him, maybe I'll find out how to save him. It might not work, but I don't know any other way."

From the light that suddenly shone in Lovey's eyes, Lauren felt confident she was on to something. But what?

"So how do I get Eugene back here?"

"Easy, just call him. He'll come."

"But what if he's gone fishing in some ice hole in Alaska, can he still hear me?"

"Of course. You're his mistress. He's tuned into your every need." Lovey giggled. "But I don't think he's that far away. He rather likes fishing on the Mississippi."

Lauren laughed as well, then unable to resist the curiosity that niggled at her, leaned forward to ask, "Lovey could I ask you a personal question?"

"Sure," Lovey answered with the childlike openness that Lauren had found enchanting at their first meeting.

143

"You said last night that you stayed with Eugene. You mentioned sharing some, ah, tender moments." She stopped, suddenly almost too embarrassed to continue, but she *had* to know. "Lovey, just before I left the store, his vase started rocking. Were you, ah, you know . . ."

"Making love?"

"Well, yes. I mean, are genies able to make love with mortals."

For the first time Lovey blushed. "And how. You have no idea how fantastic he is, although I don't think it has to do with his magical powers. I suspect it's the experience he's gleaned over the centuries. After all, he once lived in a harem where women are rumored to have possessed knowledge of erotica that would curl our hair. And then there was the brief period when he belonged to Cleopatra. Eugene says the history books are wrong when they claim her lure for Mark Antony was the Egyptian empire. Cleo was quite an accomplished woman.

"But would you believe, Lauren, Eugene says I'm the only true love he's ever had?"

As Lauren stared at the delicately freckled face of her friend, she saw wonder. She shook her head. It wasn't hard for her to believe, for it was obvious the sweet woman was aptly named. She understood true love and was one of the rare genuinely good people in an otherwise selfish world.

She hugged Lovey's ample body tightly, making a promise she prayed she could keep. "Don't worry, Lovey, if there really is a way to save Eugene, I'm going to find it." Then she brushed away her tears and said, "Okay, so here goes: Eugene Ali Simm Simm, get your ass back here right this instant."

"Right this instant" was taken literally by the genie, who appeared faster than Lauren could draw breath. "Johnny on the spot, aren't you?" she asked as soon as she'd recovered from the surprise that she suspected she'd never grow accustomed to. On the other hand, she wasn't going to have to worry about that much longer, was she? Eugene would soon be wherever it was genies faded to, or he'd become mortal and no longer capable of materializing from thin air.

"You called, Lauren?"

The bells that hung over the front door of Spice of Life jingled before Lauren could respond, and Lovey excused herself. "That's probably Crickett, my assistant. I'll just get her squared away and scoot on over to your store." She stopped long enough to plant a chaste kiss on her lover's cheek. "See you later, honey."

Eugene smiled but turned his attention back to Lauren to learn what she wanted.

"Come on, Gene," Lauren said, taking his hand. "We're going for a drive."

"Where to?"

"Just around the countryside. I stumbled on

that estate sale yesterday. Who knows what we can find together. Aunt Edna used to say she was going junking, so I guess you can say that's what we're doing."

"But why do you need me?"

Lauren shrugged, keeping her expression blank and her answer vague. "Oh, I don't know. Guess I'm hoping if I don't luck out finding antiques, you might be able to help me find something else I'm looking for."

"Such as?"

Lauren sighed with feigned exasperation. "Are all genies as nosy as you?"

"Not all of them, no, but then there aren't very many of us around today, so it's kind of difficult to make a comparison," Eugene replied, dead serious.

Lauren shook her head. "You're too much, Gene. I was joking, okay? Lighten up, and please, stop sounding like my philosophy professor at Purdue. I like you much better when you're in your hippie mode."

"Sorry," he mumbled. "Guess I'm not feeling very hip this morning."

This time Lauren's exasperated sigh was in earnest. "Come on, we've got to go in search of a miracle."

"Thought we were looking for antiques."

Lauren didn't answer, but she thought, *I've already got the antique, Gene. I've got to find the miracle to save it.*

Chapter Eight

"Fasten your seat belt, Gene," Lauren said.

"Mind if I ask where we're going?"

"Oh, I don't know. Yesterday I went to Port Sulphur. Today I thought we'd head in the opposite direction—Lafayette, maybe, or St. Martin."

"Try Lafayette," Eugene said.

Lauren looked at him suspiciously. "You using your magic powers again to locate antiques for me, Gene?"

The genie had settled into the seat and closed his eyes. He shrugged, then muttered, "Just trying to be a good assistant."

"Okay," Lauren said with more exuberance than she felt, "I'll accept your help this time, but after that, no more magic until we get back, all right? Today we're just two friends out junking and enjoying one another's company. How does that sound?"

Eugene looked sideways at her, and she was

gratified by his grin. "Sounds groovy to me, mama."

As Lauren drove down Canal Street then eventually merged into traffic on the highway, she tried to make chitchat. It wasn't difficult. Eugene matched her light tone, returned her teasing when she poked fun, and laughed with her at a story she remembered about her aunt. But the light had gone from his eyes and in spite of his effort to disguise it, she knew that his soul was filled with a profound sadness. Depression began to settle over her as well. As if sensing his failure to fool her, Eugene dropped the charade and brought up the subject of his impending doom.

"Look, Lauren, I know why you wanted me to go with you today. You think that by spending time with me, you'll find the answer to keeping me from fading. I appreciate it, but I think it's a waste of time and energy. I may only have a few weeks left, and I want you to be thinking about the wishes you want me to grant. Odds are, you'll never encounter another genie, so you might as well take advantage of it."

Lauren didn't answer for a few minutes. She couldn't. The knot in her throat had to be swallowed first. After a moment, she tried again. "Tell me about Aunt Edna. What did she wish for?"

Eugene smiled—really smiled this time—but

he wagged a finger at the same time. "Unh-unh, can't tell you that. She made me promise to keep her wishes to myself. But I *can* tell you that she was very careful about what she wished for. She was a quick study, understood at once that she could call on me for favors without blowing her wishes, and managed to keep me around much longer than most. Special lady, your aunt."

"What did she tell you about me?"

"Ah, fishing for compliments," Eugene teased. "Well, you won't be disappointed. She was very proud of you, though as I've told you before, she thought you needed to loosen up a bit. She said when you were a little girl you had more passion for life than anyone she'd ever known. *Joie de vivre,* she called it. She said you lost it somewhere along the way, and she was counting on you rediscovering it when you came to New Orleans. Are you finding it again, Lauren?"

Lauren thought about the afternoons she'd spent with Casey, about the finds she'd made yesterday at the estate sale, and the dance with Sam the night before. Had she really lost her joy of life in her pursuit of success? Were those seemingly insignificant moments of pleasure the rediscovering of that? "I don't like New Orleans, Eugene, but I can't deny that there haven't been some good times. Still, I haven't changed my mind about returning to my work in Chicago."

"Are you sure you don't like New Orleans, or

are you parroting what Charles and your mother think about it? Seems to me you're liking it more than you want anyone to know. Take the calliope you discovered yesterday. Bet you sat on that floor for an hour playing those discs, humming and smiling. And wasn't that Sam North you were dancing with last night?"

Lauren's brows knit together. "Do you see everything I do?"

"Of course not, but I'm tuned into your moods. When you're sad I feel it, and when you're happy I sense that too. Every now and then when I hear you laugh, I just take a peak to see what's caused it."

"Oh." Lauren slowed the car as they reached the city limits of Lafayette, stopped at a red light, then glanced over at the genie. "You're right. I was excited about the calliope. It was quite a find, and I can't deny it was fun dancing with Sam, but those are only fleeting moments. There's more to life than fun, Eugene," she said piously.

"You're right," he agreed amiably. "There's finding what makes you happy, *really* makes you happy. That's rarely a job promotion, or a title, or even monetary success. It usually involves love and family and friends."

"I know that!" Lauren said, suddenly annoyed. How had they started talking about her? They were supposed to be finding a way to help him.

150

As if reading her thoughts again, Eugene suddenly turned the topic of conversation back to himself. "Over the centuries I've watched men destroy themselves with ambition. Not that ambition is always bad, mind you, but as the old saying goes, Though many would be king, few have kingly qualities.

"I learned a long time ago that the small things in life are what make it worth living. Know who made me realize that? Charles Perrault."

"Sorry, you've lost me," Lauren said.

"He was a French author who became famous for his Mother Goose fairy tales. He didn't have an easy life, but he discovered early on that life was only full if one found pleasure no matter how small and passed it on to others. Millions of children have been delighted with his stories."

Lauren chuckled. "So what are you saying? I should write fairy tales?"

Eugene's frown was heavy with disapproval. "Your aunt also told me that you were anything but obtuse, Lauren Kathleen Kennedy."

"Sorry, I do know what you're saying, but, Gene, I'm happy when I'm working on an important ad account or when Charles and I are planning our future."

"Are you really? Seems to me Charles's plans center around him — oh, not that you aren't included, but I get the impression he considers you a beautiful backdrop. Think about it. *He's*

151

looking to become a senior partner in Hedges and Monroe. The two of you will marry one day when he thinks the time's right. You'll buy a house in the 'burbs—preferably North Shore—and have the socially acceptable 2.5 children who will be perfectly behaved because *he* says so. And, you, Lauren? *You'll* play hostess to all of his important clients."

"That's unfair. Charles knows I want to keep working." But she felt unease stir in her heart as she remembered the last telephone conversation with him. "I suppose you think life with Sam North would be more to my liking."

"Only you can answer that, but at least the man does seem able to spark a response of some sort every time you're together."

"Mostly anger," Lauren bit out, but then she relented. "Okay, so last night was different, but I could never respect him, Eugene. He had it all, and he threw it away. What woman would want a man who would give up everything to satisfy his own selfish needs?"

"Wallis Simpson certainly wanted King Edward," Eugene countered smartly.

Lauren laughed now with gusto, shaking her head at the same time. "I can't win with you. You've been around too long. You have all the answers."

"Wisdom is often acquired with age," Eugene agreed a trifle smugly.

"Okay, then smarty-pants, make it all easier

for me."

"I can do that. Put the wish together, phrasing it carefully so you get exactly what you want. But be sure you're right about what would make it easy, because if you're wrong, you could end up at your own Waterloo, just like Napoleon."

"I don't have the answers, Eugene. I thought I did. Now I'm confused."

"Then perhaps you should trust me. I want things to be right for you, Lauren," he said quietly.

Unexpected tears burned in Lauren's eyes. She'd forced Eugene to accompany her on this outing to find a way to help him, and instead he was concentrating on her needs.

They spotted a flea market a couple of minutes later, so conversation of a personal nature was dropped for the time being.

For more than two hours they wended their way up and down the makeshift aisles, Lauren picking up an item that looked authentically old, Eugene either giving a nod of approval or a discreet shake of his head. When at last she'd made several purchases, Eugene leaned forward and asked if she wanted him to blink them into the trunk of her car.

"No! I told you, at least for as long as we're on this outing, no magic. Just two friends

153

working together." Then she had a thought. "You weren't using your special talent to tell me which pieces were authentic, were you?"

"Didn't have to. I'm the oldest relic out here today, but even if that weren't the case, I learned a lot from your aunt."

Lauren started to say something but stopped when she noticed that Eugene was turning into a tree. She gasped, recovering a second later when she realized he was merely suffering another fading spell. The old cypress was in fact several yards behind him. "Quick, Gene, let's get to the car. You're practically translucent."

But the fading spell passed almost at once, and Eugene was restored to living color of blue and green bell-bottom pants and embroidered natural bleached muslin shirt. Only his skin remained pale, and Lauren realized that the fading spells were as frightening to him as to her. "I'm sorry, Eugene. I know this can't be easy for you," she said gently.

"The inevitable is rarely something we look forward to." At Lauren's questioning glance, he explained, at the same time loading the trunk of her car with their new acquisitions. "Death is inevitable as growing old, going through hard times, suffering sadness or loss. The good things are only to be hoped for and snatched from Fate's greedy hands—if one's lucky enough to recognize them when they come his way."

Once they'd settled in the car, Lauren tested

his theory with examples of the "good" he was referring to. "Like love? Friendship? Success? None of those are inevitable?"

"Sadly not. True love, the kind in fairy tales and romance novels, is a rare find. Success? Two men with equal opportunity, talent, drive can reach for the same brass ring, and only one may come away with it. And friendship is a word too often used when it doesn't apply."

"Is this another lesson, Eugene?" Lauren asked, just a hint of teasing in her tone in her effort to make him forget his precarious state.

"Could be, or could be I'm just reminding myself how precious my last days are." He gave a weary smile, then asked softly, "Mind if we go back now? I think I'd like to spend some time with Lovey."

Lauren started the engine, but when she pressed on the accelerator, the tires whined and spun.

"Think we're stuck, mama," Eugene said, at once back to the jaunty hippie manner of her first encounter with him. "All I gotta do is blink, and we're outta here."

Lauren chuckled, shaking her head and accepting the dare she heard in his tone. "No way. All I have to do is rock it back and forth and ease it out." But for all her confidence, the car became deeper and deeper mired in the mud caused by last night's storm.

"Now what?" Eugene asked, his expression as

155

innocent as an infant's.

"*Now* you get behind the wheel while I stick some cardboard under the back tires," Lauren said with determination. As she got out, and Eugene climbed over to sit in the driver's seat, she told him, "Don't do anything until I tell you to."

She tore strips from the cardboard boxes they'd just placed in the trunk and wedged them under the rear tires. Then leaning against the car with her shoulder and arms braced, she yelled for him to "Hit it!"

Mud and muck sprayed from the spinning wheels, but the car didn't move. Lauren swiped at her face and the front of her dress before going around to the driver's window. Eugene was doubled over with laughter. "Very funny, buster!" Lauren said, but she couldn't stop the giggles bubbling up inside her. "Okay, so it is funny, but I am *not* getting in my new car covered in mud. Give me a blink and clean me up, then get this car out of this rut."

"It's all right to use my magic now?"

"Eugene," Lauren growled.

"Okay, okay, but I'll swear, mama, Edna was much easier to understand. She didn't keep changing the rules on me." Before she could reply, he jerked his head. The mud covering her from head to toe disappeared, as did the soggy ruts under the wheels.

Eugene scooted back into the passenger's seat

without being asked, and Lauren slid in behind the wheel. She moved the gearshift into drive, but paused long enough to tell him primly, "The rules are quite simple. You only come to my aid when I ask you."

"What about if you *need* my help and don't know it?"

"You mean like if I'm about to step in front of a train?"

"Yeah, or if you're about to miss an opportunity that will only come your way once in a lifetime."

Lauren considered this. "Yes, I suppose I can see that you'd need to run interference then as well."

"Okay, just so we both agree on the rules," Eugene said, turning away to look out the window to hide his grin of satisfaction.

As they drove back toward New Orleans, Lauren was silent for several miles, then she said, "You know, Gene, this magic business is confusing. I mean, if I can ask for favors any time I need them, why do I have to worry about using up my three wishes?"

"You know, mama, that's so easy I'm surprised you haven't figured it out. I'm yours to command for as long as you need me — provided I don't fade away first, of course. I can help you do almost anything as long as it's for your own good. I *can't* do anything that would be wrong for you unless you *wish* for it. Then I'm bound by the three-wish rule, which states that I'm powerless to deny you even if I know you're wishing for the wrong thing."

"Oh, I guess that is pretty obvious."

"One more thing. Once you've made your three wishes, I become a free agent again until someone new lays claim to my lamp."

"Okay, I think I've got it now."

Eugene studied her face. She'd given him permission to run some pretty slick interference, and he hoped she really did understand. He watched for her reaction when they pulled into the parking lot behind Yesterday's Treasures.

Yep, he'd been right as rain, he thought when he saw the light that suddenly shone in her eyes as she spotted the red Corvette parked there.

"Well, I'm outta here," Eugene said. "Ask Lovey to stop in and see me before she leaves, will you." With an imperious wave of his hand he disappeared in a whiff of smoke.

Lauren looked from the trunk of her car to the back door of her antique shop, torn between carrying in her booty or going inside to see what Sam North was doing here *again*. Her curiosity won.

She found Sam sitting beside Lovey on the countertop, legs swinging. They were deep in conversation, laughing at something and oblivious to her arrival until she stood directly in front of them.

"Oh, hi, Lauren," Lovey said. "How did the

drive go?"

Lauren shrugged. "We found some great things for the shop, but I didn't come up with any answers." As Lovey's sky-blue eyes clouded, she offered a smile of encouragement. "We did talk, Lovey, and I think we have some time. Don't worry, I'm pretty damn determined, and I have a fairly good track record at solving problems."

The clouds didn't disappear, but Lovey put up a good front, even managing a thin smile. "Well, you'll be glad to know that business has been brisk. I sold that exquisite blue and lavender quilt — the customer didn't even haggle over the price, incidentally — and let me see. Oh, yeah, the butter churn, a doll, two cookie tins, and the calliope you bought yesterday."

"The calliope? To whom?"

"Yours truly," Sam said, just a trace of smug satisfaction gleaming in his wicked green eyes.

"Why on earth would you want a music box?" she asked, not bothering to hide her irritation. She'd priced it as soon as she'd brought it into the shop, but had decided during the night not to sell it. It was possibly the only antique in the world she wanted for herself.

"It's not for me, actually. I bought it as a gift for someone else."

Lauren was dying to ask who he would willingly spend so much on, but she'd rather cut out her tongue than give him the satisfaction.

159

"Well, how nice for you. I'm sure whoever it's for will be delighted." She turned away from him in a clear gesture of dismissal. "Thanks a million for standing in for me today, Lovey. I guess if I'm going to be around much longer, I'll need to look into hiring an assistant."

"I enjoyed it," Lovey said, hopping down from the counter. "Guess I'll be getting back to my place."

"Oh, Lovey, wait! Eugene asked that you see him before you leave. I think he's in the back." She winked.

"Gotcha," Lovey said. "Thanks for keeping me company, Sam. Hope your friend enjoys the music box."

"How long have you been here?" Lauren asked Sam.

"A couple of hours, I guess. Lovey seemed a bit in the dumps, so I thought I'd try and cheer her up."

That was kind of him, Lauren realized. But it irritated her that he kept revealing sides to himself that didn't fit the raffish devil she'd believed him to be. She went behind the counter to put it between them. "I'm sure she appreciated it. But I'm here now, so you don't have to hang around any longer."

"Got nothing better to do. I have to be at the club to go over some business with the manager at seven-thirty. Until then I'm free as a bird."

"Then maybe you should take the calliope to

the friend you've bought it for. *She'll* probably be thrilled." Even as she put the emphasis on the feminine pronoun, hoping he'd correct her, she could have kicked herself. Why did she care who he'd bought it for?

"No can do. It's a birthday gift."

"And today isn't her birthday?"

"Nope. I just like to plan ahead."

"Well, if you'll excuse me, I do have things to do," Lauren said.

"Need some help?"

Lauren considered. "Actually, yes, you could help me carry in some boxes from my car."

"You got it," he told her cheerfully. "But on one condition."

Lauren stiffened.

"Relax, all I want is for you to have dinner with me."

"Why on earth would you invite me to dinner?" Lauren asked. "Seems to me I remember that you said I reminded you of your ex-wife whom you abhor."

Sam came behind the counter, cornering her and standing mere inches away. He put his hands on her arms, letting them trail down the satiny flesh until they found her hands, which he took in his. "In some ways, I suppose I have to stand by that statement. She's attractive, though not classically beautiful like you. She's ambitious and driven and even mercenary, which

161

you've admitted to being."

Lauren opened her mouth to protest, her dark eyes suddenly luminous with angry passion. She'd never said she was mercenary! But Sam silenced her with a kiss that startled her so much she stood frozen on the outside though a fire was suddenly raging on the inside.

The kiss was gentle yet lingering, and when Sam stepped slowly away, he grinned. "But, baby, she doesn't taste like you, and she certainly can't dance a polka like you did last night."

In spite of her irritation at his comparison to his former wife, Lauren smiled.

Encouraged, Sam pressed on. "So, what do you say? Have dinner with me? Look, what's the worst that could happen? We could form a truce of sorts, kind of a detente." He waved an arm expansively around the store. "Thanks to my dear, albeit busybody aunts, you have enough stock to keep you around for another six months if you don't find a buyer in the meantime. So as neighbors, we're bound to run into one another on a frequent basis. Wouldn't it be nice to be friends?"

Lauren couldn't fault his logic, but she mistrusted his motives. She didn't know Sam North well, but from the few encounters they'd had in the past few days, she found it difficult to accept him at his word. There seemed only one way to put her suspicions to rest. "All right.

Dinner it is. Where shall I meet you?"

Sam consulted his watch. "It's already four o'clock. Why don't we go now? We can walk the Vieux Carré, do some browsing, even spy on your rival antique dealers. What do you say?"

"I say, I'll meet you after five when I close the shop. Like it or not, I'm a store owner, and I can't just shut down whenever I please."

"No, but you can ask Eugene to watch things for you for one measly hour."

Before Lauren could argue further, Eugene appeared from the back of the store. "Did I hear my name?" he asked.

Lauren squinted at him suspiciously. For all that he wore the most guileless expression she'd witnessed, she wasn't fooled. He'd been eaves-dropping again. Then she heard Sam asking him to man the store until closing time. Suddenly she was grabbing her purse as Sam guided her to the front door, a hand placed gently but firmly on the small of her back. Why, she was being taken hostage, and Eugene was smiling on them with the benevolence of a kindly father sending his daughter on her first date.

"We're not driving?" she asked.

"Nope, thought we'd just sorta roam awhile; work up an appetite."

They meandered through every antique shop on Royal Street, then through souvenir stores, an art gallery, and a voodoo shop. In spite of her resolve to appear uninterested, Lauren found

163

herself fascinated by the many bottles of potions, the dolls with their ugly grimacing faces, and the colorful cloth pouches that the woman behind the counter explained were *gris gris,* good luck charms. "They bring much good fortune," she said to Lauren, though her eyes kept flickering to Sam.

"Want one?" Sam asked.

"I don't think so," Lauren said, feeling inexplicably nervous. "Let's go."

But before they could leave, an ancient woman, tall and match-stick thin, with skin the color and texture of charred parchment, appeared as if out of thin air. Lauren shrieked at the sight of the boa constrictor wrapped around the woman's neck.

The woman laughed, a soft, deep cackle that sent shivers up Lauren's arms and down her spine. Her smile revealed several missing teeth and one capped with gold. "Let Marie tell your fortune, missy. I tell you if this man be good for you or if he bring sadness to your life."

Lauren cast a sidelong glance at Sam which quickly changed to a glare when she saw the challenging laughter in his eyes.

"All right," she said with more bravado than she felt.

The woman gestured with a long bony hand for them to follow her to the back of the shop.

"I'll just wait here," Sam said.

"Oh, no you won't," Lauren protested, taking

164

his hand and dragging him with her.

As they went behind a curtain, she mentally cursed herself for letting Sam provoke her into taking part in the charade. Before they left, she promised herself, she would buy a doll that resembled him to stick pins into.

"Sit there, missy," the old woman instructed. She unwound the lethargic boa constrictor from her neck and placed it on a dried bough protruding from a corner of the floor.

Fifteen minutes later, Sam and Lauren left, he guffawing, she trying to hush him. "Stop! It wasn't funny. It was . . . scary. Did you see the way she looked at me with those black eyes?"

"You just got jittery 'cause you're as superstitious as she is and believed she was hitting too close to home."

"She was. Even you have to admit she was pretty good. She knew I'd recently lost someone very dear to me, that I was in a state of limbo, even about Charles."

"Number one, most people lose people who are close to them in one way or the other. She didn't say 'death.' Hell, she could have told me the same thing with Casey leaving Tuesday to go back to New York.

"As for being in a state of limbo, that's pretty general, too. Think how many people are constantly considering career changes, a move, even a new relationship."

Lauren thought about it. "I guess so, but how do you explain what she knew about Charles? She knew about his promotion. That he doesn't want me here. She even described him to a tee, right down to his blond hair, blue eyes, and Brooks Brothers suits."

Sam laughed. "I take it back, you're nothing like Janice—my ex-wife. She doesn't have a gullible bone in her body. In fact, if you looked up 'cynic' in the dictionary, you'd find her picture."

"I am not gullible!"

"Oh, yeah. Baby, you are one heck of a pushover. Think about what she said. She mentioned a blond man who is very proud of his image. He lives in a distant city. She said there has been a strain between you in recent months, which you assumed referred to you coming to New Orleans. She didn't say he got a promotion. She said he's focused on success."

"And that's Charles."

"Maybe it's your boss. What's his name?"

"Clifton Hedges."

"Blond by any chance? Natty dresser?"

It annoyed Lauren that he was right, but she nodded, reluctantly.

"Well, there you have it. He's probably not exactly overjoyed that you took a leave of absence, thus the strain between the two of you, and he's definitely career focused."

Lauren stopped and folded her arms across

her chest. "Well, Mr. Know-It-All, you just lost your own argument. It doesn't matter if she was talking about Charles or Clifton, the fact remains, she was tuned in to the people in my life."

Sam shrugged, but his eyes expressed his disbelief better than words. "Whatever."

"You're just ticked because she didn't mention you," Lauren teased.

"Maybe she did. She did say something about you entering a magical period of your life. And if I recall, she said for you to follow the music that will guide you to happiness if you let your heart hear it. Music is my middle name, remember."

"The only music my heart hears is the grumbling my hungry stomach is playing," Lauren teased, ignoring the first part, for she couldn't tell him that the magic referred to Eugene.

"Very funny," he said, taking her elbow to guide her. They'd arrived at Jackson Square, and just as she remembered, there were artists everywhere with brushes and palettes in hand. "We'll go eat in a few minutes, but first, let's go watch. Some of them are very good."

In fact, most of the artists were exceptionally talented, and as they passed from one to the other, Lauren thought what fun it would be to have a painting of herself to send home to Charles.

Sam must have read her thoughts, though obviously the part about Charles had been lost on him, for he said, "Sit for one, Lauren. I'll hang it in the club."

"Why on earth would you want to hang a picture of me in The Jazzy Lady?"

"Why not? It will give me stories to tell of the little girl who grew up and left Peter Pan behind."

His tone was as defensive as his words, and she wondered what she'd done to offend him. But she sat obediently in front of the artist, avoiding Sam's eyes for the next thirty minutes.

When the portrait was completed, Sam stood beside her and studied it. "Not bad. He even captured the arrogant glint in your eye."

Lauren didn't answer but dug in her purse for the money to pay.

"I've got it," Sam said, slipping the man a couple of bills. "If I'm going to keep it, I should pay."

"But I was going to send it to Charles."

"What for?" Sam asked, sounding annoyed. "He'll have the real thing once you return to Chicago. All I'll have is a memory."

Lauren was about to ask why he'd want a remembrance when he was continually irritated by her, but in that instant, he pulled her against him to kiss her. This time the kiss was anything but gentle. His lips were bruising and demanding, and confusion was the only thing that kept Lauren from pulling away. At least that's what

168

she told herself. The truth was, his lips sent fire coursing through her veins and provoked a weakness that was almost debilitating. She sagged against him, and her arm lifted of its own volition to caress the nape of his neck beneath his long hair.

It wasn't a long kiss—lasting no more than a few seconds—but when he pulled away, Lauren almost stumbled. Her face burned as she caught the stares of onlookers smiling their approval.

Sam seemed equally embarrassed, for he grabbed her arm and pulled her away with such force that she tripped. But before she could fall, he caught her to him and pressed her against his chest once again. For one hopeful second, she thought he was going to repeat the kiss, but he set her away from him almost brusquely.

Embarrassed and inexplicably hurt, Lauren reacted in anger. "Sam!" she called out when he started to walk off again.

He stopped and faced her, eyebrows raised and a half-smile tugging at his lips.

"Why do you keep doing that?"

"Keep doing what?" he asked innocently.

"You know perfectly well *what*. Why do you keep kissing *me?* I'm practically engaged."

"Practically engaged ain't exactly to the altar, baby."

"Don't call me baby. You said you wanted to be friends."

"I do."

"And do you kiss all of your friends?"

The devil that lurked in his soul suddenly surfaced in his eyes. "Only the pretty ones, babe. And after the first time," he added with a cocky wink, "only those who kiss me back."

Chapter Nine

Sam saw the answering anger spark in Lauren's eyes, but it disappeared with the easy smile that unexpectedly spread across her face. She sauntered up to him, hips swinging seductively, and reached up and touched his cheek. "You know, Sam, you are a charmer. I can see why playing in a club every night has such appeal for you. I can imagine the women who must throw themselves at your feet. And I owe you an apology. I said that you hadn't grown up, but I can see now that I was wrong." Her voice was rich with honey sweetness. "Oh, you're still a boy, but a *playboy*. How nice for women who like to be teased and toyed with. Unfortunately, I'm not one of them."

"Funny, I thought you enjoyed the game as much as I," Sam drawled.

Lauren canted her head slightly to the side. "Hmm, yes, I can see how you might have thought that. I think that's typical of the playboy syndrome. You're so full of yourself, so

confident of your machismo, you wouldn't recognize rejection if it were dumped over your
head. But read my lips, buster. *I'm not a play-
thing.*"

Sam laughed as she brushed past him, stalk-
ing off across the square in the direction of her
store, but the laughter faded quickly once she
was out of earshot, and he cursed his stupidity.
Why had he purposefully antagonized her? Hell,
why had he gone to the shop in the first place?
And why in blazes had he kissed her again?

He trailed after her. Not that he was following her or thought to catch up to her. On the
contrary, if he never saw Lauren Kennedy again,
it would be too soon. She was bad news. She
was the kind of woman who crawled inside a
man, got in his blood, and invaded his senses
like a cancer he couldn't get rid of. She was
beautiful—a rare combination of sultriness and
innocence that made a man want to protect and
devour at the same time. And damn it, she was
a lot like Janice. Yes, sir, Lauren and her Chi-
cago-high-profile-executive-almost-fiancé probably suited one another to a tee. He wished them
all the misery they'd probably find with one another.

He walked slowly, giving her time to leave
Yesterday's Treasures before he arrived to claim
his car. But as lethargic as his pace was, his
mind was roiling with conflict. As quickly as
he'd condemned her for being like his ex-wife,

he remembered the sparkle in her eyes the night before when he'd spun her around the store as they'd danced the polka. Janice would never have been amused by the impromptu dance.

In fact, it was that very memory—the feel of her soft, supple body in his arms, the smell of her that was a mixture of perfume and dusty sweat, the sparkle in her eyes and her throaty laugh—that had made sleep impossible for him that day. He'd been unable to stop thinking about her and had decided to pay another visit to the antique store to set his thoughts straight about her. He'd invented a flimsy excuse about having misplaced his wallet the night before, but she hadn't been there and the excuse had gone unvoiced. Instead, he'd found Lovey True, the apple-cheeked proprietress of the health food store, tending shop for Lauren. His disappointment had been keen. And then on impulse, he'd bought the calliope.

As he walked along Bourbon Street, he shook his head. It was almost as if the fair Lauren had cast a spell over him. He couldn't seem to stop thinking about her, and when he was with her, couldn't resist the desire to kiss her. And when he kissed her, he nearly drowned in the emotional sea that the taste of her created. And every damned time, she could be relied on to deliver the slap that jolted him back to earth and safe ground where reason returned to remind him that the woman he kissed was an illusion. The real Lauren Kennedy was cold-blooded, materialistic, and predictably uptight. Exactly like the woman who had almost destroyed his life when she'd kept his daughter and refused to follow him back to New Orleans.

It was a good thing Lauren would soon be leaving. He could get back to his routine, she could marry her aristocrat, and the world would be back on track.

He had just rounded the corner when he saw her beemer turn out from the drive. Stepping back into the shadows, he watched her drive past and felt his gut tighten. At the stop sign, she paused to pull the ribbon from her hair, sending the pale gold mass cascading to her shoulders. She ruffled it with her fingers, and damn if he didn't wish it was his fingers tousling the silky strands.

By the time Lauren pulled out of the parking lot of Yesterday's Treasures, she had calmed down and composed her thoughts which had run helter-skelter since her parting from the disturbing musician.

Sam North was undeniably handsome, incredibly sexy, uncommonly charming . . . and dangerous. Any woman would find it almost impossible to avoid succumbing to the charisma he exuded. She was no different.

That understood, she vowed to keep distance

174

between them until she left the south. It shouldn't be too difficult. He was her neighbor, true, but she been in New Orleans for six weeks before they'd encountered one another. Surely she wouldn't be here much longer and could manage her schedule so that they didn't have to so much as wave in passing in the driveway.

But as she left the Quarter, turning onto Canal Street, she felt the first twinge of guilt. Perhaps she'd been too hard on him. After all, as much as it galled her to admit it, he was right about her returning his kisses. She felt the blood rise to her cheeks as she recalled the feelings his lips had evoked, the knot in her lower belly, and the thrill that had almost provoked a ragged groan. She'd been angry with herself more than with him. *She* was the one in love with another man, and kissing Sam as if *they* were lovers rather than barely more than reacquainted strangers.

Yes, she definitely owed him an apology, but that would necessitate seeing him at least one more time. Well, so what? Surely she could handle one more encounter that needn't last longer than it took her to say she was sorry for jumping on his case. She'd tell him, present her hand with the offer to be friends, then calmly walk away . . . and keep a comfortable distance between them from then on.

That settled, she leaned back, determined to let the drive home relax her. Twilight had settled over the city, and as she turned onto her street, she pushed the button to open all of the windows. Shutting off the air conditioner, she inhaled the unique New Orleans scents: the pungent fragrance of hundreds of varieties of flowers mingling with the sharp briny smell of seawater that had washed back into the Mississippi from the Gulf. It was a perfume that had stayed with her since childhood, and she drew hard on it, as one would on a cigarette and felt the same satisfaction.

She'd loved this street as a young girl. Even then the magical blend of old and new had not been lost on her. She slowed the car to a crawl, enjoying the half-mile drive as she hadn't allowed herself to do since her return. The houses that backed onto the river on one side, a strip mall on the other, were all older, two-story, and proud of a time long gone. Verandahs encircled most; some had stately pillars instead. All were well-kept. The gardens were orderly, or had been purposely left to run wild, so that vines swarmed over trees, walls, and verandas, creating an allusion of provocative abandon. But the charm that drew tourists in droves year round was in evidence wherever she looked.

As she slowed the car at the approach to her own drive, she noticed a silver Cadillac parked in front of her house. She frowned slightly in puzzlement. The frown deepened with displeasure when she recognized the woman seated behind the wheel. Nancy Landers, the Realtor who held the consignment on her house, was already stepping from the Caddy as Lauren turned into the drive. Nancy smiled broadly and waved enthusiastically as a young couple stepped out at the same time. Lauren groaned.

Prospective buyers! Odd that when she'd put the house on the market, she hadn't considered the hurt she'd experience when the time came to show it to strangers who might very well become the new owners.

She nibbled on her bottom lip as she shut off the engine, then gathered her purse and few miscellaneous books and papers she'd brought from the store. She was stalling, postponing the moment when she'd have to plant a smile in place, but she couldn't delay any longer.

"Nancy, hi," she said with as much enthusiasm as she could muster.

"Hi, yourself, honey," Nancy drawled in a cheerful sales voice. "This is a happy day for you, Lauren. I've got the sweetest couple here who are just dying to see your house. I've told them all about it, and they're almost positive it's going to be perfect." She put an arm around the waist of the young woman at her side. "Lauren Kennedy, this is Mary Kate and Tip Conners. They're newlyweds, and also new to our beautiful city. Just moving here from Georgia."

Lauren managed what she hoped was a friendly smile as she shook hands with both of them, his strong, exuberant, and bone-crushing, his bride's damp and limp. "Shall we go in?"

"Of course we should," Nancy said with the same wearying cheerfulness. "I have a key, Lauren, but I called your store a few minutes ago from my car phone, and that dear man, Eugene, said you were on your way home, so we waited. Tip is fairly chomping at the bit to see the spectacular view of the river from the master suite."

"Well, then, by all means, let's go right on in," Lauren said.

She unlocked the front door and let the trio pass.

Once inside the foyer, Nancy took over, guiding them all into the parlor. She really was good, Lauren mused as she listened to the experienced realtor describe the craftmanship that had gone into the ornately carved moldings, the hand-laid parquetry, the exquisitely woven Persian rug that covered all but a few feet of flooring, the Brussels tapestry drapes, and Venetian lace curtains.

She heard Mary Kate and Tip asking questions, but she turned away, suddenly feeling sad and lonely, as if she were saying goodbye to her Aunt Edna once again. Why hadn't she known she would feel this way?

Excusing herself, she went into the kitchen to pour herself a glass of wine. She sat at the kitchen table, listening to them move around the rooms on the lower level, then make the climb upstairs. Always, Nancy's voice could be heard chattering excitedly yet with business aplomb about the qualities that distinguished this house from most she'd handled.

As if looking around for the first time herself, Lauren studied the large kitchen where she'd spent so many mornings with her aunt. Unlike most of the other rooms, the kitchen had been modernized over the years. The counters had been tiled so that they gleamed brightly in green and white. The floor was polished brick, and hooked rugs were scattered in front of the cabinets beneath the sink, under the small table, and at the door. All of the appliances were state-of-the-art, and she could hear her aunt justifying the need for them. *I'm a businesswoman. I'm on the go from sunup to sundown. I don't have time to dilly-dally in the kitchen like some useless southern belle with nothing better to do.*

Lauren smiled at the memory and tears stung her eyes, but she quickly swiped at them with her fingertips as she heard the approach of her visitors on the stairs.

"Well, there you are, Lauren. We wondered what had happened to you," Nancy chirped. "You're going to be so thrilled to hear that the Conners think the house is every bit as divine as I promised."

Lauren raised her glass in response, but be-

179

fore she could speak, Nancy had turned her attention back to the newlyweds.

"Now, this is the *pièce de résistance*. A kitchen every woman dreams of. Utilitarian yet beautiful."

Lauren tipped her glass, emptying it, then promptly refilled it from the bottle she'd brought to the table with her. *Great impression you're giving them,* she thought, then felt her mind shrug its unconcern. What did she care what they thought of her? They weren't buying her, just her aunt's house . . . and that thought started the tears anew. With a mumbled apology that she was sure they didn't even hear, she fled the room, hurried up the stairs, and slammed her bedroom door behind her.

A few minutes later, she heard the kitchen door open and close, heard the faint rise and fall of Nancy's excited prattlings beneath the windows, and then listened to their footsteps as the three rounded the back of the house on the flagstone walkway. Tears still slipped from the corners of her eyes, but she willed herself to the window and watched as they walked the pathway to the levee. *Her* levee.

They returned a few minutes later, and Lauren heard the door below open as Nancy called to her. "Yoohoo, Lauren, we're leaving now. I'll call you in the morning, sweetie!"

Lauren didn't answer. Couldn't answer. But with the final bang of the door, she wiped the tears from her face with the hem of her skirt and marched downstairs. "I'll be damned if Mary Kate and Tip are going to move in here and erase you, Aunt Edna!"

Her gait was brisk, her destination sure as she stomped down the stairs and out the front door. The Cadillac was barely away from the curb when she yanked the 'For Sale' sign out of the ground. She placed it over her shoulder, carrying it like an angry picketer marching for a cause. At the garage, she took the lid from the garbage can and threw the offending placard in face down with the rest of the trash.

That done, she folded her arms and laughed as she glanced up at the windows of the garage apartment next door. She'd accused Sam of being childish, but he couldn't possibly produce a tantrum like the one she'd just thrown.

As she walked back toward her house, she considered what she'd just done, this time rationally, without passion. She'd have to call Nancy at once and explain about changing her mind, but as much as she dreaded the phone call, she wasn't sorry about her decision not to sell.

Nancy would be displeased, naturally, but her upset would be nothing compared to the reactions she could expect from Charles and her mother. Still, once they realized that she had changed her mind *only* about selling the house, she thought they'd understand. After all, it wasn't as if she were planning to stay in Louisiana. She still intended to return to her life in Chicago. But this way, she and Charles would always have a retreat.

As she grabbed the knob to the kitchen door, she couldn't resist the urge to look at the apartment next door once again. Wouldn't Mr. Sam Smoothtalking North be surprised when she brought her husband here for visits? Something inside her twisted with the thought, but she passed it off as hunger pangs.

Leaving the window where they'd been watching the goings-on next door, Tillie and Toots turned to face each other, incredulity giving way to happiness. "Well, I'll be . . ." Toots said.

"I do believe our Lauren has just demonstrated the first good sense we've seen since her arrival here."

Toots's grin was full of glee. "I think we may have had something to do with this, Sister."

"You mean by helping her to see what a success she is in the antique business?"

"I mean exactly that. And, of course, Eugene probably deserves some of the credit. But at least we know Edna's little niece is planning on staying. That's the important thing." She raised a hand, holding it outward as if about to take an oath. "Give me five, Matilda Crocker, and make it a high one."

Tillie giggled. "My pleasure, Mrs. LePointe," she said, and slapped her sister's palm soundly.

"Casey would be proud of us for remembering the victory signal," Toots bragged.

Tillie was about to voice her agreement when the sound of screeching tires hitting the drive interrupted her.

"Oh, dear, I do believe Sam is upset about something," Toots observed unnecessarily as they rushed back to the window.

After a few seconds, they both stepped away again, Tillie clicking her tongue, and Toots shaking her head.

"Did you see the way he stopped to glare at Lauren's house, sister?" Toots asked.

"I certainly did. Whatever do you suppose has happened between them now?"

"I don't know," Toots said ruefully before suddenly brightening. "But look at the positive side, Til. At least he's thinking about her."

Eugene was thinking about Lauren as well. Through his highly tuned telepathic sensory system, he'd homed in on her depression as soon as the first tears surfaced in her eyes. His heart ached as he tuned in visually, took in the happenings in her home, and witnessed her misery.

Sitting alone in his lamp, he drew up his knees, resting his chin on them as he watched. If only he had more time left to help her. But in spite of his words the day before about the likelihood of having several weeks left, he knew his days were numbered. He sighed heavily.

He'd counseled her to take her time with her wishes, to select them prudently. But he hoped she'd quickly recognize the direction her heart would lead if she'd only listen and use her wishes for a future with Sam North.

He sighed again, then muttered encouragement as he watched her weeping on the bed in her room.

Lauren straightened, and Eugene sat up with her, listening to the words the Realtor called to her. His chin landed heavily on his knees again as he faced defeat. The young couple were going to buy the house, and there wasn't a darned thing he could do about it unless Lauren wished it so, but she remained silent.

He closed his eyes to shut out her misery, but he slowly became aware of her footsteps landing heavily on each stair as she marched downward. He cheered as he watched the "groundbreaking" ceremony of the sign being torn from the lawn and dumped where it belonged, in the trash container. "All right, mama!" he cheered.

He was grinning as he fell back on the bed of pillows behind his head. Crossing an ankle over his knee, he folded his arms beneath his head. Now if she would just get on the straight and narrow where Sam was concerned.

Using all the concentration he could muster,

he sent a message that could only be received by her subconscious mind . . . and then only if she were receptive enough to listen.

"Go see him, Lauren. Go to Sam. I might be on my last legs, mama, but like it or not, he *is* your Prince Charming for all that he's inclined to act like a toad most of the time. Dig it?"

Chapter Ten

Lauren heard the squeal of tires on the drive as she pulled the tube top over her head. Glancing out the window, she stepped into cutoffs just as Sam climbed out of his low-slung car and raced up the steps to his apartment. He paused, breathing hard, his broad chest rising and falling heavily as he leaned against the railing of the veranda that circled the second floor of the building. His dark brows almost obscured his deep-set eyes with his scowl, and his normally full lips were pulled into a tight, grim line.

Rather overreacting to her desertion in the square, Lauren thought as she watched him spin on his heel to disappear inside his apartment with a resounding bang of his screen door. Maybe she should go over and apologize, admit her culpability in returning his kisses, and suggest they start over again . . . as friends.

She checked the clock on her nightstand. Almost seven. Would he bother to eat now that she'd abruptly canceled their dinner date? Perhaps she should thaw a couple of steaks in the microwave and offer peace with a bribe. According to the old adage, the way to a man's heart was through his stomach. She might not be after his heart, but it couldn't hurt to smooth the troubled waters that always seemed to bubble up when the two of them got together.

Twenty minutes later she rapped on his door with the toe of her shoe.

"Nobody home," Sam barked from the far side of the veranda.

Lauren grinned as she balanced the tray and walked around back to where "nobody" was sitting at a small table, legs raised and ankles resting on the wrought iron railing. "I come bearing gifts," she said lightly.

Sam cast the tray an offhand glance, then purposefully allowed his eyes to graze the length of her as he swilled liquor in a glass. "Set the food aside and let me have a better look at the gifts you bare so beautifully."

Lauren blushed but refused to allow him to annoy her. "The food is the only gift I'm bearing for you, buster."

Sam shrugged before tossing down the two-finger drink. "So she not only walks and talks, she cooks."

"Not much. Boxed fettucini, frozen asparagus, packaged béarnaise sauce, and a couple of skillet-grilled steaks. But edible." She nudged his legs from the railing with her hip, and motioned with her chin toward the bottle on the table. "Come on, move that and make room. I owe you dinner since I walked out on you, and I'm a lady who always pays her debts."

Sam sat up with apparent obedience, but he lifted the bottle only to refill his glass, then nudged the tray a couple of inches to set it back on the table with a clunk. "No offense, but I think I'll pass."

"What? Too yankeefied for you? I might have some crawfish you could bite the heads off if you prefer," Lauren teased as she lifted the bottle and turned it to read the label. "Aged scotch. Very good brand. You have expensive tastes, Mr. North."

As Sam tossed down a second shot, he grimaced, then raised the glass in salute. "If this is a preamble to another you're-a-selfish-jerk lecture, spare me, Lauren. You delivered one already, and Janice picked up where you left off."

"Janice?"

"My ex-wife."

"I remember. When did you talk to her?"

"She called me on my car phone." He reached for the bottle, but Lauren beat him to it, and held it out of reach.

"Don't you have to play tonight?" she asked. "You can't do it if you're drunk."

"Wrong," Sam said, catching her off guard as he snatched the scotch back. "That's the beauty of being a lounge lizard, baby. Nobody cares

188

what condition we're in as long as we keep the music rocking, and I can do that in my sleep."

Lauren didn't answer, but sat down in the only other chair, her hands clasped between her legs as she watched him down glass number two in as many minutes and pour another. "She really set you off, didn't she? I mean, I suppose I should take part of the credit, but somehow I didn't think I did that good of a job."

Sam laughed softly. "Oh, you underestimate yourself. You had me going, but I've been dropped on my face before. I would have recovered."

"But Janice blindsided you before you got your footing back."

"Ding-ding. Give the lady a one-way ticket back to Chicago for the winning answer."

Lauren ignored the sarcasm as she propped her elbows on the table. The anger was real, and it ran deep, but she saw more. She saw the pain in his eyes and felt a sharp twinge of compassion in her chest. Was it possible that he was still in love with his ex-wife? It must be; how else could she have the power to drive him to drink right before he had to go to work? She herself didn't know him well, but she sensed that no matter what he said, he wasn't a man used to drinking on the job . . . even if the job was performing in a club nightly.

He filled his glass for a fourth time, raising it in Lauren's direction. "A toast. To Janice North, soon to be, Ragsdale."

189

Lauren grabbed the glass before he could bring it to his lips again. "Don't do this, Sam."

He didn't answer to protest. He merely stared straight ahead over the treetops at the river. A lone barge made its way south, and he silently followed its progress for several minutes, Lauren watching him.

"Your dinner's probably ruined," he said out of the blue.

"I wasn't really hungry," she said quietly.

He moved his head slightly to look at her. "Thanks for the thought."

"Seemed like a good idea at the time. Wrong again, huh?"

"It's all in the timing, Lauren," he said, philosophically, staring out at the river once again. "Guess ours was off from the start."

"Didn't have anything to do with timing, Sam. I'm involved with someone else, and you're obviously still in love with Janice."

Sam's head jerked around, his mouth falling open. Then he laughed, not softly as before, but loudly and with gusto. "Still in love with Janice? Honey, I don't think I was in love with her in the first place. How in hell could I *still* be?"

Lauren frowned, feeling confused and embarrassed. "But I . . . I thought . . . well, that she's remarrying. Never mind, I guess I misunderstood."

"No, you understood exactly fine. She's getting married in three weeks. Marrying some jock named Kevin Ragsdale. Works for an international food conglomerate. He's some kinda big shot, from what she tells me. They'll be dividing their time between France and New York. All too terribly exciting and grand."

"But if you're not in love with her, why do you care?"

"I care, Ms Kennedy, because she's going to put my daughter in a boarding school in Maryland. All very proper and hoity-toity. That way she can grow up with the same misguided values as her mother . . . and another lady I know."

That stung, but Lauren let it go. "Why don't you just bring Casey down here to live? I mean, you're her father. You have *something* to say about how she's raised."

"Not according to Janice, I don't."

"And that's good enough for you? Just because Janice says so, you roll over and play dead." She knew that her speech had quickened, that her voice was growing emphatic, but she couldn't imagine him giving up without a fight. "I got the impression from Casey that the two of you are close. Your daughter strikes me as an exceptionally bright child, Sam. Maybe I'm wrong but I don't believe she could love you so much if she didn't think you cared in return, cared enough to fight for her."

Sam was on his feet so quickly, Lauren flinched, but she didn't back away when he turned blazing green eyes on her. Didn't retreat even an inch when he leaned heavily on the table, his sinewy arms braced on either side of the tray, and the muscles rippling with tension. "You think I haven't suggested that Casey would be better off here with me? It's been bad enough hearing her tales about being chauffeured back and forth to school only to return home to evenings alone with a hired nanny and television for company."

"Then why do you put up with it?"

Sam's answering sigh was ragged. "Go home, Lauren. Thanks for the proffered meal and your concern, but I think I want to be left alone to wallow in my self-pity."

He'd turned away to face the water again, and Lauren got up and stood behind him. Tentatively, wanting to comfort though not annoy, she laid her hands on his shoulders. "Sam, don't give up. Casey loves it here with you. Any judge in the world would see the injustice of confining her to a boarding school while her mother flits back and forth between Europe and New York when she could be here in a stable environment with her father."

Suddenly Lauren was pinned between the railing and the impenetrable, trembling wall that was Sam, and she wasn't sure how it had happened.

"You think I haven't wanted that?" he demanded, his voice hardly more than a tight raspy whisper as though it escaped through gauze. "Janice makes a better case than you give her credit for. I'm a nightclub musician, Lauren. Surely you haven't forgotten your own derision when we discussed the Wall Street practice I walked away from in favor of playing my music. What makes you think a judge wouldn't feel the same indignation?"

Lauren reached up to run her fingers lightly over his furrowed brow as if to smooth away the pain. "Oh, that's ridiculous! Nuts to apples. Your career has nothing to do with what kind of father you are. Casey adores you. Anyone could see that, and I know she wants to be here with you and the aunts."

"Of course she does, and Janice knows that, too. Why do you think she waited until Casey came home from her vacation here to tell her about her plans?" His hands fell to his sides, and he walked a few feet away before slumping over the railing in defeat. "Oh, she says she waited to tell Casey in person, to be fair, but I know better. Janice has never played fair in her life. She waited to steal the advantage. She knows I wouldn't have let Casey leave only to be shipped off to school like so much extra furniture being put in storage." He laughed harshly, unexpectedly. "She's quite adamant that Casey not be raised by two dotty old ladies, incidentally."

"She's a bitch," Lauren said with conviction, settling her arms firmly over her chest.

"No, only a woman."

Lauren laid a hand on his arm. "We're not all like her, Sam. Don't condemn our entire gender."

Sam bowed his head, squeezing his eyes tight

193

shut as he pressed them against his fists. "Aren't you, Lauren?"

Stung, Lauren couldn't answer. She picked up the tray and walked away. She'd tried to help, and he'd struck her with his words. But as she descended the steps, she wondered if his attack hadn't been justified. Hadn't she been as indignant as Janice about his decision to leave New York and pursue his music?

If only there was some way to redeem herself in his eyes, and then she remembered her remaining two wishes. She could help. She had magic on her side. But what should she wish for? Should she wish for Sam to give up his music and return to his practice in New York? Would that be best for him and Casey? Should she wish for Casey's mother to have a sudden change of heart about sending her daughter to New Orleans to live? That was probably the best bet, but as she opened her mouth to utter the wish, she remembered Eugene's words to her earlier that day when she'd entreated him to help her make the right decisions: "I can do that. Put the wish together, phrasing it carefully so you get exactly what you want. But be sure you're right about what would make it easy, because if you're wrong, you could end up at your own Waterloo just like Napoleon."

Was she sure what was right for Sam? Did she have the right to interfere in his affairs? She didn't know, but she'd wait, make sure she didn't make a wish that would hurt him. Her eyes widened at her last thought. She'd believed she was trying to help Casey, but it was Sam she'd just worried about hurting.

For the next two hours, Lauren sat in front of the television set, but she couldn't have told anyone what was on. Her thoughts ran higgledy-piggledy from Sam to Charles to Casey to Edna to Eugene and back to Sam again. How had everything gotten so confusing?

Eight weeks before, she'd come to New Orleans, all her ducks lined up in a row. She'd known exactly what she had to do.

She had to put the house and shop up for sale.

She had only to clean the store up, keep up appearances of a thriving business until a buyer was found, then return to Chicago, her life with Charles, and her profession. Simple. Nothing more than one, two, three. Three months tops to get everything settled.

Then she'd met Eugene. Complication number one.

Sam had come next. Complication number two.

She frowned, why was either one a complication?

Eugene had been left to her by her aunt, her most treasured bequest. All Lauren had needed to do was sit down, figure out three simple wishes, and wham, everything could have been perfect.

But, no, she had messed up from the first when she'd uttered that ridiculous wish about finding the perfect man.

Then there was the most important, devastating complication of all, Eugene's impending doom. She'd been determined to find an answer to save him, been convinced that the secret couldn't be that hard to figure out. But she wasn't any closer to the answer tonight than she'd been five days before. And time was running out.

Still, for all the importance of saving Eugene, Sam kept intruding on her thoughts . . . especially now that she'd met the vulnerable side of him that was in need.

Damn it! Why couldn't she help anyone?

She heard his car rev in the drive next door, and went to the kitchen window to watch him leave. What condition would he be in now? Had he continued to drink after she'd left him?

She was relieved to see him back out smoothly, then straighten on the street, and drive away with reasonable caution and speed. Apparently he'd regained some semblance of control. She sighed. One less problem to worry about tonight? Small comfort when the whole world seemed to have been turned topsy-turvy.

Nine-thirty, her watch told her. Charles had promised to phone at ten. But that was before he'd agreed to escort Natalie Wolfe to the celebration dinner. Still, Charles was a man of his word. She was confident he'd find an excuse to get away to call her, if only for a moment. Remembering the romance novel she'd bought the day before, she decided to read while she waited.

The book accomplished what her mind had been unable to do for the past several days — let her escape from chaos. When she glanced at the clock again, she was amazed to see it was already ten after the hour. Setting the book aside, she scooted to the edge of the chaise lounge where she'd relaxed for the past forty minutes. She glared at the telephone. *Ring, damn it.*

But by ten forty-five, he still hadn't called.

Lauren glanced at the books he'd been reading. The hero and heroine were shown embracing and staring rapturously at one another, passion and devotion shining from their eyes. She tried to transpose Charles's face over the dark-haired hero's, but his image refused to come clearly to mind. Instead, it was Sam's strong jaw, his full sensuous lips that were so ready to grin wickedly, his deep-set eyes, and thick straight brows that filled her thoughts.

She resolutely shoved his image into the recesses of her mind. It was Charles she was in love with.

It was Charles she was angry with at this particular moment.

It was Charles who was spending the evening with another woman on his arm. Charles who hadn't had the decency to telephone earlier and tell her that he would be unable to talk to her later as planned.

Come to think of it, it was Charles who had

197

been pressing her for weeks to turn everything over to the attorneys and return to Chicago where she belonged. How did he know where she belonged? And what gave him the right to presume to tell her? They'd been seeing each other for more than two years, and though they'd discussed marriage, he'd always been the one to postpone what he claimed was inevitable—their engagement and subsequent marriage. His excuse was as timeworn as Eugene's lamp: "We're both on the same ladder, professionally speaking, Lauren. I may be a rung or two higher than you, but we're both making the climb, and do we dare risk a slip by complicating things by formalizing our relationship? Brows have already been raised by the fact that we're involved. What's a few years in the scheme of things? We wait, play our cards close to our vests, and when we've attained our goals, we can announce our plans to the world as a team."

"Only problem with that, Charles dear, is that one of the team members is playing the game with someone else tonight," Lauren said aloud. Funny that she was more irked about his neglect to call than about his date with Natalie.

She sat down on the bed with a thud. "And in the meantime, I'm sitting here alone on a Friday night with nowhere to go."

She almost heard her aunt answer her, *"So turn around and give your behind a good hard kick, 'cause you have no one to blame but yourself."*

She grinned. "If you were here, Aunt Edna,

we'd have ourselves a good long talk. You're the one who got me into this mess. Because of you, I'm mad at Charles, worried about Eugene, and spending too much time thinking about that rebel who lives next door." With the reminder of Sam, she jumped to her feet. She didn't have to sit home alone at all. She could go to the club. See for herself if he was okay. Besides, he'd invited her before. It might be interesting to see him perform. She might even understand why he'd chucked away his life in favor of playing every night.

As she opened the closet, her grin widened. What would he think when he looked out and saw her sitting in the audience? She pulled a dress from the closet. It was a devastatingly beautiful evening dress she'd bought six months before, intending to wear it to the annual stockholders' ball with Charles. Well, Sam would be the recipient of all her glory, she thought as she slipped the metallic gold taffeta halter dress from its hanger. The neckline was daring, its contrasting silver taffeta notched collar dipping all the way to the sashed waist. As she slipped it on, she turned slightly from side to side, proud of the way the full, sassy skirt emphasized her long, slender legs.

She applied her makeup with an artist's touch, then swept her hair into a high french twist, allowing one long tendril to hang free, caressing and framing her face and chin.

As she clipped long dangling gold earrings

199

into place, she stepped back to study the overall effect.

Grabbing her purse, and slipping her feet into a pair of gold backless heels, she flicked off the overhead light.

"I'm going to knock your socks off, Samuel North," she said as she skipped down the stairs. "And you can eat your heart out, Charles Dumont."

Sam saw her as she came in. Hell, the whole room saw her come in. She was enthralling, standing in the entryway, a glittering statue of perfection. He felt his heart swell with pride, then wondered what the devil his heart thought it had to do with anything. The lady had made it quite clear, *her* heart belonged to someone else. Lucky jerk!

He didn't miss a beat as his fingers skimmed skillfully over the keyboard to the accompaniment of Hank and Malibu. But his concentration was not on the music. He watched as the maitre d' escorted her to a table, off-center but near the stage floor.

He caught her eye, greeting her with a wink, then turned his attention back to the song's finale.

When he rose a few inches from the bench to take a small bow, he looked her way again, hoping to catch her attention, but she was talking to a waiter who'd obviously been ensnared by her wide, generous smile.

The first set lasted for another twenty minutes, and though Sam's playing was faultless, he performed on automatic pilot, hitting the keys meticulously by rote, his thoughts otherwise flitting between the two blondes in his life whose primary function seemed to be to keep him in turmoil.

After Janice, he'd made a commitment to himself, one he'd found easy to live with. He would shun cool milk-skinned willowy blondes with their breathtaking smiles, fathomless eyes, and sheathed claws. Since puberty when he'd begun to notice the differences between boys and girls, he'd had a thing about blondes, from Jean Harlow to Goldie Hawn. He scowled into the audience with the thought that it had probably begun with the little girl of his childhood games, Wendy.

Now here she was back in his life, disturbing his sleep and distracting him. His attention needed to be focused on Casey and what to do to solve the dilemma of how to stop Janice from sending her away to a boarding school.

He played with vigor when they moved into the final tune, an up-tempo, demanding piece. But as his hands pounded the keys, exacting power, they metaphorically took his wrath out on the intoxicating woman whose gaze bored into him.

He stood to take his bows along with Hank and Malibu, smiling broadly, then motioned to Hank to make the intermission announcement.

201

Without glancing in Lauren's direction, he stepped gracefully from the low platform and headed in the opposite direction.

He knew she watched him as he moved from table to table, visiting with regulars, greeting strangers, exchanging pleasantries with one of the city's dignitaries. He'd get to her, but in his own good time. When his conscience nudged, he reminded himself that she disapproved of his career choice, thought it nothing more than the hobby of a spoiled playboy. She'd come slumming, curiosity getting the better of her, nothing more.

By the time he made his way to her table, less than five minutes of his break remained. Perfect, he thought as he slid into a chair across from her. She was far too beautiful tonight for him to risk spending too much time with her. "You clean up real good, Kennedy."

"Thank you," she said coolly, her displeasure obvious at having been ignored for the better part of twenty minutes. "And you're very talented. I can see why you love it."

"Gee, praise from a genuine critic."

Hurt appeared in her smoky eyes for a fraction of a second before she forced it back down inside where it could remain her private secret, but not before he'd seen. Regret tweaked at his conscience, but as resolutely as she, he buried it. "So what brings you out into the decadent New Orleans night? I thought nice conservatives from Chicago locked their doors as soon as the sun set."

"Not always. We're human, too. Every now and then our baser needs rise to the surface, and we feel the urge to explore the seamy side of life."

Sam leaned back in the chair, crooking an arm over the back as he crossed his legs and grinned with satisfaction. "And tonight the urge overcame you. Well, baby, glad to oblige, but you needn't have come all the way down here. Anytime you feel like slumming, all you have to do is stop by the apartment."

Lauren's fingers trembled as she picked up her bag, but she managed to keep her tone cool as she answered. "No thanks. I think I've had enough to last me a good long while." She stood up as if to leave, but hesitated long enough to add, "But I'm glad I came. Makes me kind of appreciate the life I've been missing in Chicago. Think I'll run on home and call Charles." She leaned down so that Sam was forced to make a decision between meeting her eyes or the silky flesh revealed by the low decolletage of her dress. The eyes lost, but only for a moment, until her smooth, husky whisper forced his gaze back to her face. "You know, Sam, you're sexy, but even with almost a thousand miles between Charles and me, he fills a need I just can't seem to satisfy here in New Orleans."

As she turned to walk calmly away, her poise and elegant reserve not slipping for a second, Sam felt remorse slam into his gut like a hammer. He'd baited her, and though she'd struck back with admirable force, he knew he'd wounded her. He caught up with her at the front door. "Look, Lauren, I'm—"

She stopped him with a hand on his chest. "Don't. Not one more word." She tilted her head slightly to meet his gaze, and he saw the tears which turned the smoky brown to shimmering topaz. "I couldn't stop thinking about you tonight. I felt so awful knowing how you were hurting over Casey. I thought I'd come down here and lend my support. Not much, I admit, but all I had. Tell me, Sam, do you always have to make everything ugly?"

He grabbed her arm above the elbow so she couldn't walk out, at the same time casting the maitre d' a get-lost look. "Don't run away, again, Lauren. I'm sorry I hurt you. You're right, I was ugly, out of line. I'm sorry."

She pulled loose with a jerk that surprised him, and wrenched open the door.

Behind him, he heard Hank bringing up the horn, and Malibu tightening the bass, but he followed her out to the street.

"Lauren, wait!" When she didn't even slow down, he shouted after her. "You know, for someone who's so damned good at giving lectures, you're not very good at staying around and facing the music. One day you're going to find the only person you're running from is yourself."

She heard him. She felt the bite of his words. But she didn't stop, for she was suddenly afraid. How could a man she didn't care about make her

204

cry? That frightened her, but what terrified her was how badly she'd wanted to ignore his insult and say yes to his invitation to visit him in his apartment.

Chapter Eleven

Lauren spent a restless, sleepless night.

It didn't help that though she tried reaching Charles by phone until well after 3 A.M., he didn't answer.

It didn't help that Sam squealed into the driveway a little after that, stopping the car a good distance from his garage to stare up at her window and wave when he saw her standing there.

It helped less that his cockiness stirred more unease than Charles's absence evoked.

The following morning, Lauren was treated to another of her mother's famous 7 A.M. chastising lectures.

"Where were you at midnight, Lauren?" Judith Kennedy was off without preamble, and Lauren felt the predictable rise of her hackles.

"Give me a break, Mother! In less than three weeks, I'll be thirty years old. I'm allowed to stay out past midnight now."

The long silence indicated her mother's shock better than words.

Leaning back on the pillows of her freshly made bed, Lauren sighed, then apologized for her rudeness. "Sorry. Didn't mean to bite your head off. I didn't sleep well. Guess I'm a bit grumpy."

"Well, at least you're safe. I was worried about you."

"Why were you calling me so late, Mom? You're almost always early to bed, early to rise."

"I had trouble sleeping as well. It stormed all night, and you know how I've always been afraid of electrical storms. As for why I was calling you, I was worried about you. You didn't sound like yourself the last time we spoke. As a matter of fact, you sounded a lot like you do this morning."

"Testy," Lauren supplied.

"Well, yes, that's exactly how you sound. I spoke with Charles again yesterday evening before he went to his reception. I voiced my concerns—now, don't get upset, he cares, too. Anyway, he agrees that you should close up that business your aunt Edna was so fanatical about and come back home to people who love you."

Lauren didn't answer as she chewed her bottom lip, but tears borne more of weariness than irritation were swimming in her eyes, and her voice was caught around the knot in her throat.

"Lauren, are you still there?"

"Yes, Mom," she managed. "I'm here."

"And you're crying. I can hear it in your voice." Judith's tone gentled. "I didn't mean to upset you, sweetheart. I know what a responsible young

207

woman you are, and I realize you're trying to do what you believe Edna wanted. But, darling, however much you loved her, you have to realize you are responsible for your own life, not for Edna's dreams."

"I loved her, Mom," Lauren said between hiccupping sobs.

"I know you did, Lauren. I loved her, too. She was my sister, after all, but for all that she was independent and zany, and though I recognize the kind of worship you had for her, she was different from you and me. Her bohemian attitude about life was fine for her. It suited her, but we're not cut from the same cloth. Come home, Lauren. Just listen to your own tears. Can't you see how this is tearing you apart?"

"I . . . I'm all right, Mother. I'm just tired."

The sigh on the other end was loud and pregnant with impatience, but her mother was trying. That was evident in her next statement. "At least think about what I've said. Edna may have had a devil-may-care attitude about many things, but she was nobody's fool. She hired competent attorneys to take care of things after she was gone. You won't be letting her down if you come back home and get on with your own life. As a matter of fact, if Edna were to see how unhappy you are, I'm sure she'd be the first one to urge you to go."

"I'm keeping the house, Mom."

"What?"

"Don't have a stroke, Mother. I didn't say I'm going to live in it. I just can't bear to sell it. I decided yesterday. Besides, if Charles and I ever do get married, it'll be a nice place to get away to."

"What do you mean, *if* you and Charles get married. You're not having second thoughts about him, are you?"

Was she having second thoughts? She didn't know the answer to that, but she did know that Charles had not spent the night at home. "I tried calling him at three o'clock, Mom. Three A.M. He wasn't home. Maybe you should ask him."

"Oh, Lauren, he and the some of the boys from work probably went out after the dinner last night. They might have gotten involved in a poker game. There are any number of possibilities. Don't go jumping to conclusions that probably have very little to do with the facts."

"Look, Mom, I've got to go. I've got to get ready for work. I'll call you in the next day or so, okay?"

"All right, Lauren, but please think about everything I've said. We want you home—Charles and I. Promise you will?"

"I'll think about it."

And she did. All the time she was getting dressed, as she drank two cups of coffee, and all during the drive to the store.

"Eugene," Lauren called, rapping on his lamp at the same time, only seconds after she'd arrived at Yesterday's Treasures. "Can I come in?"

There was no answer, not even a sign. But suddenly Lauren felt as light as air, and as thin, transparent, and wispy as if her metabolism were being transformed from solid bone and flesh into liquid smoke. She held her arms out, examining her

209

hands which were as transparent as cellophane. She watched her fingers disappear, yet felt no fright. Instead, she felt as peaceful and light-hearted as those folks she saw on Oprah, and Sally, and Donahue—the ones who had died and felt their spirits separate from their bodies before being rejoined once the life process began again.

The entire metamorphosis took mere seconds, but it seemed to Lauren as if she floated on a time-less cloud. Then there she was, appearing un-changed, yet obviously no bigger than a tiny spider, for she was seated comfortably inside Eugene's lamp.

The first smile she'd managed since leaving The Jazzy Lady the night before lit up her face as she saw Eugene seated beside her on a sea of brightly colored pillows.

"Wow," she said, the awe she felt evident in her tone.

"Awesome, huh?" Eugene said with a face-splitting grin. "Shoulda seen your Aunt Edna the first time she came in. Red as a beet and laughing as if a thousand hands were tickling her. Created a bit of a hassle for me for a while."

"Didn't want to leave?" Lauren asked.

"Kept wanting to come back just to experience the thrill of changing."

Lauren laughed, really laughed, until tears streamed from her eyes and her sides ached. "Well, I can understand it. I've never felt anything like it before," she said as soon as the fit of giggles had subsided. "Kind of like being anesthetized without going completely under."

"Well put, mama. Have to tell Lovey. She never can get a grip on what the feeling is." He waved his arm around the spacious circular room, which was lavishly decorated with colors ranging from bright fuchsia and scarlet, fluorescent green and electric blue, to royal purple and sparkling gold and silver. "So what do you think?"

Lauren took it all in, examining every detail. There was a state-of-the-art stereo system, a silver framed photograph of Lovey sitting on top of it, a television set with built-in VCR, an exercise bike and rowing machine, three guitars, and posters of Janice Joplin, The Doors, The Mamas and the Papas, Jimmy Hendrix, and the Beatles. "Its amazing. On the one hand, I feel like I've stepped into an Ottoman bedchamber. On the other, its very modern, avant-garde." She gestured with her chin in the direction of the rowing machine. "You work out?"

Eugene looked offended. "Me? Heck, no. I have a fast metabolism. Eat like a pig and never gain an ounce," he said proudly.

"Seems to me I saw a picture of a genie once who resembled a tub of lard," Lauren teased. "So it couldn't be the magic."

"It's not. It's simply good genes. My parents were both as thin as reeds. You probably saw a picture someone drew after they met my cousin, Shamu."

"I thought Shamu was a whale."

"Where do you think they got his name from, mama? My cousin was a whale of a genie."

Lauren couldn't believe how easy it was to laugh

when she was with Eugene. He relaxed her and made her feel so comfortable, so carefree. "Tell me about your parents," she said, crossing her legs and resting her chin in her hands.

"What's to tell?" he asked, but she could tell he was pleased by the question from the way he squared his thin shoulders and his eyes lit up like two black opals. "My mother was reputed to be the most beautiful woman in the land. She was betrothed at birth to the sultan, but when my father saw her standing at the river edge when she was fourteen, he fell in love with her and vowed to have her for his own."

"Where was this?"

"Persia, of course," Eugene said, looking offended at having been interrupted.

"Sorry. Go on."

"He, too, was uncommonly beautiful. My mother said he had the skin of a woman, it was so soft. She fell deeply in love with him as well. But of course when my father went to the sultan and asked him to give up the girl who was betrothed to him in exchange for wonderful, rare treasures, he denied the request."

"Your farther was a wealthy merchant?"

This time Eugene looked positively indignant. "A magician, Lauren," he answered with exaggerated patience as if explaining to a dim-witted child.

She hunched her shoulders. "Sorry. Pardon my ignorance."

"Anyway, my father and mother decided to run away, but the sultan found them, had them brought back in chains, and ordered my father beheaded."

"What did he do? Put a spell on the sultan?"

"Certainly not! The sultan had many powerful sorcerers. Even my father's amazing magic couldn't have stood up to their combined powers."

"So, okay, what did he do?"

"He did what all magicians who had become genies before him did. Before he and my mother attempted to escape, he'd crafted a lamp—this same lamp, as a matter of fact—as a contingency should they be captured. When they were caught, he simply said the secret magic words that consigned his spirit forever to the lamp."

Lauren shook her head. "I don't understand."

"Its simple, mama, Magicians, true magicians with power—not the hocus-pocus illusionists of today—were taught from early childhood that their magic must never be used for selfish deeds. If it was, there had to be a trade-off. They had to give their soul to a lamp and so became the vassal of whoever owned it. Like I told you earlier, it used to be that one person could own a magic lamp forever. Then one day genies got together and formed a union. But that's another story.

"Getting back to my parents' tale. My father used his magic for selfish reasons, to have the woman he loved, so he gave his spirit to the lamp and became a genie."

"But what about your mother?"

"Oh, she was perfectly content to live in the lamp until the day she died. She said it was their own private paradise."

213

"She died?" Lauren moaned. "Eugene, that's so sad. Couldn't she have become a genie, too?"

Eugene frowned. "Somehow I thought you were quicker."

And then it dawned on her. "Oh, I get it. She would have had to give her spirit to another lamp, and they wouldn't have been able to be together."

"Right on, mama."

But she was frowning again.

"What now?" Eugene asked.

"If your mother could live in the bottle with your father, why couldn't Lovey live here with you?"

"She could have," the genie answered quietly, his face betraying his sudden heaviness of heart, "if I'd found her earlier, perhaps a century ago when I was young. But I knew my time was running out when I met her a few years ago. I couldn't ask her to spend the best years of her life in here with me while I faded away."

"I'm sorry," Lauren said, uncrossing her legs and getting up. "If you'll just blink me back, I won't bother you anymore."

"Chill out, mama, and sit down. Ain't no big deal feeling blue and sad. Goes with life. Kinda got the impression you were feeling a little down in the dumps yourself when you arrived at the store this morning."

At the reminder of why she'd come to visit him, Lauren nodded. "I was. Am, I guess."

"Hold it," Eugene commanded, stopping the confession he sensed was coming. "Let me blink us up some tea. Got a great ancient blend that mellows the heart and soothes the soul."

214

"Yesterday," one of the Beatles' most famous hits, suddenly began playing softly from the stereo speakers just as two steaming cups of tea appeared in Eugene's hands. He handed her a cup. "Settle back against the pillows and let the music and tea do their work. Then we'll talk."

But talk was postponed a couple of hours until Lauren awakened with a jolt, disoriented and uncertain where she was.

"Feel rested?" Eugene asked.

She sat up quickly, straightening her shirt and smoothing her hair. "How long have I been sleeping? *Why* did you let me go to sleep?" And then her eyes narrowed with suspicion. "Eugene Ali Simm Simm. Did you drug me?"

"You mean like with barbiturates? No way, mama. I don't hold with that sort of thing. No, the tea and music did their stuff. Guess you just needed something to rock you away. Rough night?"

"You probably already know the answer to that," Lauren huffed primly.

"Actually, I was sorta otherwise occupied, if you can dig it." He waggled his thin eyebrows a couple of times like Groucho Marx. "Not that I wouldn't have been there for you if you'd needed me."

Lauren rubbed sleep from her eyes, then remembering the shop, glanced at her watch. "Twelve o'clock! Eugene, I was supposed to open up three hours ago."

"Its cool. I opened up, and every time you've had a customer, I've been Johnny-on-the-spot. Sold that ugly spittoon that belonged to Earl Butrum."

"Who?"

"Earl Butrum. You wouldn't know him. Just some no 'count cardsharp from San Anton'. Took a bullet in the chest after he cheated some poor farmer out of his savings. Only twenty-six years old when they laid him out — Earl, I'm talking about. But wasn't no great loss, nohow. Townfolk figured someone ought to give that farmboy a reward, and they rounded up a hundred dollars cash, some chickens, and a cow."

Lauren was laughing so hard by the time he finished his story, his accent so genuine, he could have lived — probably had lived — there during the incident he described, she couldn't get her breath. "Oh, Eugene, you're wonderful. You just can't fade away."

"Yeah, well, anyway, got you three hundred dollars for that disgusting spittoon of his. Though why anyone would want it, I don't know. Lady said she was going to plant flowers in it." Then he laughed. "Kinda fitting, don't ya think? Him pushin' up daisies all these years?"

"Ha-ha," Lauren said as she pushed herself gingerly to her feet, her legs stiff. "Sell anything else?"

"Nope. A lot of browsers. Only one buyer. Maybe this afternoon will be better. Folks on vacation like to sleep in, hit the stores later in the day."

"Well, actually that's what I came to tell you. I think I'm going to close the store early." She couldn't face him when she told him the rest, so she moved around the room, carefully keeping her back to him as she spoke. "Actually, I think I'm go-

216

ing to close the store for good, Gene. I'm going home to Chicago."

"Giving up, huh?"

She whirled around, almost falling as her feet got tangled in the jumble of pillows and cushions. She caught herself with a hand on the wall, but Eugene was at her side, holding her other arm even before she righted herself. "I'm not giving up. There has to be a fight before there's anything to surrender. I never intended to keep the store, Gene. You know that. I just thought I'd keep it running while we waited for the right person to come along and buy it. But I realized this morning that that could take weeks or months. The right person may never come along. I have a life that I can't keep on hold forever."

"So what about your wishes? You settled on them yet?"

"No, but I will before I leave." At the woebegone expression on his face, she smiled. "And don't you worry, I'm closing the store, but I'm not leaving New Orleans until I figure out the secret to keep you from fading away."

"Can't talk you out of quitting?"

Exasperated, she sighed heavily. "For the last time, Gene, I'm not quitting. I never started. I've got a life waiting for me in Chicago, and I've got to get myself back on track thinking about tomorrow."

Eugene tapped the poster of Janis Joplin. "I've never forgotten something she once said. Real profound. Said, 'You can destroy today worrying about tomorrow.' "

217

Lauren leaned forward to kiss his forehead. "Thanks, Gene, you're a good friend. You give and give and give. You need to quit worrying so much about me and start thinking about yourself. Unselfishness is a virtue, but in your case, I think you need to spend more time concentrating on your own happiness." Before he could answer, she pointed to the top of the lamp. "Whisk me out of here, please."

Lauren moved around the store, locking cabinets that held pieces of jewelry, delicate lace, and dolls, then pulled down the shades on the windows and turned the sign in the door from Open to Closed. She was surprised at the melancholy that settled over her. Tears blurred her vision, but she stubbornly held them back, at the same time wondering what she was on the verge of weeping for. She was going home. That was what she'd wanted from the moment she'd stepped off from the plane in New Orleans. Still, she was saying goodbye to memories, her childhood, and the aunt she'd loved like a second mother.

She was just turning the dead bolt when someone rapped on the door. "Sorry, we're closed," she yelled without bothering to lift the shade.

"Lauren, it's Lovey!"

With a sigh, Lauren unlocked the door, pulled it open, and raised her hand in a halfhearted wave as her mouth found a slight smile. "Hi, Lovey. Gene's in his lamp if you're looking for him." She'd turned her back on the round little woman, pretending to fuss with a stack of books on the counter as she fought new tears. But Lovey bustled to her side, bending slightly so that her face was looking up at Lauren's.

"What's up, Lauren? You closing the store on the busiest afternoon of the week?"

Lauren reached inside for bravado, but came up empty. "I . . . I'm closing the store for good, Lovey, not just for the afternoon." She saw Lovey's mouth open, the blue eyes widen in disbelief. She checked the protest she could almost hear before it was uttered with a hand held up and a shake of her head. "I don't want to talk about it right now, Lovey. Okay?" Her lips trembled as she attempted a smile. "Later, all right? I won't be leaving right away. It'll take me a few days to wrap everything up. We'll talk before I go."

"Sure," Lovey said, hurt evident in her tone. But like Eugene, she was sensitive and unobtrusive. "I'll just pop in on Eugene, then get out of your hair. Stop into my shop before you head back to Chicago. I . . . I want to tell you goodbye." She walked away, rounding the sales counter to rap on the genie's lamp, but stopped expectantly when Lauren called her name.

"I've tried, Lovey. I swear I've tried. I don't know what the secret is to save him, but I'm not giving up."

"Thanks." Her wide smile was as sincere as her tone, and Lauren felt guilt twist in her heart as sharp as any blade.

The two women stood staring at one another, neither of them able to find words to comfort the

219

other. After a long, awkward moment, Lauren hurried to the counter where she'd dropped her purse and keys several hours earlier, snatched them up, and hurried from the store.

She cried all the way home, though what for she couldn't say.

She pulled the car into the drive slowly, stopping it midway, unable to summon the energy to walk the twenty yards from garage to house.

As she got out, a sleek Porsche whizzed past up the driveway next door, screeching to a halt within inches of the parked Corvette.

Lauren watched as an exotic-looking woman with legs so long she wondered how the small car had accommodated them climbed out. Her short straight black hair was cut in a fringed cap that framed a long face and emphasized her impossibly large obsidian eyes. Her crimson lips parted in a magnanimous smile of greeting, revealing the pearliest teeth Lauren had ever seen except maybe on toothpaste ads.

"Hi," Lauren said, feeling foolish for staring, and wishing she'd dressed in something with more pizazz as she took in the other woman's chic taupe coat dress, which somehow looked both demur and sexy. "I live here," she said and wished for incisors sharp enough to bite off her tongue.

"Nice neighborhood," the gorgeous Amazon said with a voice that sounded like it had been spun from silk. "I've, ah, got an appointment. Excuse me." She adjusted the shoulder strap of her Louis Vuitton bag and wriggled scarlet inch-long nails in farewell.

"With the aunts?" Lauren asked.

"I beg your—oh, Tillie and Toots? No—"

"Hey, Alexis, come on up!"

Both women turned toward the garage apartment at the sound of Sam's voice from the veranda.

"Bye," the stranger—apparently Alexis—said, shutting her car door and starting off toward her appointment.

Lauren mumbled a reply, but her gaze was fastened on the man standing above them. Dressed in a navy blazer, blue oxford shirt, and khaki pleated slacks, his long ebony hair slicked back, he epitomized the typical thirty-something executive WASP. Her mouth dropped open then snapped shut when he lifted his arm in a greeting directed her way before turning his attention back to his approaching guest.

"Jerk," Lauren muttered under her breath, before slamming the car door with her hip and marching off toward her house without once giving in to the temptation to look back.

In the kitchen, she tossed handbag and keys onto the counter and picked up the phone. She jabbed the buttons with amazing dexterity, then silently dared her party not to answer.

Charles picked up on the second ring.

"Where were you all night?" Lauren demanded at his chipper "Good afternoon, Charles Dumont speaking."

"Lauren?"

"You were expecting someone else?"

"Of course not. What's wrong, sweetheart?" he

221

asked, and Lauren leaned against the cabinets, somewhat mollified at the slight nervous edge she detected in his tone.

"What's wrong is that you were supposed to call me last night at ten."

"But I thought your mother explained about the reception in my honor."

"Mother called, but I was certain you'd slip away long enough to give me two minutes to tell me how it was going." She heard his sigh, long and deep, then the tolerance that crept into his voice.

"It wasn't merely a social function, darling. It was a tribute, and I was the guest of honor. I couldn't simply slip away when it suited me."

"I hate the way you enunciate every word when you're trying to be impressive. Did I ever tell you that?" she asked, feeling a smidgen spiteful yet definitely better.

"No. I didn't realize that," he said, measuring his words with care, as he did any time he considered her irrational. "I apologize. Now tell me what's really bothering you. Ah, PMS, right?"

Lauren almost growled into the phone. "No, it's not premenstrual stress, Charles. I'm mad as hell at you for not calling as you said you would. And while we're on the subject of telephone calls, where the hell were you at 3 A.M ? I tried calling *you* then."

"I don't think I like your tone, Lauren."

"Just answer the question, Charles. I'm not a client you have to tiptoe around. I'm . . . I thought I was the woman you were planning to marry."

"Of course you are," he said more cheerfully, all

too clearly relieved by the change of subject, but she wasn't about to let him off the hook.

"Well?"

"Well what, Lauren?"

"Where were you until after three o'clock this morning? I've been to those boring receptions before, and can't remember any of them lasting until eleven even."

"I don't appreciate the insinuation," Charles said a trifle too piously.

"Just answer the question, Charles. Did you spend the night with Natalie Wolfe?"

"I don't think I like where this is going, Lauren. Are you sure you want to pursue this?"

She didn't answer. She took the phone from her ear, staring into the earpiece as if by doing so she could transmit the glare she was aiming at the man she'd only weeks before kissed so passionately goodbye at O'Hare airport. "No, as a matter of fact, I don't think I do."

"Good." The relief in his voice was so evident she almost laughed, but his next words checked it. "I'm glad, darling, because I don't think I like it when you act shrewish."

"Well, that works out nicely because I don't think I like you at all."

She heard his voice, but his words were lost in the string of expletives she uttered, which she hoped turned his ruddy complexion purple. She slammed the receiver back into its cradle with such force her arm tingled all the way to her elbow.

Opening the refrigerator, she reached for a soda and popped the tab.

It occurred to her as she climbed the stairs to her room to change that caffeine might be the last thing she needed, considering her ill temper and jangled nerves. Shifting a pillow in the window seat, she sat down, drawing her knees up, and decided to count to ten, or a hundred, or a thousand until her anger dissipated. But when she spotted the charcoal gray Porsche still parked below, she gulped some soda, deciding caffeine might just be what she needed to fuel her anger.

First Sam, then Charles. She jabbed a pillow with her fists. A red-letter day. In fact, she thought, as she glanced at the wall calendar, she might well commit this one to memory. It was as good a day as any to declare war on all men.

Chapter Twelve

Lauren left the house a few minutes later and spent the next two hours at the river, as she had taken to doing when she needed to relax, escape. She had brought her crawdad net, as she did on days when she sat there with Casey or with a book. Today there was no escaping the thoughts that skittered through her mind.

She thought of Charles, of Chicago, of her mother and Aunt Edna, of her job and Sam and his talent as a pianist, but she'd been avoiding the questions that really mattered.

Was her relationship with Charles really, finally over? And if so, why? Had she never loved him as she'd thought? Had she become so immersed in her dreams for security that she'd deluded herself into believing that this man, who shared the same goals as she, was the man she wanted to spend the rest of her life with?

And what of her conviction that New Orleans represented everything she disapproved of? Why suddenly was she understanding and even yearning to share the prevalent attitudes of playing hard and living life to the fullest?

And what about Sam?

When her mind skimmed over that question for the umpteenth time, she forced her thoughts to stop. *What about Sam?*

The answers were fast in coming.

He was arrogant, cocky, and immature.

Oh, there was a gentle side, a part of him that could be sensitive. She'd witnessed it the day before when he'd talked about his daughter, but then why hadn't he stayed in New York to provide for her?

He was undeniably handsome, the kind of to-die-for handsome that made a woman weak-kneed and jelly-bellied. Few women could resist those sexy green eyes or that smile that revealed little-boy charm and bad-boy fun, and she certainly wasn't made of stone. Of course she'd thought of him, too often in fact, in too vivid detail. She'd even fantasized what it would be like to let those kisses he'd given her go farther, but that had nothing to do with things of the heart.

Then why had he been able to hurt her the night before? Hadn't it been her heart that had trembled under his attack, felt as if it might crumble?

She hadn't felt the tears begin, but as she sat hugging her legs, her chin on her knees, they dropped onto her shins and trickled down to her ankles. Lowering her head so that her eyes were pressed against her slender knees, she willed them to stop, but the harder she fought, the more the pain racked her body.

Well, a good cry was balm for the soul, cleansing and soothing, her aunt had always said. And she found it was true, for after a while, she brushed the last tears from her cheeks, sniffling loudly as she pushed herself to her feet.

Picking up a long stick, she walked out on the *battue* to the bank, where she stirred the water, creating ripples that widened into ever-growing circles.

Symbolically recreating the maelstroms in her life, she thought, then laughed at the metaphor. She dropped the stick as she turned and made her way slowly up the steep incline to the levee and back toward home.

Home. Yes, Aunt Edna's house had always felt like home. Perhaps that was why she hadn't been able to sell it. She smiled, realizing that she had resolved at least one question in her mind and was happy with the decision.

But what of Charles and her job in Chicago? If in fact, she and Charles were through, could she go back to her work at Hedges & Marshall? Was that still what she wanted?

She pressed her fingers to her temples against the dull ache that was beginning a steady thrum there. Too many questions. Too much turmoil. She was a person who had always needed order, and now . . .

As she rounded the corner of the garage on the flagstone walkway, she noticed that the Porsche was gone, then spotted Sam washing his car. Her eyes narrowed as she frowned.

There hadn't been any questions, any chaos, or any confusion until he'd walked into Yesterday's Treasures six days before. Hands balled, she changed course and made for the root of her troubles.

Sam looked up at the sound of her approach, shutting off the nozzle of the hose, his other hand already half-raised in greeting when she pounced.

"For your information, Mr. North, *I'm* not the one who runs away. *I'm* a responsible adult who makes commitments and lives by them.

"You're the one who ran away, turning your back on your wife and daughter, never giving their needs a thought. Chase your rainbows, Sam. Play your games, but don't blame your wife because she's trying to secure a future for Casey. And don't accuse me of running away!"

He waited for the tirade to wind down, trying not to react, not to let her words sting. He'd noticed her tear-stained face and swollen eyes as soon as she'd gotten within ten feet of him. He didn't know what had provoked her pain, but he was willing to let her take it out on him. He only wanted to help. "Lauren—"

She jerked free of his grasp, stomping her foot in a final angry burst. "And while we're exchanging truths," she said between clenched teeth, oblivious to the fact that he hadn't said a word, or that she was the only one making judgments, "How good a pianist can you be if you're stuck in some honky-tonk every night? Were you a mediocre attorney as well? Is that why you skulked away from your career and family?"

Sighing, Sam ran a hand through his hair as he bent to turn off the tap and lay the hose aside. Obviously the woman wasn't going to listen to reason, wasn't interested in whatever answers he might give. What had provoked this tirade? Had his treatment of her the night before brought all this on? Somehow he doubted it, for wouldn't that mean she cared more than she'd led him to believe? With a grin, he straightened, deciding to test the theory. Leaning on the damp car, his elbow propped on the hood, he squinted against the sun behind her as he looked into her eyes. "You know, babe, I didn't know I'd gotten under your skin so deeply. I thought we'd just scratched the surface, and here I find out you've been giving me a great deal of thought."

"Oh! Why you egotistical baboon! I wasn't thinking about you. I was worrying about poor Casey." As she spun away from him, she slipped in a puddle of water, and was only to be saved from a humiliating fall by Sam, who caught her at the waist.

She was pinned against him, and the thrill of his bare chest and muscled stomach against her back shocked her to her toes. Jumping away as if burned, she whirled around for one last attack, determined to free herself from his spell once and for all. "Why don't you grow up, Sam? Be a man and provide for yourself and your daughter instead of living here over this garage, sponging off your aunts."

Anger sparked in his eyes, just for an instant, but long enough to give her pause. Sam took advantage of her momentary silence. "Look, I'm not going to argue with you, and I'm not even sure why you're here. Casey isn't your concern. Seems to me you told me yesterday that you're planning to marry that straight arrow up north. Hey, that's cool. He sounds perfect for you. Ambitious, focused, and boring as hell. Have a happy, dull life, Lauren, and don't waste time worrying about mine."

"I told you, I'm not worried about you. I was thinking of Casey. Do you think Janice is ever going to let her come here and stay with you if she finds out you have your . . . your women friends over here even in broad daylight."

Sam's eyes widened with the dawning of understanding, and he was amazed at how good it felt. Lauren was jealous of Alexis. Tossing his head hack, he laughed, and even when he saw her look of pure unadulterated rage, he couldn't stop.

She opened her mouth, then snapped it shut again. How dare he laugh at her. How dare he.

She turned away, this time letting prudence slow her lest she slip again, but she could hear his mocking laughter all the way to her door. Her hand on the knob, she gave him another glare. Her attention was so fully on him, she jumped when Toots laid a hand on her shoulder.

"Oh, you startled me," she said, almost managing an apologetic smile until she saw the frown on the older woman's face and noticed the ice in her eyes.

"You shouldn't have said those things to Sam, Lauren. I'm very disappointed in you, and I think your aunt Edna would have been ashamed. I'm not one to butt in, but I can't let this go unsaid. You were very nasty to him, and he didn't deserve it." Toots paused, out of breath from the rush of words her indignation had inspired.

From the corner of her eye, Lauren saw Tillie standing across the drive, nervously wringing her hands, and she felt herself flush with embarrassment at having been overheard by the two gentle sisters. But, damn it, she'd been right, hadn't she? Lifting her chin slightly, she asked that question. "Was one thing I said untrue?"

"Everything you said was untrue, Lauren," Toots said, her tone somewhat gentler now.

"Are you telling me Sam didn't turn his back on his wife and Casey, give up a promising career just so he could play music in some dingy bar every night? Doesn't it bother you that he can't afford a house of his own? Is it any wonder Janice won't let Casey come here to live with him? Why, he even has his . . . his girlfriends over in the middle of the day!"

"Yes, he did leave his practice in New York so that he could pursue his true love, which has always been music. But why not? He's one of those rare geniuses who succeed at whatever they do. He was ambitious and hungry. Graduated at the top of his class from Tulane. He got his law degree here,

231

but he wanted to practice in New York, so he worked there while he went on to get a PhD in economics. He was already married with a child, but he was a brilliant attorney who worked hard and was paid well. He invested wisely and by the time he turned thirty, he'd amassed a fortune." Toots looked down at her hands, a smile flitting across her face. "He joked about it when he came back, said he had a stock portfolio Donald Trump would envy."

"Then why does he live here in your apartment and work in that club?"

"He owns this house, Lauren. He used to come here with Janice and Casey for vacations. And when Tillie was widowed, then me a few months later, he suggested we move in here together. We didn't want to, and Janice was dead set against it, but he was adamant. He knew we'd never be able to afford to live in the comfort we have here on the small pensions left us. We offered to move out when he came home, but he wouldn't hear of it. As for why he plays at The Jazzy Lady, why not? He's happy there. New Orleans is his home, music his passion. Few people are lucky enough be able to pursue their dreams."

Lauren's embarrassment stoked a fire that she could feel burn in her face, but she pressed on, wanting to know all of it. "Okay, I was wrong about him sponging off you, but what about Janice? You can't deny that he left her in New York, ignoring her protests and thinking only of himself."

232

Toots sighed and ruefully shook her head. "No, I can't deny that he left her behind. It broke his heart when he had to tell Casey goodbye. He never said that, of course, but he didn't have to. It was in his eyes, in the way he moped around for the first few weeks after he came home. But Janice didn't give him a choice. He told her years before that one day he wanted to return to Louisiana, play his music, and spend time smelling the roses. Apparently she thought he'd forget about it or change his mind once he started making a splash on Wall Street. When she realized he was still serious about it, she started looking around for a replacement."

"A replacement?" Lauren asked, certain Toots couldn't mean Janice had been unfaithful while they were still married. Wouldn't Sam have told her that when they'd talked about his ex-wife? But she already knew the answer to that question. Of course he wouldn't. He was too intrinsically decent to malign his daughter's mother. Her chagrin complete, Lauren barely heard Toots still talking to her. Her eyes sought out the man she'd just laid into with such viciousness and unfairness, she doubted he'd ever speak to her again. But he was gone, apparently back into his apartment. As soon as she could extricate herself from his aunt, she would go to him, offer her apologies, and hope he'd find it in his heart to forgive her.

"So, my dear, as you've heard, Sam is guilty of none of your charges."

"Apparently not," she said absently. "I wish I'd

known all this before. Why didn't he defend himself?"

But before Toots could answer, the chimes that hung outside Lauren's kitchen door tinkled. Not even the slightest breeze stirred the day, yet the chimes jingled melodiously. With a groan, Lauren suddenly realized that the genie was acknowledging the wish she'd uttered without thinking.

At Lauren's moan of regret and woebegone expression, Toots impulsively hugged her to her ample breast. "We all make mistakes, dear. Sam's more than likely upset. Understandably. Give him a while then go talk to him. He's a very sweet man for all that he tries not to show it. He'll be forgiving."

Lauren smiled her thanks, waved to Tillie, letting the nervous little woman know that the misunderstanding had been corrected, then excused herself to go inside. She *would* apologize to Sam, but first she had business with Eugene.

It annoyed her that a slip of the tongue had cost her one of her invaluable wishes, but maybe not. After all, how on earth was Eugene going to grant that wish? There was no way she could have known beforehand about Sam's marriage, his successful law practice and investments, none of it.

Raising a hip, she rested it on the corner of the kitchen table, crossed her arms, and called to her genie. As always, he was there in the blink of an eye. In spite of the fact that she was getting used to his promptness, she jumped, though not as high as she would have a few days ago.

"You called, mama?"

"I sure did," Lauren said with a satisfied smile. "I got your signal that you'd heard my wish and granted it."

"Okay, so what's the problem?"

"No problem as far as I'm concerned. In fact, I'm delighted. For a few seconds there, I thought I'd blown my second wish. Then I realized there was no way on earth I could have known about Sam before. Therefore, you can't grant it."

It was Eugene's turn to smile, and Lauren didn't like the mischief that gleamed in his eyes. "Come on," he said. "Follow me."

Lauren raised a brow, but tagged after him up the stairs. "Where are we going?"

Eugene simply gestured for her to keep following. When they reached her bedroom, he motioned her toward the dresser, then magically moved from the doorway to the middle of the bed where he sat cross-legged in an instant. "Top middle drawer," he said.

Lauren eased the drawer open slowly though her mind raced trying to remember everything she'd unpacked and put in there. But there was nothing but a thick stack of letters, treasured letters written to her by Edna and kept tied with a blue ribbon. She'd brought them south with her thinking to read them while she mourned her favorite relative's passing. She'd quite forgotten them until this moment. Pulling the neat bundle out, she waved it at Eugene, her eyes asking the question.

"That's right, your aunt Edna's letters. Look at

the one with the postmark dated May 29, 1983.

Sitting on the edge of the bed, Lauren slipped off the ribbon and found the letter. Her eyes misted at the familiar bold scrawl of her aunt's handwriting, but as she unfolded the blue floral stationery and began to read, she laughed.

> ". . . *You'll remember Sam, Ralph and Carri Ann North's boy from next door. Or maybe you'd remember him better as Peter from your playtimes in Never-Never Land. Anyway, we're so proud of him. Graduated at the top of his class from Tulane just last Friday. He'll take his bar exams in July, but there's no question he'll pass with flying colors.*"

There was more, but Lauren didn't read on. She stuffed the letter back in the envelope and searched for the one Eugene wanted next. It was dated five years later, October 20.

> ". . . *Sam North is making quite a name for himself on the east coast. You'll no doubt remember that he works in New York now. Has a beautiful little girl. He was back here last month for his mother's funeral. Such a handsome young man and so well-mannered. He's very modest about his accomplishments, though of course everyone who attended Carrie Ann's funeral commented on the feature articles about him that regularly appear in*

236

every major publication. According to News-
week *magazine he's quite the most talked*
about man in the Big Apple. I can't say as
that I care for his wife, Janice, overly much.
A bit snooty for my taste, and hoity-toity, if
you know what I mean."

The letter went on to detail the sad facts about
Sam's mother's illness and death, but Eugene interrupted Lauren and wagged a finger at the letters on
the bed. "One more. December 1, 1990.

". . . So sad about Sam's marriage, al-
though as you may remember, Lauren my pet,
I didn't like her from the first. Sam's aunts
are my neighbors now. Sam insisted they
come live in his house, it being so much easier
for them as they're both widow ladies. I told
you that, didn't I? Oh, of course, I did. But
back to Sam. He's back in New Orleans now.
Moved back just before Thanksgiving. Giving
up his law practice to follow his true passion,
which is the piano. Did he ever play for you
as a child? Everyone said he was a prodigy
even then.

"I keep getting off-track, but will try to stay
on course long enough to tell you what his
wife did. She's staying in New York, has filed
for divorce, and is keeping little Casey (Sam's
daughter). That might be fine. These things
do happen. But Matilda and Petulia (Sam's
aunts, you remember?) tell me she almost

*broke Sam's heart because she was involved
with other men long before he decided to
come back to his hometown. I just feel as if
my heart will break every time I see him,
though you can be sure, Sam is too much of a
gentleman to talk about it."*

"Okay, Eugene, you win. But it's still not fair. I
blew an entire wish!"

"Sorry, Lauren," he said quietly, then, "Mind if I
get back to my pad. Feeling kind of puny today."

Lauren let the letter she'd been holding flutter to
the bed and jumped to her feet, her own selfish
concerns forgotten as she looked at how pale and
translucent the genie was. "Are you all right? Oh,
Gene, please be okay! Don't fade away yet. I'll find
the secret, I promise. Just hang on a few more
days."

His smile was bright, but she could see the doubt
in his eyes. "I'm gonna give it everything I got,
mama, but you can't blame yourself if you don't
find it. Genies fade."

He shrugged, and Lauren thought the simple
gesture of hopelessness so pathetic, she almost
cried out in protest as she bent to hug him. But she
grabbed thin air, Eugene was gone.

"Eugene!" she screamed, desperately afraid he'd
faded from earth.

"I'm still with ya, mama, but I gotta rest."

An hour later, Lauren knocked on Sam's door.

She'd washed her face, and then spent a good deal of time concentrating on Eugene's imminent danger, but it was as if she were hitting a brick wall. She'd finally decided to let it go for the time being, at least long enough to go make her apologies to Sam. But tomorrow, she promised herself, she was going to spend the entire day with Eugene and Lovey. It was the only way she knew to find the key to saving him.

"It's open," Sam said from somewhere inside the apartment.

"It's Lauren," she returned, not opening the door, but waiting.

She heard amusement in his voice. "It's still open."

"Hi," she said lamely when she spied him sitting on a sofa on the far side of the room, his long lean legs propped up on the coffee table. Lauren looked around the room. It was tastefully decorated, warm and inviting, the color scheme of burgundy, forest green, and ivory reflecting a man's preference. "Nice," she said and would have added more, but was stopped by the charcoal drawing pinned to the wall. It was the portrait she'd sat for two days before in Jackson Square. He told her that he intended to hang it in his club, but it touched her that he'd hung it in his home instead.

Sensing her unease and embarrassment at spotting the picture, Sam motioned to one of the twin easy chairs. "Have a seat."

She hesitated, for the first time noting the soft music playing in the background. Placido

239

Domingo, if she wasn't mistaken. "You're obviously trying to relax. I won't stay. I just wanted to apologize. I'm sorry, Sam. I had no right to say the things I did to you. I was rude and uncharitable and judgmental."

Sam removed his feet from the coffee table and stood up. "Want a beer?"

"Did you hear me, Sam? Will you accept my apology?"

"Only if you'll have a beer with me . . . unless you don't like beer. I've got soda, too."

"A beer will be fine," she murmured, confused by his offhand reaction to her apology. "Can we talk, Sam?"

His back to her as he pulled two long neck bottles from the refrigerator, Sam shrugged. "Sure. But sit down."

She pulled a chair from the table, and Sam slid a bottle across the honey oak wood surface.

"So you've been talking to Till and Toots," he said as he turned a chair backwards, straddling it and propping his chin on the top.

Lauren blushed. "Toots overheard the terrible things I said to you. She was quite angry with me, and I was very embarrassed. But, Sam, I was already regretting the words before she told me anything. I swear."

He swigged hard on the bottle, making a gusty sound of satisfaction before setting the beer aside and meeting her gaze. "All's forgiven. You didn't even have to come over here, though I appreciate it. But nothing you could

240

have said today would have mattered."

"Oh," she said, her tone sounding as flat as her heart which he'd just completely deflated.

Sam chuckled. "You misunderstand, kiddo. The reason you couldn't have upset me today is because I owe you one."

Lauren raised an eyebrow.

"Last night before I went to the club," he said, then laughed at her still blank expression. "When I was sitting out back, guzzling scotch? You remember? Good. Well, then you should also remember you gave me a pretty solid kick in the pants, metaphorically speaking, of course."

"I did?"

"Yeah, the lecture on how I shouldn't let Janice stop me from bringing Casey here. I told Alexis about it today, and she agrees with you."

It took Lauren only a second to shift gears and remember the tall, elegant, and sexy young woman she'd met in the driveway several hours earlier. "I'm glad *Alexis* agrees," she said, taking a quick drink of the icy beer, than standing up. "I hope it works out for you."

Sam squinted one eye as he tried to read her reaction, figure out what had set her off this time, and then he saw the answer in her eyes. Fire flamed in that beautiful dark gaze, and he recognized the jealousy that had stoked it. A spark of pleasure warmed him as well, and he grinned. "You don't remember her, do you?"

"Remember who?" she asked with exasperation until she realized he was referring to the woman called Alexis again. "Of course I remember her. I just met her a couple of hours ago. How could I forget her? How could anyone forget her? She's . . . she's very pretty."

"Very pretty? Ha! That's probably the grossest understatement of the century. She's knockdown gorgeous. And sexy as hell. My dad always said it was the Cajun in her that gave her that sex appeal that draws men to her like flies to —"

"Okay! I stand corrected. She's the most exquisite woman I've ever seen." She turned away, bumping her hip painfully on the edge of the table.

"She's my cousin, Lauren. On my father's side." He was halfway out of his chair, but settled back when he saw her stop and turn around to reclaim her seat. Her chin was still raised slightly, defiantly, but she was listening. "She spent a weekend here at the house when we were kids. You were here then, too." He smiled at a memory. "We told her she could be Tiger Lily — the Indian princess Captain Hook kidnapped?"

"I know who Tiger Lily is!"

Sam struggled not to laugh, instinct telling him that just one good guffaw would have her scratching his eyes out. "Anyway," he continued soberly, "she's an attorney, too. Guess you could say it's a family thing."

Lauren drank slowly, giving her chagrin time to evaporate as she waited for him to continue. He obliged immediately.

"As I was saying, I thought about what you said last night. I called Alexis this morning — her name's

242

Alexis Morgan, by the way. She came over and we talked. To make a long story short, she agrees with you that I have a very good chance of getting custody of Casey. She's going to call Janice's attorney today. He's probably not in since it's Saturday, but if not, she'll lower the boom first thing Monday morning."

"I'm glad, Sam. I know it'll happen for you. Casey's not a baby who doesn't know what she wants. The judge will listen to her desires along with all the other facts." Impulsively, she leaned forward, kissing his cheek and hugging his neck. "I'm thrilled."

When she let go, Sam backed off the chair, took her bottle and put it on the table, then pulled her to her feet. "Your Charles is just going to have to forgive this, but that kiss was a I'm-a-sort-of-glad peck. Not an I'm-thrilled-for-you kiss." His mouth came down on hers, possessive, yet tentative and careful until he felt the response in hers. Then his arms tightened around her until every inch of her was pressed against him.

Lauren gripped his shoulders, her fingertips blanched white with the intensity. Her head reeled even as her tongue answered the call of his.

She felt his hand roaming her back, stopping just above the swell of her buttocks, then begin the incline up her side to stop at the swell of her breast. She inhaled sharply against the rush of passion that was so intense she was immediately light-headed. She should stop this, back away, but she had neither the strength nor the will. Even when his lips left hers, and she heard his groan of desire against her throat, felt the heat from the palm of his hand as it pressed against her breast, she couldn't find the control to step away.

"I want you," he said, his voice barely a hot whisper of air against her ear.

Icy tentacles of panic spread through her at his words, putting out the fire. Extricating herself from his grasp, she looked around her as if suddenly confused about where she was. "I . . . I have to go."

He took a step closer, the magnetic pull of his gaze forcing her eyes to meet his. He touched her hair, his fingertips trailing a strand of pale gold, then brushing her cheek. "Don't run away again, Lauren. Stay with me." It was not a command but a plea, gently given.

"I need to think," she said inadequately, flapping her arms and searching her mind for logic, order. She shook her head. "I can't think when you kiss me."

"You want me, Lauren. I felt it. Admit it to yourself."

"Of course I want you," she said more harshly than she'd intended. Sighing raggedly, she tried for a smile, but managed only a trembling grimace. "I'm confused, Sam. Give me time. Be my friend first. Maybe then, *maybe* there can be more."

"I'm already your friend, Lauren. If I wasn't, I couldn't let you walk out of here now. I want you that badly."

She reached up on her toes to kiss his lips then,

244

tears brimming in her eyes. Never had words touched her more. But she knew if she stayed, lingered even one more second, she'd lose her resolve, and she wasn't ready for another mistake.

It wasn't until she was almost to her door that she realized what that last thought meant. Another mistake? Then she really had already said goodbye to Charles in her heart. Funny that it didn't hurt. She smiled as she glanced back and found Sam standing on the verandah watching her. Had her feelings for Charles simply melted away, or had Sam somehow worked his way inside her, nudging out the competition?

Chapter Thirteen

Lauren was a mental mess when she returned to her house. In one day, less than twelve hours, she'd made decisions which were conflicting and troubling. She paced the kitchen floor, moving to the living room then into the foyer, her thoughts flitting back and forth between Chicago and New Orleans.

She'd closed the shop, vowing never to reopen it but to leave as soon as possible to reclaim her life up north. Only a few hours later, she'd given Charles the kiss-off, though she wasn't sure that he understood that yet. She'd have to call him again, spell it out, for if she was certain of nothing else, she knew she would never marry the prig she'd discovered him to be.

But the upshot of that was she probably wouldn't have a job to return to. Even if Charles proved to be more man than she wanted to give him credit for, it would be awkward working together with their dissolved relationship standing between them. He was a vice president as of two days ago, her superior now.

Going to the fridge, she got a bottle of mineral water and poured some into a glass. She decided to take it upstairs, where she curled up in her favorite spot, the window seat, to arrange her thoughts and come up with some prospects for her future.

She would return to Chicago, of course. That was where her *real* life was. What then? A new job. That had to be her first priority.

And what about Sam? a voice inside asked.

"What about Sam?" she repeated aloud. But she needn't have asked the question again. She already knew the answer. She was falling in love with him, and the realization provoked a deep groan born of an even deeper pain.

She needed a good brisk jog. Exercise would calm the roiling thoughts and ease the ache.

Springing to her feet, she crossed to the closet and shed her slacks and blouse in favor of a pair of tattered jeans, hooded sweatshirt, and sneakers.

Despite the season, the air was chilly. She would need the warmth of flannel and denim.

Keeping her eyes lowered as she left the house, she hurried along the flagstone pathway until she reached the levee.

A trail had been created at the summit of the levee for joggers and bicyclists, and it was along here that she began running.

Twilight was settling over the city, the purple and pink rays of the setting sun seeming to spotlight the trail as she ran. She set a brisk pace, never slowing, but still her mind flitted with unsettling speed from thoughts of Sam to questions about her future in Chicago to Eugene and his impending doom.

Tears streaked her cheeks as her feet pounded the gravel trailway, and though she dashed them away, she couldn't escape her turmoil.

Darkness was descending, and she was winded and growing tired, though she couldn't have run more than a few miles. So she reversed her course and headed back for home.

What was she going to do?

If she went home to Illinois, could she recapture her life? Did she want to?

If she stayed in New Orleans, would Sam be a part of her future? Would her surrender diminish the enthusiasm he'd had for the chase? And if not, could she let go of her childhood fears and learn to trust tomorrows that would always be uncertain, undisciplined, and unstructured? For that was what life with Sam would be.

As always, she argued each side logically, but this time reason failed to provide the answers. Her heart was ruling her emotions, and it was an alien experience she didn't know how to deal with.

The air had grown colder and the wind, which had been only a breeze earlier, stung her cheeks. She pulled up her hood and turned her face away from the river. But even had she been watching where she was going, the trail beneath her feet was barely visible in the dark. She didn't see the small stick carelessly dropped in the middle of the pathway. As her foot came down on it, her ankle twisted painfully, and she fell heavily, skinning her hands and bruising her knees.

She didn't cry out, but she moaned loudly.

As she rubbed her ankle, then her sore knees, she felt tears of self-pity fill her eyes again. "Damn it," she muttered, then more loudly. "Damn, damn, damn!"

"Who are you damning with such fervor?" a voice asked.

She didn't look up. She knew who it was, would have recognized his voice anywhere. "You, me, New Orleans, everything."

Sam hunkered down in front of her, reaching out to rub her ankle. "Does it hurt badly?"

"It's all right. Just a slight twist. I didn't even hurt my pride because I thought I was alone. Guess that'll be bruised now as well."

Sam ignored that, though he was glad that she probably couldn't see his smile in the darkness. But then he remembered his reason for being on the levee after the sun had set, and his grin disappeared. "What the hell were you doing out here by yourself? For such a sensible woman, you didn't show much good sense tonight. Didn't your mother teach you about bad men who come out after dark to snatch little girls on lonely trails."

"I needed to think. Running always helps."

"So next time run in the daytime," he barked, gripping her under the elbows to pull her to her feet.

But she resisted, shrugging free of his grasp. "I don't want to get up yet." She knew she sounded like a petulant child, but she didn't care. She glared at him defiantly. "What are you doing here?"

"I saw you leave your house. Watched as you tore off down the levee. I waited, and when you didn't return even after it got dark, I decided I'd better come out and make sure you were all right."

"Well, as you can see, I'm perfectly fine."

"So I should just leave you out here?"

"Yes," she snapped just as a bullfrog croaked from the water's edge reminding her of the snakes and gators that lived in the nearby swamps. "No," she amended.

"Yes? No? You want me to stay or you want to go back with me?"

"I want you to stay here with me. I'm not ready to go back, but I don't want to be alone either."

Sam didn't answer as he lowered himself to a sitting position beside her. "No moon. Not exactly a night for a romantic interlude." When she didn't answer, he tried again. "Of course, there are some things that are fun to do in the dark. I—"

"Don't tease, Sam. I want to talk."

"Okay, talk."

"I first started coming to spend summers with my aunt Edna when I was only six. I came every year until I was twelve, do you remember?"

"Of course I do. I looked forward to it."

"Guess you always thought it was just summer vacation for me, huh?"

Sam shrugged. "I don't suppose I ever thought of it. Why? It wasn't?"

Lauren shook her head and Sam saw the shimmer of gold in her hair as the hood fell away and the wind picked up the silky strands to whip them around her face. "No, I came because my mom was always working. I was a latchkey kid before they had a name for it. It was fine when I was in school because I was only home a couple of hours before she got home from work. But summers, she couldn't afford to pay a baby-sitter for me."

"So you came here. That's cool. You liked it here, didn't you?"

"Yes," Lauren said with exasperation, "but that's not the point, Sam. The point is my father left us when I was five. My mom never forgave him, and every day for the rest of my life I heard the lecture about getting a good job, developing a career, and marrying well so that I would always have security."

"Your dad abandoned you?" Sam asked, surprise heavy in his tone. "He didn't help with your support after that at all?"

"He died, Sam."

"But that's hardly the same thing as walking away, Lauren. He didn't want to leave."

Her gaze flew to his, and even in the dark, he could see the impatience. "I know that, but I didn't understand it then, and all I heard from my mother was 'You have to plan for the future, baby. Otherwise, you're going to end up just like me, working for pennies and worrying yourself into an early grave.' The point isn't that he died, that he left us. The point is that he didn't prepare a safe, stable future for us. So I planned my life by a specific road map, and now I'm lost."

Sam took one of her hands in his, pressing it against his thigh. "Why? I don't understand. You have money now. I don't know what your aunt left

251

you, but just from the proceeds you'd get from the house and business alone, you'd be secure for the rest of your life even if you never worked another day."

Again the shake of her head, and now he heard tears in her voice. "I thought it was about money, too, but it's more than that. I want stability. I want an unshakable foundation." She paused, sniffling loudly and dabbing at her eyes with her free hand. "Charles wasn't home last night. I think he was with another woman."

Sam was momentarily speechless, the air knocked out of him by the pain her words had caused. So, she was crying about Charles. When he spoke, it was softly, barely a hoarse whisper as he fought the disappointment and hurt. "But you only *think*. You don't know for sure? Why not ask him?"

Suddenly, unexpectedly, Lauren withdrew her hand from his and scrambled to her feet. "Damn it, you're missing the point again, or I'm not telling it right." She waved her arms expansively as she walked in circles, and in spite of his confusion, Sam couldn't resist a grin. She looked like an angry bird — a graceful, elegant golden plumed bird.

"You're right," he said, standing up and trying to follow her meanderings before stepping aside to give her room to pace. "You're either leaving out a key element here, or I'm more obtuse than I realized."

She spun around at his words, hands on hips. "I thought Charles was everything I'd ever wanted, but he's not."

252

"Okay, I think I've got it now. You've lost the stability you thought he represented. Your man of rock turned out to be made of clay."

"No . . . well, yes, but what unnerved me to the core was discovering that I didn't care. I never loved him, Sam. If I did, it would hurt to think of him with another woman, but what hurt was realizing that I'd been building my dreams around smoke."

"Oh," Sam said as his lips spread in a wide, satisfied grin.

"Oh? *Oh?* Is that all you can say?"

He grabbed her wrist, tugging her against him. Slipping his arms around her waist, he stood with his legs braced wide apart as he leaned back to look at her face. "Oh, no, baby, I have a lot more to say to you, but it's going to have to wait. I have to get to the club. I want you to go home and get a nap, 'cause when I get home in the morning—two-thirty or three—we're going to have that chat." He kissed her then, only a quick peck, then another. "Okay?"

Lauren sighed and trembled at the same time. Was talking really what he had in mind? From the way his heart pounded against her breast, the way his eyes gleamed, she had her doubts, and the thought of what he really had in mind thrilled her . . . and terrified her.

"Okay?" he persisted.

She lowered her face, pressing it against his chest before nodding.

"Good, then let's go back."

They walked, slowly, not speaking, and Lauren

surprised herself with her contented sigh as Sam's arm went around her shoulders. She smiled at his profile as she slipped her arm around his waist, and at least for the moment, her questions about the future were stilled. For now there were no to-morrows, only hours . . . the hours that she'd wait for him to come home.

That night Sam performed to acclaim as always. But though his music was as flawlessly executed as ever, his thoughts were fifteen miles away with the most enthralling, enigmatic, and confounding woman of his experience.

He wanted to make love with her. But it was more than that. He wanted not just tonight, or a few nights or weeks. He didn't want to acquire a taste for the sweetness that loving her promised only to have it forever denied him when she left New Orleans to return to Chicago. Would she stay? Could he let her go . . . this woman who had already become an addiction?

Though Edna had long ago hired a housekeeper who came in twice a week, and the house was almost spotless Lauren found herself too restless to sit around doing nothing while she passed the hours until Sam returned home. She never could have slept. She scrubbed the expansive kitchen floor on hands and knees, scoured the bathtub and shower, and ironed tablecloths that had already been starched and pressed only days before . . . all because of Sam.

Her hands perspired, and she constantly

254

wiped them against her jeans. Her stomach was queasy with anticipation, and she tried to settle it with nibbled crackers and sipped ginger ale.

Sam North was the sexiest man she'd ever met — smooth-talking yet rough-edged — a dangerous combination for a woman who had always sought the safeness of predictable solid relationships. He'd told her earlier that he wanted her and asked if she felt the same way, and though she'd tried to deny it to herself then, she couldn't lie to herself now. But again the question that was never far from the surface, crept back: What about tomorrow? She was risking all of her tomorrows by going to him tonight. He was the fascinating and forbidden, for he represented the one thing she'd never allowed herself . . . . risk. Now she was willing to take the chance, but she wondered as she stared out the front window just after midnight, would there be tomorrows with Sam?

Just before midnight, the jazz trio took a break, but unlike most nights, Sam didn't work the floor, talking with his admiring fans. He headed straight for the bar and ordered a shot of bourbon straight up.

Hank caught up with him just as the bartender slid the drink his way. " 'Bout ready to start the last set?" he asked, slapping his friend and employer on the shoulder.

"Sure," Sam said, tossing down the liquor in one long swallow.

"Something got you worked up?" Hank asked as they made their way to the stage.

Malibu, the bass player, joined them and answered for Sam. "Methinks his pretty little neighbor lady's what's got him in a dither."

"That so?" Hank asked, his tone teasing. "Can't see any problem there. Lady's got a lot of class. Go for it, boss. Whatcha gotta lose?"

That was exactly the problem, Sam thought as he turned his back to his friends, signaling the start of the last set. He had everything to lose. He could lose his soul to this woman.

With a sigh, Lauren caught her hair up off the back of her neck to rub her aching muscles at the nape as the grandfather clock in the foyer chimed two o'clock.

Leaning against the cabinets, she sighed restlessly. Her back was to the window, so she didn't see the headlights turn into the drive next door. But she heard the purr of the engine, the protest of tires being stopped too quickly, then the slam of a car door.

Sam noted the lights in Lauren's house as soon as he turned into the drive. Was she waiting for him as he'd waited for the night to be over? Was she as nervous? As anxious?

Lauren's skin tingled with anticipation as the hot

hot water that jetted from the shower pelted her back. As she lathered fragrant soap over her arms and legs and belly, she closed her eyes and thought of Sam, imagining his fingers gliding over her skin. As the water rinsed the suds away, she smiled. She no longer had any doubts about what she wanted. Turning off the water, she hurried from the shower to pull on a satin pajama set of burgundy boxers and a short belted jacket.

She padded quickly down the stairs barefoot, the damp ends of her hair bouncing against her shoulders. She wasn't going to think about tomorrow. She was going to enjoy tonight, and she wasn't going to wait for Sam to come to her.

But moments later reality was ever so much sweeter, she realized as she met his eyes, and he reached for her hand to pull her inside his apartment.

He didn't speak or smile, but the welcome was in his luminous emerald gaze and on his lips as they found hers.

His hand trailed the length of her back, cupping her hips as the kiss she'd thought about caused her breath to catch and her heart to pound.

His tongue met hers in the beginning of the mating dance, but he surprised her by pulling away. He searched her face as he asked, "Are you sure?"

She didn't answer, couldn't for a few seconds. Barely in his arms for more than a minute and already she was breathless. She shook her head, but when he started to speak, she put her fingers over his lips. "I'm scared," she whispered, then with a soft chuckle, "but I never welch on deals."

He laughed with her, but sobered quickly as he picked her up in his arms and carried her into the bedroom. "No preliminaries," he said as they walked. "No drink, no chitchat. I'm rude, crude, and unsophisticated—a regular Neanderthal—but I've been playing this out in my mind for hours and the pleasantries are going to have to wait because, baby, I can't."

"I find your cave utterly charming," she murmured against his neck as he lowered her to the bed.

Looking down on her, her blond hair fanned around her head like golden, gossamer silk and her perfect oval face delicately flushed, he thought her the most utterly charming woman he'd ever encountered. But for the moment, words were relegated to the back of his mind as he concentrated on creating pleasure.

He pulled an end of the sash belted around her waist, his eyes never leaving hers until he pushed back her jacket. Then his gaze drifted to the perfection of her small breasts, and he inhaled sharply as he cupped them with his hands. Only then did he look back at her face, searching her dark gaze for the desire he hoped would be there. When he found it at once, hot and already pleading for what was to come, he murmured her name, "Lauren . . ."

He wore only his tuxedo slacks and the white pleated shirt, which was unbuttoned and open. Lauren reached up to run a hand over the hard muscles of his stomach. She raised herself on her elbow to continue the path her fingers wished to trail up his chest to the pulsing vein in his throat, where they hesitated. "There's something you should know before we continue," she said, her voice husky with need.

His hands which had been gently massaging her breasts stilled with her words. He didn't want to ask, dreaded the confession he sensed she needed to make—the words that would confirm his fears that she was his for tonight only. But he would give her the world at that moment if she requested it, so he met her gaze, inviting her confession. "What?"

"I love you, Sam."

His relief at the simple sentence was so great, he felt the urge to cry out in triumph. Instead, he simply smiled, unaware of the sensations his devilishly wicked grin provoked in his partner. "Then we don't have a problem, 'cause making sweet love with you is exactly what this is all about."

She pulled his face down to hers. This time there was no gentleness to the kiss they shared, only hunger, raw and hot.

He pushed her jacket from her shoulders and arms as his lips left hers to begin working their magic down her throat to her breast. He heard her gasp as his lips found a swollen nipple and suckled hungrily. But his own groan of passion almost obscured it as she ran her hands through his hair and nipped at the tender flesh just below his ear.

He sensed her urgency just as she realized his. Yet by unspoken agreement, their lovemaking was leisurely, each wanting to explore every inch of the other, to experience every measure of exquisite joy their passion aroused.

She thought him a quiet lover until he'd stripped off his clothes while she writhed with need, then parted her legs with a knee and entered her. Then his growl of satisfaction was as savage and primal as the act he performed with such magnificent gusto.

She cried out with immediate climax, but moments later, she rode with him, arching her hips and meeting each powerful thrust with her muscles holding him tight, receiving him greedily.

He brought her to ecstasy four times before he finally groaned loudly with his own release.

He didn't move off her even after he'd fallen fully over her body and lain there for several minutes. After a time, he raised himself up from the waist to look down at her face, now dewy with passion, dark eyes sparkling like wet topaz. "You are the most exquisite woman I've ever known," he said softly, accompanying his words with nibbling little kisses.

She smiled, touched by the declaration and returned his kisses with a nip on his bottom lip. Her hand sought his against her side, her splayed fingers meeting the tips of his as she forced his arm up so she could admire his hand. "No wonder you became a musician," she said, admiring the slender artistic fingers. "These hands should only be used to work magic, not wasted turning the pages of law briefs."

He laughed, and she felt the taut muscles of his

stomach ripple against her belly. "Don't leave, Lauren. Stay here with me."

She thought he must be speaking about the present, didn't dare hope for more, and nodded. "I couldn't leave now if I wanted to. You've turned my legs to jelly." The last was said with more lightness than she felt. Then, in a whisper, she expressed what she truly felt. "I'll always treasure what you've given me tonight, Sam. Always."

He pressed his face against her throat. "We gave to each other, Lauren."

She couldn't answer because of the lump in her throat.

After a time, he rolled off her but pulled her against him. "What are you thinking?"

"Nothing. Everything."

"Don't want to tell me?"

"I don't know if I can . . . don't know if I can find the words."

He waited, holding her tighter, as if by doing so he could give them to her.

"I'm happy. I'm afraid."

He sighed. "Why are you happy?"

"Because I'm here with you. Because you've just made the most beautiful love with me, I can scarcely believe it happened, except that my body still tingles from your touch, so I know it's true."

"Why are you afraid?" he asked, though he thought he already knew the answer.

"I'm . . . I'm afraid of being without you."

Her candor touched and surprised him. It wasn't what he'd expected, and even though he wanted to promise her that he'd always be there for her, he knew she never believe those words. When she'd lost her father, she'd learned that forever only happened in fairy tales. She already knew that such a promise wasn't his to make, so he gave the only answer he could find. "Give up the ghosts that have haunted you for so long, Lauren. The only certainty we can count on is always being there for ourselves. Do what makes you happy, and the rest will fall into place."

She laughed softly though she was disappointed by his words. "Ah, not only a talented musician, magnificent lover, but a philosopher as well." Then she squeezed his hand, forgiving him for what he couldn't tell her. "I'm happy to be here with you."

"Umm, babe, that definitely makes two of us." He tightened his grip around her waist with one hand, and with the other sought the soft flesh of her inner thigh.

"You're not going to get any sleep if you start that again," she said.

"I wasn't planning on getting a lot of sleep tonight. Got a problem with that?"

She shook her head. On the contrary she was delighted.

They made love again, then fell asleep in one another's arms, and as the sun began its ascent over the Mississippi, he awakened her with more urging kisses. This time their passion was more intense than before, and they both fell back exhausted and sated when it was spent.

When Lauren awakened again, she felt as if she were suffocating, then grinned sleepily when she realized that Sam was the reason she was having trouble drawing a deep breath. He was sprawled across her back snoring deeply. She wriggled free as gently as possible, but he opened an eye as the last of him—a foot—thumped heavily to the bed. "That was cruel," he grumbled.

"Sorry. Couldn't breathe. Besides, I'd better sneak back to my house before the aunts get up. Wouldn't want them seeing me leaving here dressed only in my PJs."

Sam pushed himself up far enough to check the digital clock. "Un-uh, eight o'clock. Too late. They'll already getting ready for church." He threw an arm over her stomach. "Now you have to stay. Afraid you're my prisoner for at least another hour until they've gone."

Lauren joined the game. "Then get up and shower with me, then I'll brew us a pot of coffee while we wait for my sentence to end."

"You're a heartless wench. I haven't had a decent night's rest since you came into my life, and now you're making me get up to shower with you."

"You weren't complaining about losing sleep last night . . . or earlier this morning either, for that matter."

"That's because you were being so generous," he said, as he got up on hands and knees to crawl from the bed. Once on his feet, he took her hand and led the way to the bathroom. "That's the secret to all the powers on earth, Lauren Kennedy. Giving. Remember that, and you'll find the answers to your every wish."

She giggled. "I'll make those words my mantra, Sam. I'll—" She froze. Eugene! Sam had just given

263

her the key she'd been searching for all week. That had to be it! What else could it be?

"What's wrong?" Sam asked as he reached in to turn on the shower.

"Nothing," she said. She stretched up onto her toes to kiss him. "Everything's wonderful, but I have to hurry. I have to leave."

He reached a hand into the water to test the temperature, then pulled her into the shower with him. "Un-uh. No way. You've forgotten that you're my prisoner, and I was lying about the hour. I'm going to keep you all day."

"Oh, Sam," she said, sputtering water. "I can't. I want to, but I can't. I have to go see Eugene. It's important. But I'll come back later, okay?"

"Nope," he said, lathering her breasts with soap and making it almost impossible for her to think rationally. "I'm keeping you and that's final. Besides, I'm having a party today, and I want you to go with me."

"A party? Where? When? Stop that. I can't think clearly when you're touching me like that."

"The party's on a yacht on Lake Ponchartrain. Time is one o'clock. And that's the whole idea of me touching you like that. I don't want you thinking clearly if it means you're thinking of leaving and refusing to go to the party with me."

"All right! I'll go to the party with you, but I have to go see Eugene first."

"Invite him along."

"Oh, Sam, really? Lovey, too?" At his blank expression, she reminded him of the woman who owned the health food store.

264

"Sure, Lovey, too, if you want her. But better tell them it's a theme party. Roaring twenties."

"I don't have a costume, Sam."

"Improvise. Stick a feather in a headband and wear something short and tight. Put on lots of rouge and bright lipstick, and you'll look the part."

"Okay," she agreed, bracketing his face with her hands as she pulled it down for another kiss, "But I really do have to go see Eugene. Can you meet us at the shop later?"

"I can, and I will," he said, backing her against the tiled wall. "If you'll help me enjoy my shower the way a shower should be enjoyed. Eugene can wait another hour or two, can't he?"

Yes, she thought as Sam's hands began their artful ministrations on her soap-slicked skin, Eugene would wait for the miracle Sam had given her to pass on.

Chapter Fourteen

"Sister!" Matilda Crocker called to the other elderly woman who was adjusting her hat in front of the beveled glass mirror in the entryway. "Our next-door neighbor has just come out of Sam's apartment."

"How nice," Toots replied, slowly making her way to the windows that faced the driveway and the house next door. "Perhaps she joined him for breakfast," she said.

"I do believe, judging from the way she is dressed in that cute little pajama set, that she must have stayed for more than breakfast, Toots dear."

"Oh, my," the other woman breathed as she parted the drapes at the far end of the window to peer out. "I suppose you're right." Toots sighed, the sound reflecting the satisfaction and pleasure both women were experiencing. "Isn't that nice for them, Till? And doesn't she have the prettiest legs?"

"She's quite attractive from the top of her head to her toes," Matilda agreed. "Particularly this morning with that rosy glow on her cheeks. I do think Sam is very good for our Lauren."

"Oh, I hope so," Toots said as she walked back to the mirror to finish the task of setting her wide-brimmed hat at exactly the proper angle. "Edna would be so pleased to think her plans came to fruition."

Tillie joined her, placing her own hat, a smaller, more subdued version of her sister's, on her head. She chuckled softly. "Why, Petulia LePointe, I'd say you're pretty pleased, yourself. Your cheeks are absolutely the same color as your fuchsia bonnet."

"Well, I suppose it's no secret that I've always been an ardent fan of romance. I love all those sweet novels, and it's even better when it happens in real life to two such deserving people as Sam and Lauren."

"Caution, Sister," Till said, holding up a finger to make her point. "We don't *know* that everything will end up happily ever after for Lauren and Sam. It certainly looks encouraging, but I think we should exercise some restraint before we start sending out announcements."

"Oh, of course it's going to be a fairy-tale ending for them, Till. How could it be otherwise? You're forgetting that they have magic working for them."

Matilda frowned slightly. "I know, and Eugene's record is quite remarkable, but I got the impression when we stopped by the shop yesterday afternoon that he wasn't very confident about keeping Lauren

267

in New Orleans. Remember that he did tell us she's closed the shop, promising not to reopen it."

Petulia's eyes darkened, for she did indeed remember their visit to Yesterday's Treasures the day before. Not only had Eugene not seemed too certain about Lauren and Sam's chances, he'd seemed—oh, what was the word? Dejected? No, stronger than that.

As if reading her thoughts, Tillie supplied the right word. "Not to change the subject, Sister, but I'm rather worried about Eugene. He's usually so exuberant, and yesterday, well, didn't you sense a despondency that worried you?"

"I did, Till, and he looked so pale. Genies don't get sick, do they, because I got the distinct impression that our Eugene was feeling under the weather."

"Maybe that's it, now that you mention it. He was very pale, just as you said. As a matter of fact, I had the feeling he might simply fade away right before our eyes."

Toots clucked her tongue with worry. "Well, we can't have that. Not only do we need him to see to Sam and Lauren's relationship, but he's such a fine young man. I think we should take him some homemade soup after church, Sister."

"And perhaps a few of your wonderful raspberry dumplings. Those will put color back in his cheeks faster than he can blink up another wish."

"Oh, dear me, look at the time. I think we'd better hurry if we're going to get a care package together. You know how Reverend frowns when his parishioners come in late for services."

Tillie's spine straightened as she huffed off indignantly to the kitchen in front of her sister. "Well, he might well remember that doing the Lord's work is not simply arriving for church on time. Helping one's neighbors is important work."

"Amen, Sister. Amen."

Eugene and Lovey were reclining in the sea of pillows and cushions as his well-being was being discussed across town. Their thoughts, too, were on his condition, which was worsening by the hour, though the kind-hearted genie had discouraged talk about it. He knew his time was fast running out, but his concern was for Lovey. For all his magic and intuition, he knew no way to prepare her for their imminent separation and wished to spare her as much anguish as possible.

In the background, the voices of The Mamas and the Papas filled the quiet with "Monday, Monday."

Lovey rested on her side, her head against her lover's chest. "Too bad the world doesn't appreciate music like this anymore."

"Oh, I think it does, as a whole. The world's always going to change, Lovey. Progress is as inevitable as the rising and setting of the sun. But the best of times will always last."

"Not always," Lovey said, pain in her tone and in her eyes when she looked up at him.

He kissed her forehead and smiled. "Listen," he said as he gave his head a quick, almost imperceptible jerk. The voices of a past era were replaced by Garth Brooks singing the words to "The Dance."

"Listen to the words, Lovey. They're so true."

As she listened, her eyes filled with tears. "You're right, Eugene. And I want you to know, I would never have missed the dance, because the pain isn't nearly as bad as the joy I've had since we found each other."

"I know. I wouldn't have either." He encircled her with his arms. "But just once, I wish I could have used my magic for us."

"We still have Lauren," she reminded him.

Eugene opened his mouth to answer, but was interrupted as their foundation rocked, and they heard Lauren's voice. "Speak of the devil," the genie said with a laugh and shake of his head.

"She's no devil, Eugene, but I do think she believes Sam is."

Eugene's eyes danced with amusement for the first time that morning.

"What?" Lovey asked, getting up. "Has something happened?"

"Something was about to happen last night when I tuned out," he answered, taking her hand as he prepared to blink them from the lamp. "Something very special."

Lauren was too excited to stand still as she waited for Eugene to respond to her summons. She paced the aisles of her store, her hand brushing over the treasures her aunt had loved so much. But

270

her thoughts were on the secret Sam had helped her uncover and which she fervently hoped would save the genie. But speaking of Eugene, what was taking him so long?

"At your service, Mama," he said not two feet behind her.

Lauren spun around, with a wide smile. "Oh, good, you're here. I was afraid you'd gone fishing again."

"Hey, you're getting pretty good. You didn't even jump that time when I appeared."

Lauren laughed as she wriggled fingers in Lovey's direction in greeting. "I was expecting you this time."

"So, here I am."

"Well, good, 'cause I've got a surprise for you." She was looking at Eugene, but from the corner of her eye, she saw the light of hope that sparked in Lovey's eyes. Lauren winked at her as she waited for Eugene to ask about her surprise. When he didn't, she waved her arms in exasperation. "Well? Aren't you going to ask me what it is?"

Eugene shrugged with maddening nonchalance. "Figure you'll tell me when you're ready. If I haven't learned anything else over the centuries, I've learned patience."

Lauren had been about to make the wish, test her theory on the spot, but at his words, she changed her mind.

For the past week, she'd become increasingly confused, changing her mind from one moment to the next, second-guessing every decision she'd ever made. But last night, everything—well, almost everything—had fallen into place. She still didn't know what she was going to do about Yesterday's Treasures, but she knew she wasn't leaving New Orleans until her relationship with Sam was resolved. In spite of her determination to dislike him, she'd fallen madly, profoundly in love with him. It felt *right,* and so did her theory about saving the genie she'd come to love as well. As she watched him now, she was more confident than ever that the answer she'd uncovered with Sam's nudging was going to save him. But, and the idea had come to her just now, he was going to have to exercise that patience he was so proud of. She smiled, including both of her friends. "We're going to a party!"

"A party?" Lovey repeated, her tone flat and conveying her disappointment as eloquently as the dullness in her eyes. "Lauren, we appreciate the invitation—don't we, honey? Yes, we do, but I hardly think Eugene is feeling up to a party today."

"Nonsense," Lauren interrupted before Eugene could agree with Lovey. "A party is just what the doctor calls for—the doctor being me, of course. " Her tone had been light, teasing, but it sobered now as she took their hands. "Trust me, okay?"

Eugene looked doubtful, Lovey positively stubborn.

"Okay, so I know I haven't given you a lot of reason to trust my instincts this past week, but I'm on track now. I've finally gotten things straightened out in my mind, and I just *know* this party is going to be the miracle-working medicine that you need, Gene. Come with me, please, both of you."

"I . . . I just don't know," Lovey said hesitantly. "What do you think, hon?"

Eugene looked from one woman to the other, their expressions so drastically reflecting opposing emotions, it would have been laughable had he had it in him to laugh at anything.

He walked away, circling the store as he considered the proposal while the women waited. After a time, he turned back from where he'd finally stopped and peered out the window. "You know," he said, "when I witnessed Rome burning, I didn't understand why Nero simply sat there and fiddled. Guess now I can relate. If the whole world's coming to an end, what better way to go than doing what you love, and I definitely love good music, good food, and good friends."

Lauren shook her head, not knowing whether to laugh at the analogy being made by the spry, odd little man who had witnessed centuries of history-making events or cry for the obvious implication of his words. "So, does that mean you'll come to the party with me?"

"Sure, mama. I got an itch to make merry. Can ya dig it, Lovey?"

"If it's what you want, I can dig it just fine," Lovey said tenderly.

"Great!" said Lauren. "Now, we've only got one problem."

"Shoulda known there'd be a catch," Eugene grumbled.

"Not a major glitch," Lauren assured him. "Nothing you can't handle."

"Sounds like she needs some fancy magic to me, Lovey. What do you think?"

For the first time, Lovey giggled, getting into the mood that Lauren was working to create, and that Eugene had apparently decided to join in. "Sounds very suspicious."

"Look, it's no big deal, but it's a theme party—the Roaring Twenties. Sam says we can merely improvise, but it's on board some fancy yacht, and I just wondered if you couldn't whip us up some twenties duds."

Eugene raised his hand, waved it in a circle a few times, blinked his eyes, and miraculously, all three were dressed in the costumes of the fun-filled pre-Depression era.

"Wow!" Lauren whispered, her awe almost choking her as she looked first at Eugene, then Lovey, then finally at herself in the full-length mirror on the far wall. Eugene had blinked up the most authentic and flashy twenties attire she had ever seen.

The thin man looked almost dashing in the black suit with its wide lapels, baggy trousers, and oxford shoes. "You look like a gangster," Lauren giggled.

"Well, I did make the acquaintance of—"

"Don't tell me. Al Capone?"

"As a matter of fact, yes. I sorta dug the way he dressed. Lot of flash, you know?"

"Yes, we can see." Lauren turned to Lovey. "And you must be his moll. You look fantastic, Lovey!"

274

And indeed she did. The loose-fitting bodice of the short dress was gathered by a sequined sash around her hips, disguising the plumpness of her upper torso while emphasizing her narrow hips and shapely legs. The lavender fringed skirt bounced with Lovey's obvious pleasure, and her blue eyes sparkled like sapphires beneath the matching small cap. Two dark purple plumes circled her oval face, which had widened now with her smile of pleasure.

"I do look rather splendid, don't I?" Lovey asked Lauren's reflection beside her in the mirror. "But, oh, Lauren, wait until Sam gets a load of you. He's gonna die!"

Lauren couldn't resist the small self-conscious smile, for she hardly recognized the exotic-looking woman who stared back at her. The dress of simple white satin resembled a sexy slip except for the long slit that reached as high as mid-thigh. The two-inch heels were also white and adorned with tiny straps across the instep and glittering rhinestone buckles. Her hair, normally straight and sleek, was a mass of waves that hugged her head, and she wore a slave bracelet of sparkling rhinestones on her forearm. Eugene had reddened her lips and even added the final perfect touch of a black beauty mark just below her cheek. She blushed prettily as she met Eugene's eyes in the mirror. "You're too much, buster. The only way this could feel any more real would be if Sam showed up in an old car."

The beep-beep-beep of an automobile horn sounded just outside the store, and all three rushed to look out the front window.

"Oh, gee," Lovey said.

"Holy Moly," Eugene added.

"I can't believe it," Lauren said, then looked suspiciously at Eugene, who merely shrugged his innocence. "Honest Injun, mama, I had nothing to do with that."

All eyes turned in amazement to the car: a classic Duesenberg Model A Phaeton in mint condition. But as impressive as it was, Lauren's eyes were drawn to the man who stepped out of the green convertible.

Like Eugene he wore a suit with wide lapels and baggy trousers but cut from gray pinstripes, and he'd added the authentic touch of a black homburg pulled low over one eye. He looked roguishly handsome, and Lauren felt the evidence of her thrill heat her cheeks.

"Hey, baby," Sam said as she met him at the door, gathering her to him with an arm around her waist. "You look good enough to—"

Lauren cut him off with a quick kiss as she glanced in the direction of Lovey and Eugene.

"Oh, hi, guys. Damn, you all look great. Guess we're all set to go cut some rugs."

"Where'd you get the car?" Lauren asked and stepped back as Sam held the door open on the passenger side to let Eugene and Lovey climb in.

"Borrowed. What do you think? Nice touch, huh?"

Lauren looked down to where his hand rested on her hip, then back up to meet his eyes. "Very nice touch," she said, pursing her lips prettily, and got into the Duesenberg.

Lovey and Eugene laughed at the way she'd turned the tables on him. It wasn't often that a man of Sam North's confidence was disconcerted, but his dark flush betrayed him as he hurried around to the far side of the car.

Lauren leaned over the seat, taking advantage of the few seconds before Sam could overhear, and shook a finger in the genie's face. "No fading, Gene. Promise me. This party is only half the surprise, and I need you until it's over."

"Guess that means she's decided on her final wish," Lovey told him. Sensing his tension, she gave his hand an encouraging squeeze though she felt her heart would break.

"What wish?" Sam asked as he climbed in behind the wheel.

"Oh, just one I intend to make later."

Sam laughed. "Odd how I never thought of you as fanciful. Now I find out you wish on stars. I think I'm liking you better and better every minute," he said, his gaze lazily roaming the length of beautiful flesh that the high slit of her skirt revealed.

The drive to the pier on Lake Ponchartrain took half an hour. And all four of them seemed determined to enjoy every second, as if afraid that the magic of the day would evaporate.

Eugene didn't know how long he had left before he faded into oblivion . . . or wherever ancient genies went. But he was determined to make the last days . . . or day as perfect for Lovey as possible.

Lovey was just as determined on his behalf.

Lauren, too, faced the uncertainties of tomorrow. For now, Sam wanted her with him. She hadn't failed to notice that her declarations of love had not been returned during their night of lovemaking. But if now was all she had, she was going to make it the most memorable time of her life.

Sam cast sidelong glances at the enthralling woman at his side. He'd never known anyone as complex. All week, she'd sent conflicting signals, keeping him off kilter . . . and from sleep. Everything had changed suddenly last night, but what about tomorrow? She had said she loved him, and he'd heard the truth in her tone, but was that enough for her? He hoped so, but feared that a lifetime of her mother's lectures might have been too deeply planted to be uprooted. He didn't know if she would suddenly decide that she needed her world of order and structure in Illinois tomorrow. But he was going to do his damnedest while he had the chance to prove to her that she belonged with him.

As he pulled the antique car to a stop, he pointed to a long, sleek gleaming white yacht. "There she is."

"Oh, Sam, she's beautiful. Who does she belong to?"

"She's mine. I'm the host of this whing-ding. It's an annual event which I started last year. The guest list is as eclectic as a United Nations meeting.

Mostly musicians, a few politicians, a world-famous chef, a couple of attorneys, some artists, and even an actor or two, but all friends, people you'll like."

"Sounds like fun," Eugene said.

"Good food?" Lovey's eyes gleamed.

"Are you kidding?" Sam asked Lovey, though he kept his eyes on Lauren. "A true southern belle asking if the food will be good. Cajun and creole at its best."

"Great, 'cause I'm starved," Lovey said.

"Lauren?" Sam asked.

"Hmm?" She'd been staring at the beautiful ship, "What?"

"Are you all right?"

"All right? I'm so impressed, I'm speechless. I can't believe you own that fabulous boat."

"Lock, stock, and barrel," he told her as he got out and hurried around to offer her a hand down. "But, sweetheart, it's called a ship, not a boat . . . unless we're alone. Then you can call it a raft for all I care. But as captain, I have a duty to keep you on the straight and narrow."

"Aye, aye, sir. I won't embarrass you by making the same mistake twice."

As Sam crooked an arm around her neck, pulling her close for a quick kiss, he winked at Eugene. "Ain't life grand? Two beautiful women and only one of them a smart mouth."

Lauren would have uttered another wisecrack, but just as they stepped onto the gangplank, she noticed the name painted on the ship's gleaming side: *The Jazzy Lady*. She stopped so abruptly that Eugene and Lovey almost collided.

"What's wrong?" Sam asked.

"The name. It's the same name as the club you work . . ." Her eyes widened with comprehension. "You own the nightclub as well?"

"Yeah. Why, you didn't know?"

"I thought you only worked there."

"Wow, and you still came to the party with me, even though you thought I was only a lowly musician. I'm impressed."

This earned him a punch in the arm. "I'm not that materialistic, damn it."

"Just teasing," he muttered as he rubbed his arm.

Lauren laughed at herself. "So tell me, darling, just *who* are some of the names on your guest list?"

"Snob," he said, slapping her backside lightly.

"Barbarian," she countered with a laugh.

Lauren had never imagined that a day could be so enchanting. Sam introduced them to his other guests, more than a hundred friends, some so famous that she was almost rendered speechless.

For once, Sam was off duty as a musician, having hired friends to provide the entertainment. He and Lauren danced and ate and wandered from one small group of guests to another, often drifting off to stand alone together as the ship sailed around the lake.

"Having fun?" he asked during one such private moment.

"Can't you tell?"

He kissed her, letting his lips linger on hers for a long moment before answering. "Well, let me see. Your eyes are sparkling like topaz, your beautiful laughter has been floating around the ship for hours, and you haven't punched me once or stomped off since we came aboard. Yeah, I guess I can tell."

She would have answered, but Malibu appeared suddenly, slapping Sam on the shoulder. "We have a request to play. Just one or two numbers, then you can get back to your lady." The handsome bass player winked at her. "Can I steal him for a few minutes?"

Lauren joined Eugene and Lovey at a table, her face beaming with pride as she watched Sam take his seat at the piano.

"Guess that silly look on your face means the toad's finally turned into a prince, huh?" Eugene asked.

Lauren smiled but didn't answer for a moment as she looked around the room at the other guests. A prince? Yes, she supposed he was. Everyone on board liked and admired him. That had been evident from the first moment he'd spoken with each of them. She'd seen the envious looks cast her way by the female guests as well and had felt her heart quicken with satisfaction. She looked at Eugene again, finally answering. "Oh, yes, Gene, he's definitely a prince."

281

As he had on the night of her visit to the other Jazzy Lady, Sam performed flawlessly. His audience was enthusiastic and receptive, applauding loudly, then making requests and postponing the end of his mini-concert.

"Hey, man, play "Way Down Yonder In New Orleans," requested a man Lauren recognized as a senator from Illinois.

She bounced in time to the music along with almost everyone else who stood or sat around the trio of musicians. "They're playing our song," she heard Lovey tell Eugene and felt the same possessive pride she heard in the other woman's voice. But was it *her* song as well? she wondered. The music ended before she could search deeper for the answer, and then she surprised herself by sticking two fingers in her mouth to whistle her approval.

The entire assembly of guests laughed at her enthusiasm. And though she felt the warmth of embarrassment in her cheeks, the fire intensified when she met Sam's eyes and saw the love in them.

"Encore!" someone yelled, but Sam shook his head. "No, that's enough. We'll be docking soon. You're all welcome to stay on board as long as you like, but I'm going to spend the rest of the evening with my girl."

So, it was almost time for the fairy-tale day to come to an end, Lauren thought. As Sam joined her, she saw Lovey and Eugene slip away from the table to walk arm and arm along the deck. It was time to test her theory. Nervously, she wrung her hands, following the couple and testing the words

282

in her mind to make sure she got them exactly right before she said them aloud.

"What's wrong, Lauren?" Sam asked.

But she didn't answer. Instead she said softly, "I wish Eugene could share his life with Lovey and know the kind of happiness with her that I've had with you today."

Sam reached for her, drawing her against him with a hand around her waist. "I don't know what brought that on, but I'm glad you feel that way."

Lauren smiled but didn't look at him. Instead, she kept her gaze focused on the man who walked with Lovey's hand tucked possessively in his.

"Lauren?"

"Oh, happen, please," she whispered, and then it did. There was no miraculous transformation. Eugene halted suddenly and turned to meet her gaze as church bells began to sound. One, two, then three, four, and at once it seemed as if every bell in the city clanged and pealed together in some magic, mysterious celebration.

The guests all rushed to the railing, and Sam led Lauren after them to investigate the wonderful phenomenon.

The bells continued to ring, and Sam hardly noticed when she slipped her hand from his and joined Eugene and Lovey.

"We did it," she told the genie.

"You did it, Lauren," he said. "But how did you know?"

"The secret? That giving was the secret to life? Sam told me this morning. Oh, he wasn't talking about you or magic or wishes, but when he said it, I suddenly knew." She took his hand and drew it to her face. "And you showed me, too, Gene."

"I did? But I couldn't. That was against the rules," he protested as if afraid he'd somehow be blamed and lose the gift of mortality she'd just given him.

She smiled, shaking her head. "I don't mean you were giving me clues on purpose, Gene. You showed me by example, by how good and giving you are. No matter how much you dreaded the fate that you knew was getting closer and closer, you kept watch over me, giving and never asking in return.

"Then I knew. I had to give away my last wish to save you. That's what magic is, Gene. Giving love."

Lovey hugged her tight even as the bells continued to ring as if they'd never stop. "Thank you," she whispered, too touched to know what else to say.

Sam joined them then. "Really something, isn't it? I've never heard anything like it. Wonder what's happening?"

"It must be magic," Lauren said, laughing with her friends.

"Ah, so my lady does have a whimsical side. I thought you'd forgotten about magic when you grew up."

She leaned against him, circling his waist with her arms. "I just about had."

"We've docked," Eugene observed. Extending a hand, he thanked Sam for inviting them to the party. "You throw one heck of a bash, brother. I think Lovey and I are going to take a walk around the city before the sun sets."

The next fifteen minutes were spent saying good-bye to the other guests who, amazed by the miracle of the tolling bells, were still talking about it when they walked down the gangplank.

Sam looked around him at the empty deck. "Guess that just leaves the two of us."

"There's still the crew," she reminded him.

"They'll stay discreetly out of the way until I give the signal," he said, his hands drifting slowly, artfully up the sides of her hips to her waist.

She captured his fingers in hers. "I've got something better for you to do with your hands right now."

At his doubtful expression, she crooked a finger, leading him to the piano. "Sit. I want you to play for me."

She scooted onto the bench beside him, resting her head on his shoulder as his skillful fingers trailed the keys, sighing contentedly.

"You enjoyed yourself today, didn't you?" he asked.

In spite of the relaxed moment, she felt a knot of fear in her stomach. Was it already over? What now?

Sam stopped playing, his brow raised at her hesitation. "You did, didn't you?"

"Of course I did, but now it's time for Cinderella's coach to turn back into a pumpkin."

Sam shook his head, his fingers beginning their

light passage over the keys again, creating soft, peaceful music. "Oh, no. You forget, Wendy. This is Never-Never Land. I lost you once, let you get away. This time, you have to stay forever."

"Don't joke, Sam. Not now."

"Who's joking?" He swiveled around to face her. "I've never been more serious in my life. I want you to stay here with me in New Orleans. Don't go back to Chicago. Okay, so you don't like the antique store business. That's okay. You can sell the shop, and find a job in an advertising firm right here, or I'll set you up in your own company, if you like. But don't go, babe."

"You want me to stay?" she asked, the soft wonder in her tone reflecting her amazement and joy.

"Of course I want you to stay. What did you think last night was about? Today? Hell, yes, I want you to stay. I've never wanted anything so badly in my life."

Lauren clenched her fingers in her lap as she sighed wistfully. It all sounded so simple. "Do you believe in magic, Sam?"

"What? The kind your aunt Edna was always talking about? With magic lamps and genies?"

Lauren's eyes rounded with surprise. "You know about that?"

"Sure. I used to hear her talking with Till and Toots. But in answer to your question, Lauren, no, I don't believe in magic spells and carpets. I believe in the kind of magic we created in bed together last night, the magic that was between us today when we danced, and I kissed you." He kissed her then.

286

"In other words, sweetheart, I believe in the magic that happens when two people are right together, like you and me."

Before she could answer, he pushed the bench back a few inches to stand up and lift her into his arms. He sat her on the gleaming back of the piano as he kissed her lips, letting his lips linger there before moving to her ear, then her throat.

Lauren could barely breathe under the loving assault, but her thoughts were clear and unjumbled for the first time in days. She knew now how powerful Eugene's magic had been when he'd brought Sam into her life. She'd never tell Sam about Eugene's secret, for Sam was right about the rest. The real magic came with falling in love with the right person, and she knew now just how right Sam was for her. He was intelligent, and, yes, ambitious in his own way, though most importantly, he was unafraid of following his dreams.

"Say you'll stay," he whispered against her throat as he lowered her so that she lay across the piano top.

She smiled, turning her head so she could kiss his ear and whisper her own demand. "Say those three little words that will convince me."

His laughter, a soft low rumble, tickled her brow as it stirred her hair. "If by those three little words you mean 'I love you,' you didn't have to ask. That was my next line, babe. Hell, yes, I love you." Tilting back his head, he shouted it again to the city that had finally quieted. Then holding her face with his splayed fingers, he met her dark, passionate gaze, and his tone was quiet and sober when he spoke again. "I love you, Lauren, with all my heart."

The piano keys tinkled several notes of their own volition, startling both her and Sam. Suddenly she understood. Her wishes were gone, and Eugene was mortal now, but just for a time, magic still lingered in the air. Her delighted laughter floated around them along with the music from the piano.

Sam stared down at her, confused both by the music and her amusement.

"What can I say, darling?" she whispered. "We make beautiful music together."

"I didn't touch the keys," he said, holding up both hands to prove it, though of course he couldn't possibly have touched them from where he stood.

"I know," she said with a radiant smile. "You didn't have to. You're playing the perfect music right here when you kiss me. Play it again, Sam."

Epilogue

"There she is!" Lauren said, leaning slightly to the left. She pointed through the crowd at the little girl with her swinging blond pigtails who was just stepping from the exit ramp amid a sea of deplaning passengers. "Casey! Over here!"

Casey spotted her father and Lauren, and her expression of doubt was replaced with one of incredible, unrestrained joy. Feet flying, arms waving, she wove her way through the crowd to fly into Sam's arms.

"Welcome home, jazzy lady," Sam said as he hugged her.

Lauren saw the tears in his eyes, knew how much this reunion meant to him, and felt her own eyes blurring with her joy. So Casey was the jazzy lady the club and yacht were named for. She'd never known, though she'd wondered about it and not without a pang or two of jealousy.

Less than twenty minutes later, the three of

them were seated in the BMW, Lauren and Sam laughing as Casey hung over the front seat, talking a mile a minute.

"I just can't believe it. I'm really here! Forever—except for vacations when I have to go back to New York or to France. You ought to see him, Dad. What a phoney-baloney. I walk around with a finger stuck in my mouth pretending I'm going to puke just to make Mom mad. It works though."

"I just bet it does," Sam laughed. "So, did they get off to Europe?"

Casey hunched her shoulders. "I dunno. Probably. Whats-his-face almost had a stroke when he saw all Mom's suitcases. They had a fight. But they were all lovey-dovey when they saw me off. El jerko even acted like he was going to miss me." She giggled. "Like a nail in the foot, as Aunt Toots would say."

"Well, we're glad you're here," Lauren said reaching up to squeeze Casey's arm affectionately.

"Me, too," Casey said, then slapping her dad's shoulder. "I didn't think you were going to pull it off in time for the wedding tomorrow, Dad. I would have *died* if I'd missed it."

"We would have postponed it if we hadn't gotten the papers signed in time."

"Yep, well, it's all official now. Like it or not, you guys, I'm irrevocably yours."

"Irrevocably?" Sam asked, his tone teasing.

"Pretty fancy word. Where'd you pick that up?"

As father and daughter talked, Lauren let her thoughts drift back over the last four months, the most amazing four months of her life.

Lauren had decided to keep the antique store going until she could find a job in advertising, which she knew had pleased Sam's aunts and Eugene. Especially Eugene. He was working for her now as her assistant. She'd thought she'd find something else within a few weeks, but the more she'd interviewed, the more she'd realized how much she enjoyed being her own boss. Besides, she was getting quite knowledgeable about antiques. It looked like she was going to continue as an entrepreneur indefinitely.

Sam's cousin and lawyer, Alexis Morgan, had filed a petition on Sam's behalf with the courts for permanent custody of his minor daughter. Janice had fought tooth and nail for the first couple of months before inexplicably giving up suddenly. It had been decided that Casey would stay in school in Manhattan until the Christmas break, then fly to New Orleans the same day her mother and new stepfather left the United States for Europe.

Lauren would never forget the day Sam had received word that Casey was going to be coming to live with him full-time. He'd called a friend to fill in for him at the club—a first for him—then taken Lauren to dinner at Antoine's.

"Guess you know what this means," he said as

he sipped his Drambuie after the tables had been cleared.

Lauren had reached across the table to squeeze his hand. "Of course I do. It means everything to you. It means a lot to me, too, Sam. I couldn't be happier if she were my own daughter."

"Well, actually that's what I meant. Casey and I, we have a special bond, but there are some things little girls just can't tell their dads." He was rubbing her hand, absently it seemed to Lauren until she felt the cool circle of metal that he was slipping onto her third finger.

Her eyes grew large when she saw the ring, the band of yellow gold and the oval canary yellow diamond solitaire. "Sam?"

"She's going to need a full-time mother, too, Lauren."

"You're . . . you're asking me to marry you?" she stammered.

"No. I was just explaining the way things are going to be." He scooted his chair back as he stood up and walked around the table. Lauren followed him with her eyes, confused, yet excited and flustered.

"Sam, what . . ."

He fell to one knee beside her chair, taking her left hand in his to kiss the back of it. "I'm not usually a very traditional guy, Lauren, but I do understand that there are exceptions to everything. This happens to be one of those times. So . . . Lauren Kathleen Kennedy, would you do me the honor of becoming my wife?"

Tears filled her eyes, yet laughter bubbled from her lips at the same time. Sam had just uttered the most beautiful words she'd ever heard, and he posed a picture of dashing hero from a long-ago era complete with ponytail and dancing gold ear-ring. But she'd seen the glint in those devilish green eyes and knew that his true nature of ro-guish impudence was lurking just beneath the surface, waiting to escape. Giggling again, she decided to let him off the hook. "Would you stand up! People are staring."

Sam feigned hurt but got up immediately, pull-ing her to her feet as well. "I'm stung, Lauren. I've been practicing that for weeks, and you're laughing."

She shook her head. "You're incorrigible, but I apologize. It was a beautiful proposal."

"Just not really me, huh?"

She laid a hand on his cheek, her eyes serious now. "I love you, Sam."

"I love you, too. But you're right, people are staring, so I suppose we'd better do this the right way, *my* way."

But before she could ask what *his* way was, he pulled her into his arms, pressing her tight against his chest as he looked into her eyes.

"I'm mad about you, babe. You've crawled into my skin and started an itch that's going to require a lifetime of scratching. *And* I'm damned tired of sneaking back and forth between your place and mine for the sweet loving we share every night." His tone sobered as he added, "I want to make babies with you and grow old together."

From the corner of her eye, Lauren could see heads turned could hear the hush that had fallen over the room. But she hardly registered it as she met her lover's fiery gaze. "I love you, too, Sam, and I want everything you want."

Sam turned to the waiter who was standing a few feet away. "Guess we're getting married, buddy. Bring us some champagne. Hell, bring some for everyone!"

She heard the applause, the laughter, and the sudden loud buzz of voices. But it was all distant and unreal as Sam kissed her, his lips hot and demanding on hers. After a moment, she pulled away to whisper in his ear. "Pay the check and grab the bottle. I want to celebrate in private."

Their "private" celebration was as perfect as the evening that had preceded it. They made sweet love, all the sweeter for the realization that they'd have a lifetime of nights like this. Before Sam led her to the bedroom, he made her sit on the couch, eyes tightly closed. He had an engagement gift for her.

At his words, her eyes flew open. "But, Sam, you already gave me the perfect gift. This ring is all I want."

"I think you'll like the other one, too. Now close your eyes."

Lauren heard him leave the room, then return. She heard him set something heavy on the floor by her feet, and heard the sound of rustling cardboard, a squeaky hinge. "Sam!" she protested though obediently not peeking.

"Just one more sec—"

Her eyes flew open again at the familiar tinkle of the calliope she'd purchased a few months earlier at an estate sale. "I'd forgotten." She frowned, perplexed. "You said you bought it for a birthday gift."

"I lied," he said simply.

"But then why did you buy it?"

He hunched his shoulders. "Was the only excuse I could find for coming to see you that day. Besides, I knew it irritated you. I was going to give it to you later, maybe as a farewell gift if you'd gone back to Chicago. When you didn't leave, I decided to save it for Christmas. But an engagement is a much more special occasion."

She was deeply touched, not just by the gift but by his admission about needing an excuse to see her even when he knew she'd be annoyed. Her eyes misted, and she framed his face with her hands as she kissed him. "I love you, Sam North."

He grinned as the lilting music played. "I know."

Lauren filled Eugene and Lovey in on their

plans the next day. They were thrilled for her, of course, but she didn't miss the look of disappointment that passed between them when she told them the date they'd selected for the wedding.

"What's wrong? Is that a problem?"

Again the silent communication, then Lovey's bright smile when she answered. "No. That's fine. We'll be there with bells on."

"I know you're glad for me, but something's wrong. What is it?"

"It's nothing, Lauren, really. Where is the wedding going to be?"

She told them about the tentative plans she and Sam had discussed, but after Lovey left she pinned Eugene down. "Okay, something's not right, and I want you to tell me what it is."

"It's no big deal, Lauren. Lovey and I are getting married, too. We were planning on telling you when you came in this morning. We just didn't want to rain on your parade."

Lauren squealed with delight, squeezing the wiry man to her. All at once it hit her what the problem was. She stepped back, and put her hands on her hips. "You picked the same day, didn't you? That's why you were both upset."

"Yeah, but like I said, it's okay. We'll just reschedule. What's a month or two here or there when we have the rest of our lives thanks to you."

"A month or two?"

296

"Or three. Whenever my cousin can ⸺
schedule again."

"I'm missing something here, Gene ⸺
and start over. What does your cousin ha⸺
with this? Which cousin are we talking abo⸺
cidentally?"

Eugene hefted himself up onto the counter
"Lovey and I can't get married by a preacher.
don't have a birth certificate. So Shamu agreed to
come in and perform the ceremony the first week
in December. He was a priest before he became a
genie, so we figure it's the same thing, legal or
not."

"Then that's the day it'll be. Sam and I can reschedule easier than you can."

"You really don't mind?"

"Of course not."

Eugene's face looked as if had been lighted
with a thousand candles as he jumped from the
counter. "Could you do without me for a few
minutes? I just want to tell Lovey the news."
He laughed. "For such a free spirit, she's
getting quite proper since we found out about
the baby."

He was halfway to the door when Lauren
stopped him. "Baby! Eugene, wait! What baby?"

"Oops. Guess we forgot to tell you about that
in all the excitement of your news." He tucked his
thumbs under imaginary lapels, sticking his chest
out, and grinning from ear to ear. "Yep, the old
man's gonna be a daddy. Lovey was a little wor-

297

ecause she's almost forty, but the doctor
everything's hunky-dory."

ithout another thought, Lauren turned the
in the window from Open to Closed. "I'm
ing with you!"

It was brisk out of doors the morning that
Lovey and Eugene were married, but the small
gathering hardly noticed as the couple exchanged
their vows.

Shamu, who Eugene had once described as a
whale of a genie, definitely looked like one today
as he stood in the middle of the park, dressed in
the ensemble of black and white tuxedo, complete with top hat. Lovey and Gene were dressed
in typical beatnik attire, she in ankle-length, embroidered muslin, he in denim bell-bottoms and a
bright red blouse. They each wore love beads
around their necks and flowers in their hair.

The ceremony lasted less than fifteen minutes.
Then the guests, "preacher," bride and groom, all
piled into cars for the short trip across town to
the cathedral where Lauren and Sam would exchange vows in a more traditional ceremony two
hours later.

It was Sam who had suggested that they marry
on the same day. In fact, he'd even wanted a dou-
ble ceremony. But Judith North had become almost hysterical at the prospect of watching her
daughter marry on a park lawn. And Eugene had

adamantly refused a formal affair. A compromise had been reached. First the park, then the cathedral complete with all the trappings: satin gown, ten-foot train, and tulle veil for Lauren, white tuxedo for Sam, bridesmaids in apricot silk and satin, flower girl in mint green, and hundreds of flowers.

It was a perfect day, Lauren thought as she stood off to the side, alone for a few seconds for the first time in more than ten hours. Even her mother seemed satisfied, she noted as she watched her mother seated on the far side of the large hall talking with Tillie and Toots. They'd had a minor altercation when Lauren refused to give up the idea of a Cajun reception following the weddings that would be a celebration for the four newlyweds. But as the band kicked up music for the *Fa da-do,* and Sam crossed the room to draw her onto the dance floor, she saw her mother join in with the aunts, clapping her hands in time to the lively tempo.

"Having fun, babe?" her husband asked as they joined the other dancers.

"The best," she shouted above the music. Conversation was impossible for the next several minutes, for even when the song ended, she was too winded to speak.

Sam led her to the table they shared with the other newlyweds and his daughter. Looking down at Casey, he asked her the same question.

"Oh, yeah, Dad, it's great. I've decided that

when I get married, I want to look just like Lauren, but I think I want Shamu to perform the ceremony in the park. I really dig the way Gene and Lovey wrote their own vows," Casey said, proud of the hip-sounding vernacular she'd picked up from Gene. Then remembering her father's feelings, she added tactfully, "Of course, I want a husband who'll write a song for me like you did for Lauren. He can play it at the reception just like you did."

"Think you can find a man who'll go along with everything you want?" her father teased, meeting his wife's enthralling gaze over Casey's head.

"Sure. Shamu says all you gotta have is a little magic."

Lauren smiled, turning her head to include Lovey and Gene. She lowered her eyes to her lap at the former genie's wink. *And three wishes, Casey,* she added silently.